CORPSE AT THE CARNIVAL

ALSO BY GEORGE BELLAIRS

Littlejohn on Leave
The Four Unfaithful Servants
Death of a Busybody
The Dead Shall be Raised
Death Stops the Frolic
The Murder of a Quack
He'd Rather be Dead
Calamity at Harwood
Death in the Night Watches
The Crime at Halfpenny Bridge
The Case of the Scared Rabbits
Death on the Last Train
The Case of the Seven Whistlers
The Case of the Famished Parson
Outrage on Gallows Hill
The Case of the Demented Spiv
Death Brings in the New Year
Dead March for Penelope Blow
Death in Dark Glasses
Crime in Lepers' Hollow
A Knife for Harry Dodd
Half-Mast for the Deemster
The Cursing Stones Murder
Death in Room Five
Death Treads Softly
Death Drops the Pilot
Death in High Provence
Death Sends for the Doctor
Corpse at the Carnival
Murder Makes Mistakes
Bones in the Wilderness
Toll the Bell for Murder
Corpses in Enderby
Death in the Fearful Night
Death in Despair
Death of a Tin God
The Body in the Dumb River
Death Before Breakfast
The Tormentors
Death in the Wasteland
Surfeit of Suspects
Death of a Shadow
Death Spins the Wheel
Intruder in the Dark
Strangers Among the Dead
Death in Desolation
Single Ticket to Death
Fatal Alibi
Murder Gone Mad
Tycoon's Deathbed
The Night They Killed Joss Varran
Pomeroy, Deceased
Murder Adrift
Devious Murder
Fear Round About
Close All Roads to Sospel
The Downhill Ride of Leeman
Popple An Old Man Dies

CORPSE AT THE CARNIVAL

AN INSPECTOR LITTLEJOHN MYSTERY

GEORGE BELLAIRS

ISBN: 978-1-5040-9244-9

This edition published in 2024 by Open Road Integrated Media, Inc.
180 Maiden Lane
New York, NY 10038
www.openroadmedia.com

TO

CHARLES AND MARIE JOWETT

With Happy Memories

CORPSE AT THE CARNIVAL

1
THE DEATH OF UNCLE FRED

It was like a summer day on the Riviera. Not a cloud in sight, the hot sun pouring down, the air humming with the heat, white sails on the calm blue sea...

The long curving promenade of Douglas Bay shone in the sunshine and the two massive bastions of Douglas and Onchan Heads, which seemed to hold the bay in their giant arms, looked to be two-dimensional, like scenes on a backcloth.

The tide was in and the sea was like a sheet of glass. The waves gently beat the shingle and, now and then, one larger than the rest struck the promenade wall and cast a fine salty spray over the baked asphalt. The Tower of Refuge on St Mary's Rock in the middle of the bay looked like a sham cardboard castle through the trembling heat.

A horse-tram, half full of people, halted to take on two girls who looked naked under their flowered sun-frocks. The horse lazily watched them mounting, relieved himself voluptuously of a pile of droppings, and moved off with a jingle of harness when the conductor rang the bell.

From a side street, an elderly man, short and thick-set, round-faced, and with a thatch of white hair, came in view. He walked slowly and unsteadily as though either drunk or ill, putting his feet down hesitantly, one arm hanging loosely by his side, the other holding together a raincoat flung casually across his shoulders like a cloak. He wore a suit of shabby blue serge and had an old panama on his head. Now and then, he paused as a spasm of coughing or nausea shook him, and then he gathered himself together and moved on. There was nobody about. All the people had formed a mass like a swarm of bees farther along the promenade, where something unusual was going on. The old man didn't seem interested...

A tall, hungry-looking photographer in a light, stained suit and down-at-heel brown shoes, instinctively took a snap of him for want of something better to do, and handed him a ticket. The old man absent-mindedly slipped it in his pocket and deliberately shuffled to what must have been his favourite spot, leaned wearily over the promenade railings, braced himself against them, and gazed blankly out to sea. A coal-boat was approaching the harbour of the old town, strings of little freshly-painted pleasure-boats bobbed about on the water, and an elegant private yacht, large, white, and self-conscious, appeared opulently from behind the pier and put out in the direction of Liverpool. On the skyline, the faint smoke of passing ships...

At the old man's back, the casino-like Villa Marina and its cloister of shops were almost deserted. The great dome, too, shimmered with the heat and inside, the staff with nothing much to do, were looking through the windows as though expecting something to happen.

Fate, the monstrous scene-shifter, was setting the stage for the death of Uncle Fred, the elderly man.

In front of the Palace, farther down the promenade, things were much livelier. What was going on there had drawn the vast holiday crowds which normally packed the sea-front and the beach from end to end. An actress, famous for little but her unctuous figure, was crowning the holiday queen. Miss *Mannin-*

veen... Miss dear Isle of Man! And when the ceremony was over, there was to be a carnival. Already the procession was forming. Huge tubular figures, with little human legs and grotesque faces, were bobbing about and, in the decorated horse-tram, they were pushing the queen and the actress, all curves and dentifrice smiles...

Everything seemed to wake up at once. People began to move in the direction of Uncle Fred; first a thin trickle of them, then a river. In no time, they had formed a solid pack on each side of the wide causeway of the promenade and began to cheer and clap as the procession slowly rolled along. The old man found himself torn from the rails by the sheer surging power of the good-natured mob and engulfed in the thick noisy mass. A light breeze swept from the sea like a refreshing breath, and then all was hot and sweltering again.

The tall, grinning carnival figures led the way. Then a brass band, and the floral horse-tram, with the queen in a white bathing-costume and a bit shy and embarrassed by the commotion she was causing. She wore a white silk sash with her name embroidered in gold on it, across her body. Miss *Mannin-veen*. By her side, the actress, all bosom, hair and teeth, sat confident that she was the main attraction. Then, a procession of vehicles bearing tableaux of all kinds, and a crowd of competitors on foot and in fancy dress, already sweating and following the decorated lorries like a long convulsive tail. Finally, a bagpipe band. A policeman's helmet here and there, cameras clicking, merry-makers in false noses and paper caps. And among them all, Uncle Fred, fighting to get away and find a place where he could be quiet and watch the fabulous blue sea.

The carnival and the onlookers slowly moved down the promenade like bees clustered round the queen. Close-knit, buzzing, humming, clinging together. In the distance, the hands of the Jubilee clock stood at five minutes to three. Two sleek white boats of the Isle of Man Steam Packet Company, due to leave at four, were moored at the pier, their smoke gently rising straight from their funnels. The procession moved towards them, a thick nucleus and then a lot of loose tentacles, with stray spectators running here and there on the fringe, trying to find places where they could see and join in the fun.

As the showpieces trundled past the Villa Marina and left it behind, the crowd thinned and faded out as though swept away by a huge invisible brush. There was nobody left but Uncle Fred, the waitresses at the windows, and a little Manx cat without a tail, chasing a piece of toffee-paper, and which by some miracle had not been trampled to death. The cornets of the brass band could be heard all over the town playing a popular hit from the latest film... *I left my heart in the bluegrass country...*

And then, in the wake of the comedy, tragedy started a little side-show. The old man on the empty promenade died, without a complaint, a convulsion, or a single sound. He just gently sagged to his knees, extended his body, slowly rolled over on his back, and it was all ended.

A waitress saw it from the window of the Villa Marina, and was within a few yards of him when Uncle Fred quietly died. She ran wildly, calling as she went.

'Uncle Fred!'

She was followed by the doorman and a man who kept a tobacco shop in the arcade.

'He's fallen in a fit or something. It's the old man who comes down here every day. Uncle Fred. The crowd must have been too much for him...'

He didn't look dead. His face was calm and there was a tiny smile on his full lips. His eyes were closed and he might have been enjoying a pleasant snooze.

The tobacconist, an elderly man with a large moustache and dressed in an open-necked white shirt and flannels, to whom the waitress had appealed, didn't quite know what to do. He rescued the panama, which had rolled a few feet away, and laid it down beside the body.

'Is he all right?'

A crowd had begun to gather and the tragedy soon developed in active competition with the organized comedy now winding round the Jubilee clock in the direction of the shopping centre. You could see people running from one to the other. The old man, peaceful in death, was spoiling the pantomime!

'Carry him across to the doctor's... Somebody telephone for the ambulance...'

A young policeman, with a red face and athletic muscles bulging from his tunic, appeared.

'What's going on here?'

'The man we call Uncle Fred is ill.'

'Well, is nobody doing anything?'

Those who knew him looked at a loss for an answer. Uncle Fred was a familiar figure round the Villa Marina. It was his favourite spot. He would sit on the seats facing the sea or lean on the rail of the promenade, motionless, for hours, and pass the time of day or crack a joke with anybody who greeted him. Now, somehow, they all seemed afraid of him, as though they scented death and were afraid of that, too.

'We thought it might be dangerous to move him. Somebody's gone for the ambulance and to get a doctor.'

A taxi drew up and the driver, a man with a profile like a greyhound's, sat in his cab watching it all. Charabanc owners were seeking fares for trips round the island. They did it cautiously, for touting was illegal. They were too busy with the job to notice Uncle Fred, his eyes calmly closed, his face turned full to heaven.

'Here's the ambulance.'

The vehicle drew up with businesslike precision, the attendants dismounted, and slid out a stretcher. The crowd was now enormous, and two more policemen were needed to keep a space round the body and make way for the ambulance men. They gently manoeuvred Uncle Fred to get him on the stretcher.

One of the attendants raised his hand and looked at it in stunned horror. It was covered in blood.

'He's been stabbed... And he's dead...'

Women began to scream and faint. The doors of the ambulance closed on the body, and the vehicle tore away, with its bell clanging, to the hospital, although everyone knew now that Uncle Fred was past all help.

The plane which had been droning over the bay turned to the airport at Ronaldsway, glided into the wind, and made a perfect landing.

Superintendent Littlejohn, of Scotland Yard, was almost exactly overhead when Uncle Fred died. He didn't see it happen, of course. He had his eyes closed. He was feeling liverish.

The International Police Conference had just been held in Dublin. Littlejohn had been invited. It had depressed him. It had made him feel his age. Most of the old faces had gone. Schwenk, of the FBI, had been shot by a gangster; Luc, of the Sûreté, had retired to a house his mother had left him near Flers, in Normandy; Sanchez, of Madrid, was in disgrace... A lot of young men Littlejohn had never seen before had taken their places. They'd all treated him with respect, almost reverence, but he couldn't help feeling that they regarded him as a venerable old buffer all the same... an elderly uncle with out-of-date ideas. They'd asked him to lecture on his methods. It had shocked them to discover that he hadn't any.

'Have a good rest,' his wife had told him as she saw him off at London Airport.

He'd had that, right enough... But the wrong way. Receptions, conferences, banquets. Good food, good company, and no exercise. He could still taste the Irish whisky in his mouth.

Then, providentially, he'd had a letter forwarded from his old friend, the Rev. Caesar Kinrade, Archdeacon of Man.

When are you coming over? I want to see you, and celebrate your promotion to Superintendent.

It only took half an hour from Dublin to the Isle of Man. That was, according to the time-tables. But it was August and there were so many planes in the air and claiming a landing at Ronaldsway, that Littlejohn's pilot was told to take a run up the coast and back and wait his turn. So, Littlejohn was overhead, sleeping off his torpid liver, whilst Uncle Fred was being murdered.

Yes; it was murder. They found a wound through the heart when they stripped the body at the hospital. The doctor said it might have been inflicted by a bread-knife.

As the plane taxied to the airport buildings Littlejohn could make out his old friend the Venerable Archdeacon. The fine white head held high, the froth of white whiskers, the pair of sturdy gaitered legs... When they opened the door of the plane, a salty gust of Manx air blew through, and the Superintendent felt better already.

The Archdeacon began to wave excitedly as soon as Littlejohn's head appeared from the plane and when the two men met, a handclasp seemed inadequate. They gripped each other by the shoulders in a half embrace. Passers-by in the crowded waiting-hall watched the pair of them enter; some who had met Littlejohn before greeted him; and the sergeant-in-charge at the airport made for his office and picked up the telephone. 'Give me Inspector Knell, Douglas Police...' Nobody ever enters the Isle of Man without somebody or other sending a message to interested parties on the Manx grapevine!

Superintendent Littlejohn, of Scotland Yard... friend of the Archdeacon... People nudged one another and it went round the airport. A group of spectators, half expecting the distinguished pair to be met by the Governor's car, were amazed to see them climbing into an old rattletrap of a vehicle, spotted by the white exclamation marks of hens and seagulls, and driven by a man in a cloth cap decorated with the hair of the cows he milked and with his two front teeth missing.

'*Kynnas-tha-shu*... and how are ye at all, Inspector?'

Teddy Looney, the driver, bared the gap in his teeth.

'Fine, Teddy... *Brauw, brauw*.'

'He's Superintendent, now, Teddy, and mind you remember it.'

'Whatever he is, it's good to be puttin' a sight on him again.'

The old car staggered noisily into the sunny interior of the island. *Grenaby*. The same little signpost apparently pointing to nowhere, and the quiet country road leading to the hidden village in its hollow sheltered by trees, with the river driving its way under the bridge beside the deserted old mill... Littlejohn felt he'd never been away from the place and he remembered how, in the heat and noise of London, he'd often thought of it and been refreshed.

The old gate, the walk under the trees, the broad, pillared door with its wide fanlight, and they were there. The old housekeeper, Maggie Keggin, met them in the hall. She was undemonstrative in her ways and expressed her feelings in her cooking. They were soon sitting down to roast partridge, shot for the occasion by a farmer of the parish who said he'd forgotten the date. And they had cherry tart to follow.

All through the meal, the parson questioned Littlejohn about himself and his affairs, his bright blue eyes sparkling whenever crime was mentioned and Littlejohn got the impression that this good old man could have wished for just a little murder to happen to give the pair of them an exercise to do together.

'And now, I've a present for you. I've had it a long time, and I don't get any younger, you know. I'll give it to you to celebrate your promotion and at the same time ease my mind that it's in good hands... It's in the other room.'

The Archdeacon rose and led the way.

'There it is, and it's all yours, with my deepest regards.'

It was a picture hanging over the fireplace, a work by the Manx artist, William Hoggatt. *The Black Sunbonnet.*

Littlejohn felt a lump rise in his throat as he looked at it. The wide hilly landscape rising to the Sloc in the south of the Island. A Manx farmstead nestling in the hollow, and the smoke of the stubble fires floating in the air over the little, brown autumn fields. In the foreground, a sturdy Juno of a peasant girl in a black sunbonnet looking with quiet longing in the direction of a ploughman with his team. At her feet, an old woman grubbing in the potato rows. A prophecy of what the girl might become in another forty years.

There was a sudden sharp knock on the front door. Maggie Keggin could be heard greeting someone angrily.

'He's only just come... Can't ye leave the poor fellah alone for even an hour?'

The housekeeper entered the room followed by a tall, thin, grinning man with large prominent teeth and an uncontrollable quiff of hair. Detective Inspector Knell, of the Manx C.I.D. He looked bashful after the housekeeper's onslaught, and delighted to see Littlejohn at the same time.

'Knell! And how are you? You're putting on weight.'

'I just thought I'd call round, sir, and congratulate you on being made a Superintendent.'

Littlejohn had happy memories of collaborating with Knell on previous cases. He was a good sort. Knell himself thought even more than that of Littlejohn. In fact, he boasted that he owed his own promotion to the Superintendent, who was also godfather to his baby son.

The Archdeacon searched Knell's eager face with his keen blue eyes.

'Well?' he said at length.

'Well what, Archdeacon?'

'What else, Knell? I can see you're excited, and it's not about the Superintendent's promotion.'

Knell tried to look nonchalant.

'This was just by the way of a social call, Master Kinrade. You see...'

'For heaven's sake, Knell, stop beating about the bush! Out with it man. What's wrong?'

'Well, Archdeacon, there *has* been a murder in Douglas today. An old man's been stabbed on the promenade in the middle of the carnival.'

'And...?'

'And I'm in charge of the case, sir.'

'Have a good rest, Tom,' Mrs Littlejohn had said as she kissed the Superintendent good-bye at London Airport!

2
QUITE A DAY

'Perhaps we'd better put a sight on the scene of the crime first. Then, you might like to see the body?'

Somehow, Littlejohn always felt sorry for Knell. He was so modest, earnest, and anxious to please, and, although eager to enlist the Superintendent's help and advice, he was a bit afraid of making a nuisance of himself. His face now wore the pleading, ingratiating look of a dog eager to be taken for a walk.

'Do you want me to come back to Douglas with you?' Littlejohn had asked him, and the way Knell's face had lighted up was answer enough.

Unofficially, of course. Littlejohn was used to that on the Isle of Man. He wanted to be free to make a holiday of it as well as a case, and he liked to think that Knell might reap some benefit from any work they did together.

The Archdeacon was disappointed at losing his friend so soon, and Maggie Keggin was in a tearing rage. 'I don't like that Knell fellah. Him and his murders. I do believe every time the Inspector comes here, that Knell fixes up a murder to bother him and to get the Inspector to himself.'

She refused to address Littlejohn as Superintendent. It took her a long time to get used to anything new. Besides, Inspector sounded more like a good policeman; Superintendents belonged to Sunday Schools.

As they reached Douglas, Littlejohn was lolling in the police car, feeling thoroughly in the holiday mood again. *Traa-dy-Liooar,* too. Manx for 'Time enough'. The tempo of life had changed down to a leisurely pace. Knell, as a token of his affection, had brought Littlejohn a cigar and the Superintendent was smoking it. Knell was smoking one, too, with the band on, until they reached the outskirts of the town, where he threw it away as unprofessional.

What weather! It was just turned seven o'clock and the sun was beginning to set and throwing a golden glow over the gentle green hills behind Douglas. Not a cloud in sight and the peaks sharply etched against the evening sky. The quayside and promenade were packed with holiday crowds, all in light summer clothes and with red sunburned faces. A procession of people strolling up to Douglas Head and another coming down. All enjoying the end of a perfect day and killing time until the night's fun began.

The police-car rounded the clock tower at the end of the crowded promenade. It looked like a football match, with hardly room to squeeze in another. The policeman on duty saluted smartly and peered in the car to get a look at Littlejohn. There was a horse-tram there, ready for off.

'Where was the body found, Knell?'

'A good stretch along the prom, sir. Near where you can see the tall memorial, there... The war memorial...'

He slowed down the car and pointed. The horse hitched to the tram gave Littlejohn a familiar kind of stare. Somehow, they always looked that way at the Superintendent. Cabhorses, dairymen's ponies, ragmen's donkeys and those in the turnouts of pearly kings... They all gave him the same sort of brotherly look, almost a wink, as though they recognized a pal when they saw one. Sometimes, they even neighed at him.

The tram-horse neighed!

'What the 'ell?' said the driver. 'I've never 'eard' im do that before, all the time I've driven 'im.'

There was nothing else for it. It must have been the holiday feeling!

'Let's park the car and take a ride on the horse-tram, Knell.'

Poor Knell! He agreed, just to please his companion, for whom, without asking why, he'd have thrown himself fully dressed in the harbour or shinned up the radar mast of the harbourmaster's office. But he hoped nobody would see him gallivanting along the promenade on a tram! He'd never hear the last of it if anybody in the force spotted him. Knell pulled down the brim of his hat to disguise himself a bit.

Had it been in Nice, Littlejohn's friend, Dorange of the Sûreté there, would have said 'Let's have a drink first, old man...' and they'd have sat and watched the crowds go by. As it was, Knell was almost teetotal and bursting to get working.

Clop, clop... The muffled beat of hooves on the asphalt. It was years since Littlejohn had ridden behind a horse. He remembered his father bundling them all in the cab when they went on holidays in long-forgotten days... How transitory and sad holidays were when you looked at them from the outside... All these people thronging the place, eagerly squeezing every drop of joy out of a week or a fortnight in a kind of make-believe... Clop, clop... Littlejohn shook himself. He was growing sentimental in the sunset and sea air.

Along the fine broad promenade, with the gardens down the middle all looking their best. On one side, the still blue sea and the Tower of Refuge like a painting on a backcloth against the skyline. On the other, a row of neat, prosperous-looking boarding-houses, with people sitting on the steps, lolling at ease and enjoying the evening beauty. A sea of cheerful faces everywhere, the tram starting and stopping, and Knell on tenterhooks.

At last! They dismounted in front of the Villa Marina. A

charming building, surrounded by gardens and flanked by arcades of shops selling souvenirs, sticks of rock, views of the Island, or vulgar picture-postcards featuring drunken red-nosed men or henpecked husbands with enormous ugly wives... Bathing costumes and paper-backed novels... *Send your friends at home some Manx kippers by post from here...* Charabanc drivers touting for evening mystery tours with flashy new vehicles drawn up at the kerb.

'This is where the body was found.'

It brought Littlejohn back to earth.

There wasn't anything to see! Uncle Fred was completely forgotten. The jolly crowds were walking over the very spot he'd died on. A woman in a paper cap tried to kiss Knell and he clawed her off. She left the shape of her lips on his cheek in red lipstick and, as Littlejohn wiped it off for him, he smiled and thought that anybody more unlike a couple of detectives he couldn't imagine.

Dancing was starting at the Villa and at the Palace farther down. Already you could hear the bands jigging away and people were flocking in. After that, when it was dark enough to put on the coloured illuminations on the promenade, there was to be another carnival and a torchlight procession. No time at all for Uncle Fred, now lying in the town morgue waiting for justice to be done.

'Shall we go and see the body?'

Again! It was like the passing bell, reminding you of death and destruction just as you were beginning to enjoy yourself.

Littlejohn gave Knell a blank look.

'The body?'

'Uncle Fred...'

'Yes, of course.'

A buxom woman passing by handed Littlejohn a stick of rock marked with the Three Legs of Man, and walked on with a smile. Just for nothing at all... A gesture of goodwill. And a girl, mistaking the pair of them for elderly philanderers on the prowl, gave Littlejohn the glad eye... After all, that was what they *were* doing. Prowling...

The body didn't matter very much in the case now. It seemed stupid and ironical, but it had ceased to count. Instead, they were concerned with someone among the vast crowds in Douglas, perhaps someone dancing in the carnival, who had reduced Uncle Fred to a pathetic inanimate occupant of a mortuary refrigerator.

All the meagre evidence was at the police station. The contents of the murdered man's pockets revealed nothing, not even his name. Just Uncle Fred. A wallet containing ten pounds in notes and a worn photograph of a fox terrier dog sitting on its haunches, begging, with the hand of somebody off the picture held out to keep the dog's attention. Some small change, a pen-knife, an old pipe and a worn rubber pouch half-full of what looked like Cavendish, a door-key, a clean folded handkerchief, and a coupon from a photographer.

Flic Studios, 26b Promenade Arcade, Douglas. Your picture will be ready today after 5 p.m. Copies 2s. 6d. each.

'We've picked up the snapshot. Here it is... '

One of Knell's satellites, a strapping big detective-constable called Skillicorn, had been on the job.

He handed over the postcard photograph. Uncle Fred, panama, heavy serge suit, raincoat slung over his shoulders dramatically, like a cloak. He'd evidently just looked up and grimaced at the tout in either pain or anger as he found him snapping him.

'We've had copies of the picture sent to the daily papers across the water. Somebody might recognize him. We've asked them to emphasize that he's not yet been identified.'

Uncle Fred was a mystery. Nobody seemed to know who he was or where he lived. Which was perhaps not surprising in a place like Douglas at the very peak of the holiday season. One lonely man, probably a stranger, on his own among thousands of other strangers, birds of passage, here for a week or two, and then gone for ever. A picture in the morning papers with a caption

Who's Uncle Fred? would probably bring a quick answer to the question.

Meanwhile, Skillicorn had closely interviewed the staff of the Villa Marina.

The waitress who was there at the death, knew Fred well. He came for his morning stroll every day. He'd buy a paper and perhaps some tobacco from the man with the big moustaches, and sit down and have a smoke as he read the news, and then he'd lean across the rails looking out to sea, lost in his thoughts. He was never seen with anybody.

'And how did you know his name?'

The waitress had an easy answer to that one.

'Sometimes, when it rained or was misty, he'd come in for a cup of coffee, black without sugar, and sit by the window reading his paper and looking out to sea as though he might be expecting somebody... Just like he did outside on fine days. I once called him "sir". He didn't seem to like it. "Call me Uncle Fred", he said to me, with that pleasant smile he had. And we always called him that among ourselves ever after.'

'You talk as if you'd known him quite a long time.'

'We have. He's been coming on and off for several years. Sometimes he'd vanish for a day or two, and then he'd turn up again.'

'You say you never saw anybody with him?'

'No... Never.'

The waitress, a pleasant, homely little married woman, who worked on the job and did very well at it in the summer, and hibernated somewhere at the end of the season, was quite upset about it all.

'It's as if we'd lost an old friend. I've known him by sight ever since I started working here four years ago. The staff are always coming and going and I've been here the longest, on and off. We all liked him. He was so civil and pleasant. You got the feeling that he'd do anybody a good turn.'

'But nothing else...? He never talked or told you anything

about himself.'

'No. Somehow, he never encouraged conversation. I don't know what he did in the winter months. I usually give up at the Villa in October and come back at Whitsuntide when the season's starting.'

'Would you say he was fond of the women?'

The waitress just gave Skillicorn a motherly smile.

'They usually all are at that age. Especially if they're on their own. Nothing wrong with it. They get lonely and you see them looking longingly sometimes as though they wondered what it would be like to have a woman to look after them and sit by the fireside with them and keep them company after dark. It must be awful going home to diggings or an empty house with nobody to bid you welcome back. That's how I look at it. Others might think different accordin' to the state of their minds.'

'He gave you that impression?'

'Yes, sometimes.'

Just Uncle Fred. That was all. Unless someone recognized his photograph or missed him, he might sink into the limbo of the forgotten and his murder go unavenged. Somebody would get away with it.

Littlejohn picked up the photograph again and studied it. Of its kind, it was quite good. And suddenly 'Uncle Fred' became more than a mere label. A round, refined, clean-shaven face, with troubled eyes looking from under his old panama hat. A look difficult to assess. Blank, or stony, or even pleading... In the inanimate snapshot Littlejohn couldn't tell which. A good-natured face, even if convulsed with pain or annoyance at the time. An educated man, perhaps cultured... One above the average, at least.

The Superintendent awoke from his reverie and looked closely at the picture again. He might have been imagining things, just flights of fancy. All the same Uncle Fred seemed more flesh and blood now.

'Where's the raincoat, Skillicorn?'

'He wasn't wearing it when they found him and we didn't find it when we searched the neighbourhood near where he died. It's funny... but then, the carnival crowds had just passed by and might have kicked it about and even pushed it over the promenade into the sea with their feet.'

'That may be. What newspapers did he read, Skillicorn?'

The constable's eyes lighted up.

'Funny you should ask that, sir. I'd forgotten to mention it. He'd three papers; the *Daily Cry*, which comes over by plane first thing in the mornings, and the London *Times* and the *Financial Times* of the day before. He probably got the day's news from the *Cry* and the rest from the other two which arrive later by boat.'

Littlejohn might have expected it! Uncle Fred was a cut above the average.

'As for the *Financial Times*... I don't know whether the deceased was a monied man or not. There were ticks against some of the investments quoted.'

Littlejohn looked through the papers which had been tucked in Uncle Fred's pockets when he died. They'd been opened and obviously read. Nothing of interest in them, except, as Skillicorn had said, some ticks on the back page of the financial paper. Investments in tobaccos, oils, and rubbers... BATS, Ultramar, Anglo-Asian... and calculations in pencil in the margin of the paper, as though Uncle Fred might have been counting up his gains and losses. The figures were well made and neat.

He studied the figures. According to what he could make out, there was about £257 involved in the three holdings, and Uncle Fred had made £11 by fluctuations in prices. If that was all the money he'd got, he certainly was no tycoon!

Knell and his assistant looked hopefully at Littlejohn, like two dogs expecting a bone. It was obvious they were waiting for something oracular. Like the respectful young detectives he'd left behind at the conference in Dublin. Had they been here, perhaps they would have been busy with a vacuum-cleaner taking the dust from Uncle Fred's trousers bottoms for examination, or testing his suit and panama hat to deduce where they came from. Photographing the body from all angles for the records, having it cut up by the surgeon to see if it had any peculiarities. After all, it was *one* way of getting to know Uncle Fred.

'Two hundred and fifty-seven pounds... And eleven pounds profit.' Littlejohn sighed and Knell nodded loyally at Skillicorn to show that if his underling didn't understand the workings of the famous detective's mind, he, Knell, did.

That seemed to be all for one night. Until the photograph appeared in the morning papers or somebody missed Uncle Fred and reported it to the police, they were at a dead-end.

'I think we'd better be getting back to Grenaby, Knell. The Archdeacon will wonder whatever we're doing.'

Outside, the streets were more crowded than ever. It was a real day of carnival. Knell drove Littlejohn to the end of the promenade and back, by way of relaxation, a bonus for his night's exertions.

It was still sultry. The sun had set and lights were going on here and there. The villas perched among the trees on the wooded slope above the promenade were illuminated and some were floodlit. In the dance-halls the bands were hard at it drumming like mad. Crowds strolling along the seafront, singing, laughing, shouting, and lovemaking.

'Do you know where we are, sir? We've left Douglas Head behind us. That's Onchan where the road goes up the hill and round the bend, and it follows the coast almost all the way to Ramsey. It's a lovely run.'

Littlejohn was ready to admire it all. The hundreds of people, all happy and enjoying themselves, seemed to diffuse such an atmosphere of irresponsibility and fun that he found himself caught up in it. He couldn't take it seriously. He couldn't believe he was on a case.

'I wish we knew who Uncle Fred was. It makes you wonder

how long we'll be in the dark about him.'

'Oh, yes... Uncle Fred... '

They were both smoking cigars again. Knell produced them like a conjurer pulling rabbits out of a hat. Littlejohn hadn't the heart to refuse. Knell's brother-in-law was in the wholesale tobacco line in Liverpool and sent boxes of samples over now and then. The sort which are bought on holidays when a gesture of opulence is called for. Not much to speak of, but which give satisfaction because they make you feel good to have them in your mouth.

Somebody threw a paper streamer and it wrapped itself round the bonnet of the car.

'That place belonged to a millionaire who went bust... And there was an internment camp there in the war... '

Knell was changing the subject because he thought Littlejohn was bored with Uncle Fred.

The fun-fair at Onchan Head was going full blast. Screams from the scenic railway, rifles cracking in the shooting-range, and somebody playing a sentimental song on a harmonica...

You could hear the waves washing on the shore; the sea air came across in little invigorating gusts; the moon was almost full, hanging in the east over Douglas Bay. A treacly tenor singing an Italian song somewhere... A really sentimental evening. Lovers walking arm in arm or else hugging one another closely, forgetful of everything else. Littlejohn felt like snuggling down in his seat and having a nap...

And then they suddenly switched on the illuminations, like a flash of lightning travelling right round the bay. A string of coloured lamps, decorations all the way from Douglas Head to Onchan. Hotels floodlit, advertisement signs in neon. You could hear the crowds draw in one huge delighted breath... AH...

A couple of policemen frog-marching a Teddy-boy to the lock-up for hitting someone over the head with a bottle... The ambulance shot past ringing its bell...

Littlejohn felt guilty. Parson Kinrade would be sitting up, waiting eagerly for a full account of the investigation. And all Littlejohn could say was, he's called Uncle Fred, this is his photograph, we think he might be a bit fond of the ladies, he's a good sort, reads this paper and that, and seems to have investments totalling £257 on which he's just made a capital profit of £11... Ridiculous!

They drove back in the moonlight, the beams of their headlamps catching the frightened eyes of little creatures crossing the deserted roads. It was past eleven and already the villages through which they passed were silent and asleep. Crossing the Fairy Bridge at Ballalonna, both men raised their hats like good Manxmen.

'Good evening, little people... '

Littlejohn smiled to himself as he dutifully puffed his cigar. What would Chipchase, the forger, Craggy Knowles, the bank-robber-with-violence, or Sammy Thewless, the lady-killer in its literal sense – real toughs Littlejohn had put behind bars – say if they could see him now, raising his hat to propitiate the fairies! They'd think he'd gone round the bend properly!

They skirted the vast dark mass of Castle Rushen, rising monolithically above sleeping and dimly lighted Castletown, and turned off on the old familiar country road.

Not a sound in Grenaby but the rustle of the trees, the rush of the stream under the bridge, the hooting of an odd owl, and the distant barking of dogs. Two worlds a few miles apart. Douglas, all lights and gaiety; and the hidden village already asleep.

Knell was strangely silent. As a policeman, he wasn't supposed to be superstitious or afraid. But, as a Manxman, he had other feelings in his blood from days gone by, an inheritance from ancestry, remembrance of stories told round fires long ago. Driving on the lonely highway, with deserted crofts and gaunt ruined homesteads, the *tholtans,* etched against the moon, and with the silent fields of Ballamaddrell and the wastelands around

Quayle's Orchard and Moainey Mooar stretching out to the lonely hills, he shuddered.

Knell had never read of Kipling's 'oldest land, wherein the Powers of Darkness range', but he knew all about it by the way the hair rose above the nape of his neck!

The Archdeacon insisted on Knell's coming in for supper, and they told him the little they'd found out since they'd left him, over sandwiches and coffee.

It had been a long day for Littlejohn, the culmination of a series of late nights and over-eating in Dublin. He could hardly keep his eyes open. Add to that the air trip, the drive to and from Douglas, the promenade, the lights, the laughter... And on top of it all, Uncle Fred. Quite a day!

The telephone bell rang. Maggie Keggin entered; she wasn't at all pleased.

'It's for Inspector Knell. I don't know why, but whenever he comes here there's always commotions... Bells ringin', stoppin' up late at nights, murders bein' done. It's as if the place is bewitched, as though somebody had put the Eye on us... It's Douglas police on the telephone, and I'm goin' to my bed. So, I'll wish you all good night and I hope you sleep well, though I have my doubts about it.'

Knell was quick there and quick back. He looked pleased with himself.

'Somebody's claimed Uncle Fred! The owner of a boarding-house just off Broadway, where he lodged, heard there'd been a murder on the prom, and when his lodger didn't turn up for tea or supper, he reported it. Just after we'd left, he called at the police-station.'

'It took him long enough!'

'Well, they're busy in the high season. They can't pretend to be counting heads all the time. Trimble, that's the man's name. He's identified the body. So now we know what he's called and where he lives. That's a start, at any rate.'

Knell rubbed his long, bony hands together in a kind of energetic glee.

'What *is* he called?'

'Sorry. In the excitement, I'd quite forgotten. Fred Snook... '

Snook! What a name! It seemed to spoil it all. Littlejohn much preferred 'Uncle Fred'. It suited the man in the panama far better. The Superintendent had had an Uncle Fred of his own once, and had almost adopted the murdered man as a relative. It added a bit of homely incentive to the affair. Now... Fred Snook... Just a name on a case-file... Well, well...

They saw Knell off in the moonlight and then talked a bit more. Littlejohn rang up his wife, thinking again in sleepy mood, of the cable crossing the ocean above strange fish, subterranean rocks and caves, and the lost isles and cities of which the Archdeacon had told him legends, the Manxman's *Hy Brasils*, which rose once a year from the mists and the bells of which you could sometimes hear across the still sea.

'I've found another case waiting here for me, Letty... A man called Fred Snook murdered right on the promenade at Douglas in the middle of a crowd... Yes... Snook... '

All he could hear as he got ready for bed was the ticking of the clock in the hall and the creak of old timbers settling down for the night. He opened the window wide and muffled sounds entered from the moonlit countryside. The river and the trees again and the rustle and squeak of wild things. Grenaby, where many waters meet, was a haunted place. Large spectral cats with flaming eyes, the *Purr Mooar* or great pig, fairy music... Littlejohn listened, yawned, and climbed into his large four-poster. Only one thing haunted him... The face under the panama hat... And a name. Fred Snook. It didn't fit. It was silly...

He fell asleep as soon as his head touched the pillow, and he dreamed he was driving with Uncle Fred in a horse-tram, only they weren't running on the lines. Instead, they were clop-clopping along the narrow road to Grenaby behind the horse with the knowing look.

3

'SEA VISTA'

Knell and his satellites, photographers, fingerprint men, and technicians hunting for clues, had overhauled Uncle Fred's lodgings immediately after breakfast, and gone. Over the telephone, Knell had invited Littlejohn to call at the place as soon as he got to Douglas, and let him have his views and impressions. The Archdeacon, eager to be of use, accompanied him.

'A parson! Is he after conducting the funeral? They haven't arranged the burial yet, have they?'

Mr Trimble answered the door and, without so much as a how-do-you-do, started asking questions right away.

The proprietor of the boarding-house was easily classified. He looked disappointed and defeated. Small, podgy, bald, and pathetic, dressed in a shabby waistcoat and trousers, and in his soiled shirt-sleeves. Apathy and failure written all over him. He had a large moustache of the Italian operatic variety, and a fringe of dark thin hair round his tonsure. Brown, liquid, exophthalmic eyes, like those of a spaniel. He walked with a limp and a rigid jerky gait. A man who, at some time in his prime, might have been strong and muscular, now gone to seed.

The house itself stood in Whaley Road, just off Broadway. One of a row with small front gardens and wrought-iron railings. Georgian frontages, some of them spick-and-span and fresh with new cream colour-wash, and their railings freshly painted for the season. Others were forlorn and shabby as though publicly admitting mediocrity and despair.

A brass plate on the gate. *Sea Vista*. On the glass fanlight over the front door, MRS TRIMBLE, APARTMENTS. A card hanging in the window, VACANCIES. Uncle Fred's room was already in the market! Instead of a front lawn, some lazy and ingenious owner had, at one time, cemented the garden over and now grass was struggling and sprouting in the cracks.

Nothing very cheerful. The kind of commonplace lodging-house you find in dozens clustered round large city stations. The front door was open and the glass door of the vestibule closed. Littlejohn rang. Trimble himself appeared. He'd been disturbed in the kitchen where the lodgers' midday dinner was on the boil. He had red eyelids and the besotted look of one who'd missed several nights' sleep. He seemed to mistake the pair of them, in his sleepy way, for an undertaker and his attendant chaplain.

'We're from the police.'

'Oh. The parson, too?'

'He's simply keeping me company. May we come in?'

Trimble stood aside and waved them along.

Not a big house. Three storeys, with attics. A long, dark corridor with a bamboo hatstand half filling it and a painted drainpipe for umbrellas. An aspidistra in a pot and a lot of old raincoats, soiled hats, shabby umbrellas and a coloured parasol cluttering up the place. To the left, doors to the dining-room and lounge; on the right, stairs, with large knobbed newel-posts, climbing up the wall. Beyond them, the kitchens, whence the smells of cabbage, cooking meat, gravy and floor-polish emerged and battled with the odours of soiled bed linen, cosmetics, stale tobacco, cheap scented soap, and naphthalene lavatory disinfectant which flowed down the stairs.

Linoleum on the hall floor, a worn red carpet on the stairs, held in place by brass rods. Through the open door of the dining-room an anaemic girl laying places for lunch at one single long table, distributing soiled table-napkins in wooden rings, the last stand of respectability and seedy elegance...

A woman shepherding three small children, all under ten, turned the landing and started to descend the stairs, her hands full with her unruly brood.

'Why isn't daddy coming?'

'I said he'd gone to see a friend. Can't you be told?'

'But why?'

'Oh, shut up, do! I can't never have a bit of peace on my 'olidays.'

They were carrying buckets and spades and the eldest boy held a small fishing-net. He was picking his nose. The woman looked tired, thin, and fed-up. Trimble ignored them as they passed into the street, still questioning and quarrelling among themselves with a punctuation of whimpering, slaps, and lamentations.

Sounds of whispering in the lounge, and a man emerged followed by a woman. He carried a leather suitcase, well worn and plastered with labels, and wore a flashy grey suit and a grey felt hat to match it. Middle-aged and furtive-looking, with a fleshy red face and mouth, a small dark moustache, and poached brown eyes. His thin receding hair was glued to his head with brilliantine. The woman, an unctuous blonde, was tall and handsome, with a veneer of vulgar sophistication. The man addressed Littlejohn.

'Did I hear you say you were from the police?'

'Yes.'

'Excuse me. Here's my card.'

O. FINNEGAN, F. INST. B. CON.
BUSINESS CONSULTANT

'I've got to get away on the one o'clock plane to Manchester. A business appointment. Important clients I daren't miss seein'. Means big money to me. You've got the address on the card there if you want me later... '

He was obviously anxious to be off, and, judging from the way Trimble was eyeing him, Littlejohn could guess the reason. Had the limelight of publicity and journalism been turned on *Sea Vista*, as they probably would be any minute, somebody somewhere would ask what Mr Finnegan was doing there posing as the husband of the blonde Juno, when all the time his wife and family thought he was elsewhere business consulting! The same, sordid old tale...

'Did you mention this to the Inspector who called earlier?'

'Yes. But I thought maybe you were a senior man and would understand my position better... '

'And go over his head? What did he say?'

Mr Trimble couldn't wait. He didn't want the serpent to sneak out of *Sea Vista*; he wanted to kick him out later.

'He told him not to go till the police said so.'

'Well, you'd better wait then, Mr Finnegan.'

'But

'I'm sorry. I can do nothing.'

The man retreated, abashed and muttering to himself, into the lounge again. More whispering behind the door, voices raised, shouts and reproaches. Then the blonde emerged, slammed the door with Mr Finnegan inside, and stormed into the street.

'Could we see Mr Snook's bedroom?'

'Yes. It's just as 'e left it, except the bed's been tidied and the place dusted. The police said not to touch anythin', but we'd already made the bed and...'

The whining voice kept on and on as they climbed to the first floor. A dark landing, and a corridor with four doors leading off and a bathroom at the far end. From behind one of the doors came a noise like someone chanting or saying prayers and responses.

'It's the pair we call the honeymooners. They're middle-aged, but we think they're newly-weds, though they haven't let on. She's at least ten years older than 'im, but then she 'as the money.'

Trimble's drone merged with the chanted conversation going on behind the door marked '3'.

'They're packin' up, ready for off, as soon as you fellows'll let 'em go. This Uncle Fred business has done us a lot of 'arm; spoiled the season for us, in fact. People don't want to spend their 'olidays at an 'otel where somebody's been murdered, even if it *did* 'appen off the premises. Mrs Mullineaux keeps askin' if they're bringin' the body back 'ere... Says she won't stop... They'll 'ave to pay for the whole week, of course, but...'

'Is that the name of the pair in No. 3?'

'Yes. Mullineaux... '

He pronounced it Mullinaxe.

Up another flight of stairs, this time narrower and more seedy. No carpet covered this lot; just worn oilcloth. Trimble climbed slowly, mounting crabwise on account of his lameness.

'Mr Snook lived on the first floor out of season when we'd no visitors. The rooms are cheaper then. In July and August and the first week in September prices go up, as you well know. So Mr Snook went up, too... To the second floor where the cheaper rooms are. Here we are.'

A long dismal, shabby corridor, with another bathroom at the far end of it. Four more doors. Trimble opened *No. 5.*

'Inspector Knell left the key and we didn't lock it in view of the fact that you was comin'. He said nobody'd to go in. I saw to that.'

'Very good... Lead on.'

A stuffy room lighted by sash windows, one at the front and the other cut in the gable-end of the house. An austere place with soiled cream walls relieved by cheap prints in Oxford frames. More oilcloth on the floor and a small rug on each side of the bed.

The latter was of dark oak, the sort you can pick up in sale-rooms any day. It had already been stripped of its linen and now merely held an old spring-mattress and a cheap down quilt. An old armchair in faded green plush; a chest of drawers with its top badly marked by cigarette burns; and a rickety dressing-table with a mirror out of control and wedged in place by an old cigarette packet. A large old-fashioned wardrobe, with nothing in it but a shabby raincoat, a spare shirt, and a pair of worn-out bedroom slippers. A small antiquated wireless-set on a tumbledown bamboo bedside-table, and a cane chair. Under the bed, an empty battered fibre suitcase...

Littlejohn strolled to the front window and looked out at the monotonous row of roofs and windows opposite, with the sunny blue sky above them and the street just visible below. Then to the one in the gable-end. Thence, he could see a small triangle of the sea, like a blue pocket-handkerchief, between the sloping slates of other properties. *Sea Vista.* This must be the vista! Another better-class street below, with prosperous-looking boarding-houses lining it and people in their holiday clothes sauntering about, casual and carefree, or lounging in the front gardens, anointed with oil, sun-burning themselves.

Littlejohn turned to the Archdeacon, who stood beside him looking out, too. The parson had been silent for a long time, not wishing to interfere, leaving all the questions to the expert. His face showed no disgust at the sordid set-up in which Uncle Fred had spent his last years. In the clear blue eyes there was just wonder at yet another example of human behaviour and endurance.

'Where was everybody when Uncle Fred died, Trimble?'

'All except me and Susie, the maid, was out at the carnival.'

'Nobody else indoors?'

'Not one of 'em, Superintendent. It's the event of the week, you see.'

A clock below struck twelve discordantly. Lunch-time in the

offing and hungry visitors beginning to forage for food. By stretching his neck and standing on tiptoe Littlejohn could see from the side window the back-yards of *Sea Vista* and its immediate neighbours. Dustbins, plumbing climbing up and down the back walls, washing festooned on lines, wet towels and bathing-costumes draped on window-sills, a dog chained to a kennel gnawing a bone, a sandy Manx tomcat sprawled on top of a wall...

In a room along the corridor someone started to play an accordion softly and sing a refrain.

I left my heart
In the blue-grass country,
Where my buddy
Stole my baby from me.

'I've asked 'im not to keep on playin'. It don't seem decent. But he won't be told. You see, he's entered for the personality competition and he's practisin' his act.'

'Did he always pay for his room promptly?'

'Who? Oh, Snook... Yes, weekly, on the dot.'

'Did he seem to have plenty of money?'

'He wasn't without. I don't know where he got it from. I never knew of 'im goin' to a bank... Never saw a bank-book, either, for that matter. It seemed to me that when he was runnin' short of the ready, he'd go and get more from somewhere. He'd go away for a whole day and come back smellin' of drink and then he'd be flush with money for about a month, and then go off for more.'

'Perhaps he had a pension of some kind.'

The Archdeacon made the suggestion, and Trimble jumped to hear him speak. He scratched his bald head.

'I wouldn't know about that, bishop... I take it, sir, you *are* the Bishop of Sodor and Man.'

Trimble looked at the gaiters with respect. He was going to tell the guests about this visit.

'No. Just Archdeacon.'

'Oh... Well, sir, yore friend there is, I see, takin' a look round at the late Uncle Fred's belongin's... As the Inspector wot was 'ere earlier found out, there's not a single letter, paper, bill, or book of any kind bearin' Mr Snook's name. I've no proof it *was* Snook. That's wot he said it was when he came 'ere years ago and he asked all the visitors who got a bit friendly with 'im, to call 'im Uncle Fred.'

He was right. Littlejohn had been opening and closing drawers. They held very little. A change of linen, collars and ties, a nightshirt, shaving tackle, toothbrush, a few patent medicines. That was about all. No jewellery, except a gold hunter watch in a drawer still ticking away. Uncle Fred seemed to have just the suit he was found in, and the few essentials for keeping himself clean and neat. Finally, a few books. Littlejohn examined them carefully and passed them to his friend, who raised his eyebrows. *The Private Papers of Henry Ryecroft*... It might have been the story of Uncle Fred himself... A lonely man on his own, to whom death finally came quickly and quietly...

Two more books. Gill's *Manx Scrapbook* and a copy of Trevelyan's *English Social History*. They were all soiled and well-thumbed, but contained no names on their flyleaves. The Archdeacon carefully and patiently examined the pages of each. Nothing, except two single-page timetables of Manx buses and trains... Yes, Uncle Fred was certainly a cut above the average.

Trimble was getting fidgety.

'I'll have to be gettin' down. Dinner's on the boil and the girls are sure to spoil it if I'm not there.'

There wasn't much point in staying longer. Outside the door of the room, Littlejohn halted a moment.

'How many lodgers have you in at present?'

'We've seven rooms and our own. Four on each floor and the girls sleep in the attics. We've sixteen boarders, all told, if you include Snook.'

'How are they spaced?'

'On this floor, there's four young men in one room next to the bathroom... That's where the fellow's playin' the accordion. Then, next door to them, Miss Arrowbrook, a young woman who's not strong, or says she's not, who comes for several weeks every summer. Then, the missus and me in room No. 6, which 'appens to be vacant just at present, otherwise we'd be in one of the attics and the girls would 'ave to share a bed.'

'And below?'

'The 'oneymooners, the Mullinaxes, in No. 3... The Finnegans, in No. 2. They came as man and wife, but from what I've learned lately, they aren't. If the police 'adn't insisted on Finnegan stayin' on, he'd 'ave been out on 'is neck. This is a decent 'ouse. No carryin's-on 'ere. As soon as you chaps give the word about Finnegan... *out*.'

Mr Trimble made a chucking-out gesture.

'Number One's occupied by a regular customer. Our best room. Mrs Nessle. Widow of a foreign gentleman, who comes every year for a month or so. Rollin' in money.'

Trimble's eyes grew greedy as he imagined a sort of Ali Baba's treasure-house owned by his favourite lodger.

'The rest... Room 4. The big one. Occupied by the Greenhalghs. Father, mother and three children. Double bed and two cots. Best we can do. He's a bookie, I think. Makes a good thing out of it. Out most of the day boozin' with his pals while his missus looks after the kids. Little 'orrers, Mrs Nessle calls 'em. But busi-ness is business to us in the season.'

Littlejohn caught the Archdeacon's eye which was twinkling. They both seemed to be imagining the same thing. Sixteen people, plus Trimble and his three women. All in *Sea Vista*, packed like sardines, breathing, fighting, scheming for the bathrooms, scrambling for food, joking, frisking, quarrelling, lamenting, gossiping, slandering. And then, packing-up and off, leaving their litter and their ghosts behind to haunt the empty winter house when the season was over. Only Uncle Fred had stayed on with the Trimbles.

They went downstairs again. The musician was still playing the lament about the blue-grass country. It was the top hit of the season. Everybody whistling or humming it, dance-bands playing it. A guitar accompaniment from a recent film... The air had been ringing in Uncle Fred's ears as he died.

As they passed No. 3, a head was thrust out. The honeymooner. A man in his mid-forties with a cunning sallow face, big ears, thick lips, and thin greying hair plastered back from his narrow forehead. He wore heavy horn-rimmed glasses.

'Sorry, Mr Trimble... I wanted to see you, but it'll do when you're not engaged... ' The door gently closed.

'As I thought. He's goin' to say they're off, and try to get away without payin' for the whole time they booked the room. Some 'opes!'

Down below an argument was going on. A man's rough voice, and then a woman's.

'No need to spoil everybody's pleasure because the old chap's dead. We all come to it.'

'Don't you argue with me. I've said he's not stayin' for dinner, and I mean it. We've enough of your family to look after without you bringing in strangers as well.'

Trimble could hardly get down fast enough.

''ere, 'ere. Wot's all this?'

A tallish, swarthy, pudding-faced man, half-drunk already, with another who looked like a pal, smiling awkwardly and trying to persuade his friend to let it drop and take him away.

The woman was annoyed and her anger enhanced her good looks. She was tall, plump, and blonde, and had all the poise and sophistication of a superannuated actress. She was between forty and fifty, looked after herself well, and was dressed in a skirt and a jumper of a daring cut which showed her fine arms and as much of her bosom as decency would allow... and perhaps a little more.

Her antagonist was Greenhalgh, father of the children, and he was wanting his friend to stay to lunch. The woman was winning hands down. Greenhalgh couldn't keep his eyes away from her arms, her figure, and the centre of gravity where the jumper ended and the white flesh began. It put him quite out of countenance.

'Oh, all right, then. But it's a poor sort of treatment for a holiday, Mrs Trimble.'

So this was Trimble's missus. Littlejohn instinctively looked at two framed old portraits, one above the other, to the right of the cluttered-up bamboo hall-stand. One showed Mrs Trimble in tights, presumably as principal boy in a pantomime; the other, Trimble himself, handsome then, in tights as well, standing at the foot of a trapeze. He'd been an acrobat!

It was all there in black and white. The handsome acrobat and the principal boy. Retired and in the boarding-house business, perhaps at first prosperous through taking in stage friends and followers. Trimble hoping for an easy life, whilst his wife did the work. Instead, she'd turned the tables. He did the work and she managed the place and strolled along the promenade when the fit took her. He'd gone to seed, and she'd kept up appearances in spite of it. Now, she despised him. It was obvious from the way she looked at him when he descended on the quarrel. She ignored him until she'd settled Greenhalgh. Then...

'What about the dinner? What do you think *you're* doing?'

'The police called again. This is a Superintendent.'

'Is the parson the police, as well?'

Then she caught the Archdeacon's eye.

'I'm sorry, sir. Don't mind me. I'm just in a bad mood. High season, a lodger murdered, everything upset, and that Greenhalgh chap wants to bring a half-drunken friend of his in for dinner. I won't have it. We've enough on as it is.'

In spite of the weather, she looked cool and well made-up. She had obviously been out to the shops and carried a large straw bag with parcels in it and two library books showing on the top.

'Have you any news about Mr Snook, sir? I hope it's soon settled. We're booked up for another month and with this happening, well, it doesn't do us any good. If our clients knew, they'd give back-word, cancel the rooms, I'm sure. People don't want mixing up in this sort of thing on holidays.'

'I quite agree, Mrs Trimble. I'm only on this job unofficially, but the case is in good hands and they'll be most discreet and considerate, I know.'

'It'll get in all the papers. That's what's worrying me. I expect reporters along any minute.'

'You'll know how to deal with them, I'm sure.'

'You bet.'

She was putting it on a bit. Adapting herself to the company, a Superintendent of police and a nice old gentleman who looked like a bishop. She wondered what the bishop was doing there at all. Perhaps, like the men she read about in books, he was a famous amateur detective who tagged along with a professional and solved the crime when the police were stumped.

Littlejohn smiled to himself. She had perhaps been the same with Uncle Fred, the man a cut above the average. She could deal with the Greenhalghs and the Trimbles adequately in their own vulgar idiom. Strutting and striding like a principal boy, she'd have them off the stage in no time, like a pair of wicked uncles or the traditional broker's-men. But for others she thought to be 'class', like Mrs Nessle, the Archdeacon, Littlejohn, and maybe Uncle Fred, she'd turn on the manner in which she used to address the fairy queen and the pantomime king.

'Is there anything I can do to help, sir?'

'I see you're busy with lunches just now.'

'Mr Trimble will look after it. If you want to know anything from me, just say the word. We'll go to our private room.'

She almost dragged them after her into a small cubby-hole, a kind of office with three chairs and a desk full of papers, between the lounge and the kitchen. It was stuffy and smelled of boiling vegetables.

She gave them chairs and sat down herself, crossed her legs, and made a display of sumptuous principal-boy calves, now a bit over-weight, in sleek nylons.

'May I offer you a drink or a cigarette?'

She spoke in a posh voice, very different from the one she used on the Greenhalghs of life. She nervously lit a cigarette, and inhaled deeply.

'No thanks, Mrs Trimble. We won't keep you long.'

''That's all right, sir. What did you say your name was?'

'Littlejohn. Superintendent Littlejohn. This is Archdeacon Kinrade.'

Her large blue eyes opened wider.

'Well! Not *the* Superintendent Littlejohn? I've read about you in the papers. They've been quick *and* lucky getting you over from London, sir.'

'I'm on holiday. I'm just helping the local police unofficially.'

Her voice was even more posh.

'I see. This is a pleasure, and an honour, I'm sure. And the Archdeacon too. I've heard of you, sir, as well. Well... I can't get over it. To think that...'

'Did you bring in some pepper? We've got none.'

Trimble's head appeared round the door. There were beads of sweat on his forehead. His wife gave him a killing look. Pepper at a time like this!

'Why didn't you tell me this was the famous Superintendent Littlejohn, and Archdeacon Kinrade, Ferdy?'

'I didn't know. I never asked their names. We got busy as soon as they arrived here. We're honoured, I'm sure. Pleased to meet you both.'

He looked completely put out and didn't know what to say, which was something new for him.

'Well! The pepper's in my basket in a paper bag. I won't be long. You'd better get on with seeing to the serving. They'll be in shouting for their dinner any minute.'

She said it with contempt, as though anxious to suggest to the present company that the whole set-up wasn't much in her line, but that Trimble had somehow deceived her into taking it on.

'As soon as ever we can, we're getting out of this. I'm fed up with the whole business. I beg your pardon.'

She returned to the courtesies of the pantomime royal court.

'Ask me anything you like.'

It was a job to know what to say. Littlejohn hesitated.

'I've always been interested in crime. I read a lot of thrillers in bed after we've shut up for the night. It relaxes me. Funny thing, too. I've said to myself quite often, when I've come across some ham-handed detective in a book, "Littlejohn would have solved this in no time". Are you sure you'll not take something to drink, gentlemen?'

'No, thanks. We must be going.'

'You must excuse the way we're upset here. My husband in his shirt-sleeves and not shaved. We're very busy. But from what I can gather from reading about you, Superintendent, you won't mind. You seem to put everybody at their ease.'

Trimble had left the door open about an inch and a blast of fried potatoes entered. Along the corridor they could hear the tramp, tramp of lodgers entering the dining-room.

'Who do you think murdered Uncle Fred? You'll excuse the name; he liked it and wanted everybody to be friendly and call him by it. Such a nice gentleman... It's a damned shame. You'll excuse me, reverend, but it makes me wild to think of such an innocent and harmless old man coming to such an awful end.'

The front door slammed and they could hear the voices of a group of youths joking and shouting. Presumably the three room-mates of the accordion player. One of them was whistling. *I left my heart in the blue-grass country*. It was becoming Uncle Fred's theme song.

'As far as you knew, Mr Snook had no enemies?'

The large eyes opened wide again.

'Who? Him? Why no. A nicer man you couldn't have wished to meet.'

'And no friends?'

'Well... if you mean pals, men he went about or had a drink with, no. He was the solitary sort. Regular as clockwork, he'd take his morning stroll round the town and down to the same spot on the promenade. Down for breakfast at half past eight. Out at half past nine; back again at just after twelve. Then another stroll after dinner. He liked a snooze before tea, and after, he'd often go to the pictures. He was fond of them. We have high tea here at five-thirty and then a drink and biscuits or such for supper when the people come in for the night. He was regular for meals and never gave any trouble.'

'Did he get any letters?'

'Never.'

'Completely solitary.'

'Absolutely.'

She was astonishingly fresh and what some would call appetising for her age. Intelligent, too. She had a quick straight answer for everything.

'How long has he been coming here?'

'He arrived in the autumn, five years last November. He walked in, asked for a room, paid in advance, and settled down. Now and then, he's gone away for a few days. Never more than a week. We didn't know where he went and he never told us. I don't know whether he crossed to England or not. If we tried to pump him about his trip, he evaded it and shut up like an oyster. So we didn't press it.'

The door again. This time the children and their mother.

Shouting, whimpering, quarrelling still, and then all hustled upstairs.

'So you know nothing about him, except that he lived here most of the time. Nothing about his family or where he came from?'

'Not a thing. A complete mystery. But his company and his money were good. So who were we to bother him with our curiosity?'

'You've nothing else to tell me, then? Was he ever ill or did he ever get drunk? Anything like that?'

'He enjoyed very good health. I think his liver bothered him a bit now and then. He used to doctor himself with pills. I've seen them about his room, but he never said anything about being off colour. I never saw him drunk, although he liked his glass of beer with anybody.'

And that was that. Just a blank.

They followed Mrs Trimble to the front door and she told them to call again if they wanted anything. The delicate lady, Miss Arrowbrook, was coming in as they left. She wore a set, self-pitying look, and was dressed in a serge frock and carried an umbrella. Her eyes were ringed in dark shadows and she looked down at the floor as she passed them.

They hadn't seen the staff, the two girls Trimble had mentioned. Littlejohn had briefly noticed the young maid who looked like an orphan of the storm, laying out the table-napkins. Now, as they stood in the vestibule, the other one appeared, carrying a pile of hot plates into the dining-room. This was no waif! She looked like an Italian. Tall, with an easy languid stride, full of energy, conscious of her attractiveness. Dark and fine-featured, with an ample figure – almost too ample.

'Italian?' asked the Archdeacon.

'Yes. Her name's Maria. She's been here six weeks and as soon as the season finishes, she finishes, too. If it hadn't been so hard to get staff, I'd have shown her the door long since. As it is, we have to make the best of it. She's too familiar and sexy. I have to keep her in her place.'

Mrs Trimble looked very capable of doing that. She was venomous about Maria and Littlejohn wondered why, if relations between them were so poor, Mrs Trimble didn't give the girl the sack and get on with some work herself. She seemed to have plenty of time on her hands.

Maria returned from the dining-room empty-handed and quickly glanced at the group in the vestibule. She looked to have been weeping. Her eyes were red-rimmed and her classic face the colour of old ivory.

They said good-bye and promised to return if necessary. Littlejohn almost gulped the fresh sea air outside. Most houses have their own characteristic smell, and a little of the sensual, stuffy *Sea Vista* went a long way!

At the police-station, where they called to report to Knell again, they found him waiting excitedly for them. He handed Littlejohn a telegram. It was dated from London that morning, at 9.30.

CAN IDENTIFY DECEASED PHOTOGRAPH IN DAILY CRY. NAME FREDERICK BOYCOTT. MY FORMER HUSBAND. CROSSING AFTERNOON PLANE. MARTHA BOYCOTT.

First Snook, then Boycott! Uncle Fred had certainly been an unusual type. And, judging by appearances, he'd probably had a sense of humour, too.

4
THE ARRIVAL OF MARTHA BOYCOTT

Knell was right. It *was* a funny case. And the victim was even funnier. Uncle Fred to begin with. Then, Fred Snook. And now, Fred Boycott. Ridiculous! It looked as if Uncle Fred had assumed the names to suit his sense of humour. Now, some woman or other was on the way to claim him as her husband. Littlejohn wondered what she'd look like. He could hardly wait.

'You'll be passing the airport on your way home to Grenaby, sir. Will you both call with me to meet Mrs Boycott there? We can have a talk with her at the airport police-post. You needn't come back to Douglas.'

So now they were on their way to Ronaldsway, an airport which Littlejohn liked immensely. You could see and hear all that was going on, it was cosy and compact, and everybody there was polite and friendly. They took the same route back; Santon, the Fairy Bridge, Ballasalla... They all raised their hats to the fairies again.

'Good afternoon, little people.'

'I hate to spoil the fun,' said the Archdeacon, 'but you are now really raising your hats as you cross the bridge into ancient monastery lands. The fairy bridge spans the stream which defines the demesne of old Rushen Abbey and the pious used to bare their heads in respect whenever they entered. It's much more romantic, however, to think you're saluting the little people.'

Knell grunted. Abbey lands or not, he was sticking to the fairies. He wanted all the help he could get in the case of Uncle Fred and a bit of the supernatural wouldn't come amiss.

Littlejohn didn't care which it was. He felt half asleep. The rhythm of the police-car, the strong air, and the days of celebrations in Dublin... He sat with his eyes half closed. He imagined Uncle Fred and his routine on just such another warm, languid day as this. Regular as clockwork, but *Traa dy Liooar,* time enough, of course. Up on the dot in the morning, pottering round in his old bedroom slippers which he kept in the tumbledown wardrobe. Easy enough in winter, of course, but in summer when the holiday crowds invaded the place, they moved him up to the second floor and he had to struggle for the bathroom and eat his meals with a flock of noisy, boisterous bores at the long table in the dining-room of *Sea Vista*. Then, off for his stroll on the prom, back for lunch, out again, a little snooze, tea, the pictures, and now and then, he'd vanish and come back smelling of drink and with money to spare.

Someone in Eire last week had told Littlejohn that if he stayed there much longer, he'd find he never wanted to return to England. The charm of the atmosphere seeped into you, sapped all your powers of resistance, and you just settled down without a care in the world, like a glorified beachcomber. A new sense of proportion, fresh standards of values and of what mattered and what didn't, a new start in life. Things just didn't matter.

Perhaps Uncle Fred had been like that, and the Isle of Man had cast upon him the same potent spells they said were abroad in Ireland. Littlejohn admitted to himself he felt it at Grenaby – reputed to be 'queer', it was true – after he'd been there a few days.

If it weren't for Letty and the dog at home and the accrued pension rights which the Home Office owed him, he might find himself settled for ever there, like Uncle Fred was in Douglas. Just dreaming the hours away, lotus-eating without a care in the world. There was such another chap living near the parsonage at Grenaby. Joe Henn. Littlejohn had watched him wandering bemused round his rambling garden, with his trousers and coat drawn over his nightshirt.

'What do you think of it, sir?'

'Eh?'

'The death of... of...'

'Call him Uncle Fred, Knell... It was murder, of course...'

A chuckle from the back seat, but when Littlejohn turned, his old friend's eyes were closed. Then, one opened, regarded him searchingly, and closed again. He felt the Archdeacon had read his thoughts and thoroughly understood them.

Littlejohn feared they were on the brink of another anticlimax. He somehow resented the intrusion of Martha Boycott, who even now was in mid-air like an old witch on a besom, flying over to claim Uncle Fred. Coming to disturb his rest. Alive, Uncle Fred mustn't have wanted her. Perhaps he'd fled from her for a bit of peace and changed his name to make sure. What good would he be to her dead?

They were at the airport. The forecourt was full of spectators and visitors arriving from the Manchester and Belfast planes. Airport buses filling up, people meeting one another, loud-speakers controlling passengers with refined politeness. The London flight was due in fifteen minutes. Knell's little party attracted a lot of attention. The police-car, an aged person in gaiters, and two obvious police officers with him. Surely, not a clerical confidence-trickster? The sergeant-in-charge at the airport saluted briskly and made, in addition, a little obeisance to the Archdeacon. The crowd seemed relieved, but couldn't make out what was going on.

'Move on, there.'

The loudspeaker was getting fed up with waiting for people to do as they were told instead of pottering around Knell's procession, and tersely ordered all who were going to Douglas to claim their luggage and get in the waiting bus forthwith.

The constable shepherded them all off and took Mrs Boycott's reception committee to the police office. The sergeant had cups of tea waiting for them. A nice, polite chap with whom the Archdeacon was very cordial because he'd christened him forty years ago, married him ten years since, and was now watching other parsons baptizing his growing family.

When they emerged again to meet the London plane, the crowds knew all about them. The grapevine had been at work.

'It's the famous Littlejohn from Scotland Yard on the case of the carnival murder yesterday. Somebody stabbed an old chap called Snook in the back in the crowd.'

Three small boys approached with autograph albums.

'Can we have a statement, sir?'

Reporters now.

'Nothing to say yet,' replied Knell, who was up early next morning, however, to see what they'd put in the papers.

> Superintendent Littlejohn, who is staying on a brief holiday with his friend the Archdeacon of Man, at Grenaby, is assisting Inspector Knell, in charge of the case, and with whom he has collaborated several times in the past. There is, so far, no official report, but Inspector Knell is following up several lines of inquiry which he is sure will be fruitful. Photograph on back page.

A photograph of Knell, Littlejohn, and the Archdeacon, with one of the airport constables grinning over Knell's shoulder as though there were something comic about the whole set-up! It gave Knell quite a jolt. He'd reprimand McJoughin for this. All the same, it wasn't so bad. He ate a huge breakfast after it.

They watched the passengers from the London plane gingerly descending the ladder. Littlejohn mopped his forehead. What weather! The flags over the airport hung lifeless and everybody seemed to move slowly about in a haze of heat. A middle-aged woman, heavy, medium-built and self-important, detached herself from the stream of arrivals and made for the policeman who was watching them as though looking for smugglers or secret agents.

'Take me to the Chief of Police at once. Is he here?'

She must have expected a top-ranking reception in reply to her telegram.

The bobby couldn't hear a word owing to the roar of an outgoing plane to Blackpool.

'I'm Mrs Boycott. I'm expected.'

'You must be the one Inspector Knell...'

They were still shouting and bawling at one another when Knell intervened.

'Mrs Boycott? I'm Inspector Knell.'

She eyed him up and down as though questioning his credentials or thinking him an hotel tout. She wondered if he were high-ranking enough to deal with her affairs.

Mrs Boycott was well dressed in a dark blue thin serge costume and a little hat like an inverted bucket, with a half veil over her eyes. She struggled to push back the veil to get a better view of Knell. She wore a lot of jewellery – rings, ear-clips, a gold chain round her neck. A heavy coat of make-up, too, which did not, however, conceal her age. She was a bit raddled, with tired lines round her eyes and a hanging dewlap under her double chin.

'This way, madam.'

'What about my luggage?'

The porters were unloading bags and boxes and putting them on a trolley. She indicated two large expensive hide pieces; a travelling wardrobe and a large suitcase.

'Those are mine. The charge for excess luggage was disgusting. I shall complain.'

She looked, judging by her luggage, to have come for a month or more. She followed Knell to the door, where he introduced her to Littlejohn and the Archdeacon.

'The famous Superintendent Littlejohn? Indeed!'

She bucked up considerably, began to preen herself, and started to boss the porters about.

'Just leave those two bags there, my man.'

She tapped Knell on the arm.

'Are you the Superintendent's secretary? Kindly see my bags to a taxi... Or perhaps you've brought a private conveyance?'

Knell pretended he hadn't heard. Secretary, indeed! He looked round to see if anybody else had overheard it. No? Good! He motioned to P.C. McJoughin to take and load the bags in the police-car. He'd teach him to hang around looking as if the whole affair were a joke!

Mrs Boycott didn't quite know what to make of the Venerable Archdeacon. Was he there to add dignity to the reception, or to offer her the consolations of religion in connection with the loss of her husband?

'I'm Mrs Boycott, the widow of the dead man.'

She fished in her expensive leather handbag, turned over purses, wallets, cosmetics, bottles, and pieces of paper, and finally held aloft the cutting from the *Daily Cry*. She pointed to the picture of Uncle Fred, who looked annoyed.

'That is my late husband. I believe, according to what the paper said, he was known by the ridiculous name of Uncle Fred. His real name was Frederick Mandeville Boycott.'

Littlejohn felt he wanted to laugh outright. He had grown fond of Uncle Fred and everything about him. His many names, Snook, Mandeville, Boycott, all seemed to have a comic twist about them, an eccentric touch of humour, as though Uncle Fred were still laughing at everybody.

'He was registered at his hotel in the name of Fred Snook!'

'What!'

She almost wept with annoyance and Littlejohn took her by the arm and led her into the small police office. On the way she talked in a voice almost incoherent with rage.

'It was his idea of a joke trying to humiliate his family. His photograph in the papers was bad enough. An old hat and looking like a tramp. And then to call himself Snook, and Uncle Fred, like some vulgar, familiar old reprobate. It's intolerable... '

The crowds in the airport watched their every move, as though some international criminal were being seized and put through a third-degree. There wasn't room for everybody in the party in the police-post, so they had to take over the newly-painted customs-shed, which was empty for half an hour pending the arrival of the next plane from Dublin.

'Now, Mrs Boycott... '

Knell rubbed his hands and waved her to a chair. Then the rest sat down, too.

'I'm Mrs Frederick Mandeville Boycott.'

She said it again. She spoke with a faint Irish accent. Knell nodded to show her he knew her name already.

'We were surprised when we heard from you. The dead man's name was, according to our records, Fred Snook.'

Mrs Boycott looked to be coming up for air after long immersion. Eyes popping, gasping and making gurgling noises in her throat. She looked at Littlejohn and the Archdeacon as though beseeching them to silence this underling who kept rubbing in the indignity.

'Snook! Nonsense! I ought to know. I was his wife.'

'Are you sure you've got the right man? After all, it was only a newspaper picture.'

Knell almost begged her to change her mind. She dived in the handbag again, produced Uncle Fred's photograph, and waved it about.

'Of course it's the right man! I'd know him anywhere. I've not seen him for ten years, but I'd know him. Besides, I want to see the body. I'll identify him. He has marks on his back which I shall recognize. He fell from his horse heavily one day in the hunting field and got severely torn on some barbed wire. He used to say in his silly way – he had a perverted sense of humour – that he looked like an ex-convict who'd had the cat-o'-nine-tails.'

She had a way of taking a deep breath and talking on and on until it gave out. It was like watching a pair of bellows expand and contract to see her breathing.

Littlejohn smiled gently as he smoked his pipe. Uncle Fred! A huntin' man, now. What next?

'He disappeared ten years ago. Just walked out one day and left me. I've often been tempted to get a divorce for desertion, but there were complications... His estate and our daughter. He left a letter saying he was going away for good and I could keep all he left behind.'

Knell was quite out of his depth. The vagaries and infamy of Uncle Fred were too much for him. He gave Littlejohn a weary look and shrugged his shoulders. Over to you, he seemed to suggest.

'Where did all this happen, Mrs Boycott?'

She actually smiled back. Here was a man who understood all she'd suffered.

'It was in Sussex, not far from Horsham. He had an estate there. He and his late father were members of a large firm of mining engineers.'

And Uncle Fred had, when he died, been busy with investments worth £257, and showing an all-round capital profit of £11! Well, well...

'It was monstrous the way he left me. I've spent a fortune in trying to trace him, to say nothing of lawyers' fees. The courts declined to allow me to assume he was dead. It seemed as if, not content with leaving me, he wanted to make my life a hell on earth as well. Just as my lawyers looked like establishing death, he sent me a vulgar postcard... a horrible thing. "There's life in the old dog, yet. Kind regards."'

Littlejohn turned to watch an outgoing plane just to hide his smile. Then...

'Was your late husband a wealthy man?'

Mrs Boycott pulled herself together and spoke proudly.

'He left about a quarter of a million pounds behind. He must have been mad! I always said he was highly eccentric before he ran away.'

'And after you have identified him?'

'We can assume death. It will, at least, put an end to the interminable litigation and help me settle up the estate.'

She paused, wiped her lips carefully, applied more lipstick, and turned and gave Littlejohn a cunning look.

'Has anyone else arrived to enquire or claim the body?'

'Not so far as we know. Should there be someone else?'

She hesitated.

'There were rumours that my husband had been seen with another woman just before he vanished. I didn't believe a word of it. He always seemed happy with me. You see, I am telling you all this unpleasant past history quite frankly in the hope that you will understand my difficulties, the shocking way he treated us, and give me all the help you can in the matter. I never believed the rumours about his infidelity.'

Of course she did! You could see it in her every gesture. She hated Uncle Fred for running off with another woman in preference to her, but she was going to have all the pickings in spite of her hatred.

'I was his wife and have first claim, although Victoria will, I'm sure, be putting forward her own views.'

'Victoria?'

'My daughter. She married and went to live in Hampshire. We don't see much of each other. She always seemed to be on her father's side. He spoiled her. If she arrives here, her name is Rudd.

I disliked her husband intensely. If you meet him, you will know why. A vulgar man. She will probably use the ridiculous nickname her father called her. He objected to Victoria. He called her Queenie, and she was known as such to all her friends. My husband delighted in thwarting me whenever he could.'

She paused for breath, like an organ when the blower stops.

'Where did my late husband live?'

'In a boarding-house in Douglas.'

She looked blankly around as though living in a nightmare.

'Snook! Boarding-house... I was right. I knew it! He went mad. That was why he left home. He had aberrations and loss of memory. He had forgotten who he was.'

'From what we can gather about him, he was quite normal. Are you sure you've got the right man?'

'Of course I am. Please don't ask that stupid question again. This is the picture of my late husband. Frederick Mandeville Boycott.'

There was nothing else for it. They'd have to take her to see the body and settle it.

'Perhaps you'll kindly take Mrs Boycott to identify her late husband's remains, Knell. You can let me know developments over the telephone. I'll be at Grenaby.'

The party broke up. Knell looked reproachful as he drove away with his haughty passenger. Mrs Boycott wasn't his cup of tea at all and he'd rather have left her entirely to Littlejohn. Her and her jingling bangles, her rings, her uppish ways, the smell of expensive scent which surrounded her... And the way she looked down her nose at the neat little police-car as though she usually rode about in a Rolls Royce. It put Knell out of countenance.

Littlejohn and the Archdeacon climbed the staircase to the balcony which gave a splendid view of the runways and all that came and went at the airport.

'Shall I order tea, parson?'

The Venerable Archdeacon lowered himself slowly into a basket armchair.

'Ever since I was a child, I've loved ice-cream. It was known as hokey-pokey, then. I think I would like the largest ice-cream you can buy. I've a sweet tooth and, at my age, I believe in humouring it.'

Littlejohn returned with two large ice-creams and they sat there, like two schoolboys on holiday, enjoying themselves and watching the planes come in, and then watching them all go out. In the foreground, the control-tower, then the green turf and the runways seeming to go right out to sea. Langness and Fort Island in the distance, with the old fort and the ruined oratory where the murdered priest was supposed to wring his hands and moan after dark. Beyond, the blue water, calm as a duckpond, with little boats and white sails close in and the smoke of passing great ships on the far horizon...

The holiday feeling again! The torpor of relaxation fell upon Littlejohn. His eyes closed... More than an hour later the airport policeman gently shook him awake. The Archdeacon was still asleep.

'Inspector Knell would like you on the office phone, sir.'

Knell had first taken Mrs Boycott to the mortuary. On the way there from the airport, they had made very heavy weather together and hardly a word was spoken. She'd seemed to regard herself as a V.I.P. and Knell as a very subordinate person. Whenever he had tried to open a conversation, she'd showed she didn't want to talk.

'You'll excuse me, but I'm tired with the journey and all the delayed shock of this frightful affair. I wish to rest.'

And she closed her eyes. Once or twice she spoke as if to herself.

'I'm sure it's Boycott. I'm sure... And to think of him hidden away on this island and my knowing nothing of it. The money I've spent on tracing him and his living here as Fred... Fred Snook. Ah!'

Then at the morgue. There was no fuss. She was as hard as nails there. They showed her the body. She was quite unmoved.

'Yes. I'm sure it's Boycott. Please let me see his back.'

It didn't seem decent, but the attendant gently moved Uncle Fred so that his back was visible. Yes; there they were. The marks Uncle Fred said made him look like a criminal who'd had the 'cat'.

'You're sure it's him?'

'Of course. I'm prepared to swear it. Older, more fleshy, but I'd know him anywhere.'

They took her back into the open-air.

'Would you like a cup of tea, madam?'

Knell was trying to be decent about it.

'Why? I've seen worse things, my man. I was a V.A.D. officer in the war. Let us get this business over first. Then you'd better find me a good hotel and I'll have a meal there.'

'You'll be lucky if you get in anywhere. This is the high season and they're all full up.'

'Even the best hotels?'

'Even those.'

She softened and smiled with difficulty.

'Surely. For the police... and in my present circumstances, my distressing duty, they would stretch a point. You or that nice Superintendent Littlejohn could *order* them to accommodate me. Which is the best hotel?'

'Fort Anne.'

'Please telephone them then.'

Knell was thoroughly nettled. He objected to being pushed around. In any event, he knew now why Uncle Fred had run away. A lifetime of Mrs Martha Boycott was enough to drive anybody off...

'Meanwhile, I would like to be taken to my late husband's hotel.'

Hotel! That was a good one! Wait till she saw *Sea Vista*. Knell felt a wave of satisfaction surge through him. He gave instructions to a constable about booking a room for Mrs Boycott and hoped the hotels were all full up.

'I'll drive you to *Sea Vista*, madam.'

'*Sea Vista*? Whatever's that?'

'The boarding-house where Mr Snook... ahem... Mr Boycott lodged.'

'Incredible!'

She said it again, too, when they pulled up at the boarding house, and again when Mr Trimble, still in his shirt-sleeves, opened the door to them.

All the boarders were at home eating high tea. A room full, with the orphan of the storm and the Italian maid running in and out with cups of tea and plates of bread and cakes. The Greenhalgh children were in full blast. Mrs Boycott and Mrs Nessle, the star boarder, met face to face on the stairs. They both looked alike, powdered up to the eyes and decked-out in finery. They might have been sisters, and eyed one another scornfully up and down. Mrs Nessle thought Mrs Boycott was a new arrival, nay, a competitor for the best room, opened a pair of lorgnettes, and examined her rival through them. To keep up the spirits of his fellow-lodgers, the accordionist, now second-prize winner in the personality competition, was giving them a tune and they were singing the chorus through mouthfuls of bread and butter and ham.

I left my heart
In the blue-grass country,
Where my buddy
Stole my baby
From me.

Maria, the Italian, thrusting her voluptuous bosom well before her, cannoned into Mrs Boycott with a pile of empty plates.

'Incredible!'

Trimble thought that now was the time to offer condolences.

'I 'ear you're Uncle Fred's missus. Please accept the sympathy of all of us. We're collectin' for a wreath. I shall miss 'im. We were pals. We used to go fishin' together sometimes.'

'Indeed! Incredible!'

Mrs Trimble thought it better to take over.

'Follow me.'

She was speaking posh, but eyed Mrs Boycott aggressively. Now and then, she smiled slightly as though thinking of Uncle Fred and what a missus he'd chosen for himself.

Mrs Boycott had started her tour of the house by disdainfully eyeing the interior. Mrs Trimble was ready to tell her off and ask her who she thought she was, if she got the slightest chance.

Once in her husband's room, Mrs Boycott started to take more interest. She looked disgusted at his choice of surroundings and his taste in companionship, but she remembered, too, that she was there on business.

'I suppose he had private papers somewhere.'

She made for the chest of drawers, but Mrs Trimble was there first.

'The police said nothing's to be touched.'

'The police?'

'Are you aware that Mr Snook was murdered.'

'Mr Boycott, *if you please*.'

'He was Uncle Fred or Mr Snook to all of us here, and that's what he'll always remain.'

Mrs Trimble's eyes flashed in her best principal-boy manner, the way she'd faced the wicked fairy long ago.

Mrs Boycott hesitated. Knell was sure she was after the spare cash and any will Uncle Fred might have left behind. She drew herself together.

'I find it impossible to deal with such incredible people. I would like to see Superintendent Littlejohn again. He will understand. Take me to him, at once.'

Mrs Trimble wasn't going to let that pass.

'I wouldn't have thought the Superintendent was your sort or on your wavelength at all. He's a gentleman, is the Superintendent.'

Knell jumped in to prevent the opening of hostilities in earnest.

'He's finished for the day. He's off duty.'

'Very well. Please inform him and ask him to arrange with this person...'

Mrs Trimble's opulent and half-naked bosom heaved with rage.

'Let me tell you...'

Knell, who in the course of duty would deal intrepidly with the huskiest and hardest malefactors, was scared.

'I think we'd better be off.'

He winked at Mrs Trimble, who winked back, and tapped her temple to show she understood what he was getting at. Mrs Boycott was barmy. That explained it all. She could never be Uncle Fred's missus! Just another crackpot of the kind who always turned up whenever there was crime and publicity. The next thing, Mrs Boycott would be confessing she'd stabbed Uncle Fred herself!

She saw them to the door and closed it emphatically behind them. From the windows, the lodgers watched them go; some of them were grinning.

On the step by the gate stood a woman. She was looking at *Sea Vista* from top to bottom as though expecting a window to open and someone to hail her. An elderly woman dressed in her best black. Obviously not a holidaymaker; more like a native from somewhere in the country. Small, with a thin apple-cheeked face, a modest almost frightened look. White hair and honest blue eyes and the rather bent jaded frame of one who has worked hard all her life. She was clutching a black, imitation leather handbag.

She was nervous; a simple type who didn't wish to intrude, but she had come for a set purpose and was determined to see it through.

'Excuse me.'

She spoke to Knell, who, in his usual kindly way, stopped to answer her. Mrs Boycott swept past without a look. She thought the woman was going to start a pitiful tale and ask for alms.

'Excuse me.'

The newcomer opened her bag and took out the now familiar newspaper cutting. She pointed at Uncle Fred's picture with a small forefinger which might have belonged to a child.

'Could you tell me...? The paper said he died yesterday...'

'That's right. Did you know him?'

'Yes. You see...'

She paused.

'You ought to go to the police-station. That's what it said in the paper, didn't it?'

'Yes. I knew he lived here, though. I was a bit scared of goin' to the police. I've never been to the police-station in Douglas before. I thought I'd inquire here first, just to make sure.'

'Well, I'm a police Inspector, so you can tell me.'

'You're Manx, aren't you?'

'Yes.'

'I thought you were.'

She seemed happy again, confident in one of her own people.

'Well, I just called to say that I knew him. The paper said anybody who knew him was to tell the police. My husband's been bedfast for nearly twelve months and couldn't come, but he said I ought to do it. It said in the paper, the Douglas police, else I'd have gone to the Port St Mary police.'

'And you've come all this way?'

'It said Douglas.'

'It's very good of you, Mrs...'

'Mrs Costain. My husband used to be a boatman till he had his illness. I must get back home, too. He'll want me. I can't leave him for long.'

'Did you know Mr Snook, then? Or did he call himself Boycott?'

'No. I never knew him as that. Fred Snowball we always knew him as. That was the name he used on his private papers.'

Knell raised his hat and scratched his head. This was getting quite out of hand. Snowball now!

'Look here, Mrs Costain. I'll take you with me to the police-station in the car. I've got to drop off the lady you see sitting in it. Then I'll run you down to where you live. Where is it? Port St Mary? Come on... '

Mrs Boycott looked down her nose again at the modest intruder.

'Who is this person?'

She whispered it to Knell loud enough for all to hear.

'A friend of mine,' said Knell, and then he boiled over. 'And I'll ask you to be civil about her.'

'Incredible!' said Mrs Boycott to some invisible person.

'Thank God!' said Knell when, at the police-station, he learned that Fort Anne could take Mrs Boycott. 'Take her in the spare car. I'm going to see Superintendent Littlejohn again. Get him for me on the phone at Grenaby parsonage.'

Eventually they traced Littlejohn to the airport.

'What's he been doin' there all this time?' said Knell as he took over the instrument.

'I badly want to see you again, sir. Can I call and pick you up where you are? I'm bringing another witness. This time a fisherman's wife from Port St Mary. Decent Manx, she is. No... Oh, no. I don't know how she's connected with him, but she doesn't know him as Uncle Fred... or Mr Snook... or Mr Boycott... No... Fred Snowball... '

The answer was a roar of laughter.

'What did you say, sir? Oh... Good old Uncle Fred... I see...'

Knell's face was a study as he put down the telephone. Was he, Knell, going off his chump, or was everybody else going mad?

'Is it all right?' asked the patient homely woman waiting for him.

'I suppose so,' he sighed. 'Yes, I suppose so...'

5

THE INVALID OF CREGNEISH

At the airport, the strain left Mrs Costain's face as soon as she saw the Archdeacon.

'Aw; Master Kinrade, I'm glad to be puttin' a sight on ye. I've been that bothered gettin' mixed up with the police, and all.'

'What's the matter, Mary?'

The Venerable Archdeacon was on Christian-name terms with most of the local people. In his long life, he had been associated with them all in one way or another.

'Himself... my husband... said I'd better call and say the man... the photo in the paper... was a friend of ours called Fred Snowball. He'd often come and see us at Cregneish. My husband said I was to bring the police down. He took to his bed last winter and hasn't been about since. Mr Snowball often had business with my husband, and himself wanted to help them find who murdered him.'

'You yourself don't know anything?'

'I'd rather John told you. It's really no business of mine.'

The Archdeacon smiled.

'I'd better come with you,' he said to Littlejohn. 'Otherwise, you'll get nothing from a crowd of questions. It takes a Manxman to quiz a Manxman.'

They left the airport, skirted Castletown, and took the road which Littlejohn thought gave the loveliest view he'd ever seen in his life, in spite of the fact that once, a frightened man had tried to pot him with a rifle there. The sight of Carrick Bay from Fishers' Hill...

Evening was drawing on, the air remained hot and still. As the car turned the corner by the sea, the full view of the south of the Island came to meet them. The coast road, the Mull Hills and Peninsula, with Bradda Head and Barrule in the background, and in front, the vast stretch of blue water. They turned in at the Port St Mary road, climbed steadily up a broad highway, and entered Cregneish, the most southerly village of the Island, and the most characteristically Manx. It spread itself like an encampment in little clumps of clean whitewashed, thatched houses about its hill-side. A small church, a farmstead or two, clusters of cottages. Here, with the sea ahead, and the rough roads climbing the hills, farm fields running down to a magnificent rocky coast, horses and cattle grazing almost on the doorsteps and sheep looking over rough walls at passers-by, time might have stood still for centuries and left the little community untouched.

Dark, sturdy people, sprinkled liberally among the inhabitants, gave rise to a tale of an Armada galleon wrecked on Spanish Head. Only all the wrecks were accounted for long ago and there never was one at Cregneish!

Work had finished for the day. Groups of men stood gossiping at corners. Inside the cottages, shadows moved about or else sat immobile listening to the radio. Old people had brought their chairs outdoors and sat enjoying the last of the sunshine. A chara-banc full of trippers on an evening run passed by on its way to the Sound across which the Calf of Man lay peacefully remote.

The car just managed to squeeze to the front of an old thatched cottage, the green-painted door of which was open. Mrs

Costain led the way in. There was only one floor; two rooms and a small lean-to for a scullery, with a loft-room, reached by a ladder, between the ceiling and the thatch. Littlejohn could touch the rafters with his hand.

They went straight into the living-room, a cosy place packed with old-fashioned odds and ends and dominated by a broad hearth with a wide chimney and chimney corners, the *chiollag*. A large, sandy Manx cat, snoozing by the small fire, took no heed of them. Littlejohn bent to stroke it and it began to purr without even opening its eyes. Old cottage furniture, a grandfather clock, a chest, and a dresser full of old ornaments. A disused spinning-wheel in one corner. Really beautiful antique pieces, which would have made a dealer's mouth water.

At first, Littlejohn thought there was nobody in the clean little house. Then, momentarily, he became aware that someone was about, silent, holding his breath.

'Who's there?'

'It's me. I've brought the police.'

The inquiry came from the next room, entered from the living-room by a door on the right. Mrs Costain's reply caused a commotion. One after another, four Manxmen emerged, good honest workmen, including a fisherman, looked a bit sheepish, politely greeted everybody, and went out at the front door.

Every evening, John Costain's friends gathered round his bed for a gossip, a *li'l cooish*, and to retell the events of the day. It was like a club, and sometimes as many as eight or ten men would crush themselves in the small bedroom. One or another shaved the invalid every day and cut his hair when it needed it.

'Good everin', missus... Good everin', Master Kinrade... Good everin'...'

They greeted Mrs Costain first, then the parson, and then the other two. It was obvious they were a bit surprised at the arrival of the Archdeacon, whose presence would stamp the Costain house with respectable notoriety like a benediction for a long time to come. Knell and Littlejohn they silently scrutinized and summed up ready for a lot of talk and opinions about them in the days ahead. Already the eyes of all the village were focused on the cottage and tongues were starting to wag.

The bedroom was bright and cream-washed and completely dominated by a large bed covered by a colourful patchwork quilt, and with fittings and large knobs of brass. A chair with a rush bottom, a washstand, geraniums on the windowsill, and the flowers of a large fuchsia bush climbing in through the open window. Flowers all over the room, in fact. The invalid was fond of them and his friends never came without some. They stood in jam-jars on every available shelf.

John Costain was sitting up in bed looking as fit as a fiddle. A smooth, round pink face, with pale blue eyes, stiff grey hair with a bald furrow from his brow to the crown of his head, a firm broad chin, and a long inquisitive nose. His eyes twinkled with good humour and he had a look of plain untarnished integrity.

The winter before, on a stormy day, one of the occupants of the Calf of Man had signalled that a doctor was needed. The Sound race is a formidable current in calm weather, but Costain had offered to row the doctor over. The boat had been swamped on the way back, and Costain himself had needed the doctor since then. Like most fishermen, he couldn't swim, and the doctor had only just managed to hold him and drag him to safety. After that, he'd had him as a patient with rheumatic fever, and Costain had been in bed ever since. He would get up a little in the autumn.

A collie dog lay across his feet on the bed, barked as the party entered, turned round twice, and fell asleep.

'Good day to ye, Master Kinrade, and how are ye at all?'

His eyes fell on Littlejohn.

'Good day, sir. I've seen your photo in the paper today. You're the Superintendent from over... from London, sir?'

He seemed delighted to have more company, fresh people to talk to.

'Get them a drink o' tea, missus, an' some soda cakes.'

The newcomers didn't protest; they all knew it was part of the native courtesy and to refuse would be taken badly.

The room was full of smoke. In spite of the doctor's orders, Costain liked his tobacco and was already filling his short pipe with dark flake from a jar from which he first removed the piece of potato which kept the contents in good condition. He kept glancing at Littlejohn and nodding.

'Never thought I'd put a sight on ye in the flesh, Superintendent. I've read about you a lot in the papers. I read all the time... Crime tales and Wild West... Never thought I'd ever be a reader... Now...'

He indicated a pile of paper-backed crime and Western stories which filled a chair.

'Move that lot on the floor, Archdeacon, and sit ye down. The other two of ye can sit on the bed... We've no room here for another chair.'

They made themselves comfortable. Littlejohn glanced round the clean walls of the room. There wasn't much space available. Photographs everywhere. Wedding-groups, the fashions of which gave the dates without need for comment. A large one of Mr and Mrs Costain, a bit faded but in which they were plainly recognizable. She laced up in a ribboned wedding frock; he miserable in his best clothes, with a high starched collar and a bowler hat with a tall crown... Four framed pieces of embroidery done on canvas. One a sampler, with a little house and all the letters of the alphabet in red wool. The others, biblical texts or exhortations. *Worthy is the Lamb that was Slain... Rock of Ages Cleft for Me... Give us this Day our Daily Bread...* You got the impression, knowing the people who lived there, that they were more than ornaments for the walls.

Costain never asked any of them the purpose of their visit. He had taken a fancy to Littlejohn and set about getting to know all about him.

'How long have you been on the Islan', sir?'

And then how did he like it? how long he'd been a detective? did he like that? was he married? where did he live? did he like London?

Finally, to bring Knell in the picture...

'I suppose this young fellah's your sort of apprentice... learnin' the trade.'

The Archdeacon thought it time to intervene.

'You know, Littlejohn, you'll never learn anything about John Costain and he'll know all about *you*, if you go on this way. Get busy. Ask *him* some questions now. I can't promise you'll get any answers, because he's a Manxman and distrustful of inquisitive come-overs. When an invader arrived and asked where the nearest church was and then burned it down, or when he asked where the money or food was kept, and then carried them off, the Manxman grew a bit cunning and cautious, and remained so.'

He turned to John Costain.

'What can you tell us about Fred Snowball, John?'

'Aw... '

Costain shuffled in the bed to find a comfortable spot and stroked his chin. *Traa dy Liooar*. Plenty of time. They were in for a long session. The Archdeacon didn't approve.

'Now, John. No more hemming and hawing... You want Fred's murderer laying by the heels, so just be a little more brisk and informative.'

Mrs Costain entered with a huge tin tray laden with large cups of tea and a plate of buttered soda cakes enough to feed a multitude.

'Help yourselves.'

They had to get it over, for Costain had a vast appetite and would indulge in nothing but small-talk and personal questions about Littlejohn and Knell until the platter was clean and the second and third cups of tea disposed of.

'I first met Fred Snowball seven years since... He came to ask if I'd row him over to the Calf in my boat.'

'Yes?'

'He said he was a minin' engineer, interested in the 'istory of minin', leck. Now it is said that a chap called Bushell, as had been seccitary to a Lord Bacon, in England, come over to the Calf about 1650 and did some prospectin' there. There was copper and silver to be had, they say. Fred told me all that. He'd read it. He wanted to see for himself. Well, I rowed him over a number of times... He didn't seem to get much about Master Bushell, but he did get powerful fond of the Calf... Of course, it's a lovely spot in the good weather. Quiet and peaceful and...'

The Archdeacon reined him up and put him back on the rails again.

'You became good friends, John?'

'Aye. Tuck a fancy to one another. He went back over and came every year... Then, about five years ago, he said he was stayin' on the Islan' for good.'

'Where did he stay when he came over for holidays?'

'Down in Douglas. He was a queer sort. He liked peace and quiet, an' yet when he was quiet and peaceful, he wanted people. A bit contrary, leck. He said a time or two, if we'd had another proper room here, he'd have settled and lodged with us. But he'd never 'ave stayed long that way. Cregneish is no place for a restless fellah like Fred. So he lived in one place and spent a lot of his time in the other. Eddicated man, he was, too. Knew a lot about things. Terrible interested in the birds on the Calf... Sit for hours watchin' the puffins there and laughin' away at them.'

'Did he ever talk to you about his personal affairs?'

Costain's face took on a stubborn look.

'I know you listened and kept your own counsel about Fred, John. But now he's dead, it's your duty to tell us all you can and help us to find who killed him.'

'Aw... I suppose it is, Master Kinrade. But it's a bit hard, leck.

Doesn't seem decent... He'd run away from his wife, you see. Said she was a tartar. Admitted that she was a good-looker at eighteen and he let his heart run away with his head. Actually said when he asked her dad if he could marry her, the old fellah ups and warns him, leck. "I never been able to mannidge her myself, Fred," he says. "The good Lord knows how you'll mannidge 'er. You're takin' on a rare handful." Plain as that, the old fellah put it. But poor Fred didn't find out till it was too late. He once told me there wasn't much loose in his house, across, that his old lady hadn't thrown at his head one time an' another. Terr'ble temper...'

'So he left her?'

'Aye, he left her. Said she wasn't a woman; just a block of ice.'

Costain started to look sheepish, as though beginning to tread on delicate or unholy ground. With the religious mottoes on the walls, there seemed to be certain things he thought unspeakable.

Littlejohn filled his pipe and waited. *Traa dy Liooar*. Plenty of time. He felt the same. The slow, low-geared mood was on him. He could stay there until the cows came home! But the Archdeacon was hot on the trail. His eyes shone and his froth of whiskers jutted aggressively from his chin.

'There was some other woman, then?'

'Aw...'

'Come on, John. Out with it.'

'What's the missus doin'?'

'She's talking outside with the woman next door. What has that to do with it?'

'She might not like me talkin' about it. Specially with you bein' the Archdeacon of Man.'

'Well, tell Littlejohn then, if you're so squeamish.'

'Aw... Yes, there was another woman. I told Fred when he started to talk about her, it wasn't right and I didn't approve. "A man's got to have a woman who understands him," he said to me, so pitiful, leck, that I let him go on with what he was sayin'. Inside, I hoped he found some good one to comfort him for the one that threw the things about the house at him... But no. The second was as bad as the first. She didn't throw things at him. In fact, he said she was a gentle lovin' sort. But I recollect him sayin' she was most gentle and lovin' when it was a fur coat or a diamond ring she was wanting. A rale monkey of a woman. In the end, Fred saw the light an' left her.'

'And came to live over here for good?'

'Aye. He settled down in a boardin'-house in Douglas and lived the life of a bachelor.'

The Archdeacon looked at Littlejohn questioningly. The Superintendent took up the inquiry.

'Did you ever have any reason for thinking that Fred was still fond of the women?'

Costain rubbed his chin nervously and shuffled about in his bed. The dog leapt to his feet protestingly at the disturbance, barked, turned round twice, and settled and fell asleep again across his boss' feet.

'Aw... Now why talk ill of the dead, master? Why not let him rest?'

'I'm not asking out of idle curiosity, John. If we're to find out who killed him, we must know all about him. There aren't any clues of the kind you perhaps read about in your books. We've got the hard task of bringing Fred Snowball to life and almost asking him who killed him.'

Costain nodded.

'Some men take to the drink and get to be proper sponges full of it; others take to the money and grow into misers; and some's fond of eatin'... We've all got our faults. Fred's weakness was the women. He'd always an eye for a good-looker... Some sort of intoxicated him. Nothin' wrong as far as I knew. Just he couldn't resist them. He liked to talk with a pretty lass or a good-lookin' woman an' he might tap her on the cheek or give her a li'l cuddle or, if she was a bit forward, leck, slap her on the behind... Aw, it's not right to be talkin' like this of the dead.'

It was quite enough, though. Another little piece in the jigsaw of the complete Uncle Fred.

Through the window, between the geraniums and the fuchsia flowers, Littlejohn could see the orange and red of sunset showing in magnificence over the sea in the direction of Bradda. The charabanc parties were returning from their evening trip to the Sound and singing on their way home.

I left my heart
In the blue-grass country,
Where my buddy
Stole my baby
From me.

He thought of Uncle Fred and John Costain down at the Sound, bringing in the boat after a trip to Calf Island. Two elderly men, idling the days away, one busy with his boat, and the other perhaps looking about the place, admiring the view, and his eyes suddenly lighting up as he spotted a fine figure or a pretty face emerging from a charabanc.

'Did you know Fred went under two or three different names?'

'Aye. I believe he'd once been called Boycott. He told me one time, when he was sittin' lookin' across to the Chicken Rock from the Calf on a peaceful night like this. He said he'd never any wish to cross the water to England again. "I left all my troubles behind me there," he says. An' then it all came out. He just walked out on his first missus an' he tuck another name so she couldn't trace him, leck. Started a new life. "Mind you, John," he sez, "I left her most of what I'd got." And he tells me she'd the best part of a coupla hundred thousand pounds to enjoy the income of. I couldn't believe it. To see him sittin' there in an old suit an' a pair of worn shoes an' with a hole in his sock, you wouldn't have thought he'd have two hal'pennies to rub together... But I never found him tell a lie. And he was a well-spoke, eddicated man.'

'And he'd changed his name to Snowball?'

'Yes. A chap with a queer twist o' humour, you see. Snowball was the name the second woman knew him by. So, he told me he'd changed that, too, so he couldn't be traced. Snook, he was known by in Douglas. Snowball was after a black fellah from America he knew in the first war. A black they give the nick-name to... Always made him laugh, he said. An' Snook... In his comical humour, he said he'd once heard of a fellah of that name, and he thought it funny, and as good as any other for his purposes.'

Littlejohn smiled. Uncle Fred had been quite a card, with his funny sense of humour and his women.

'Did he ever mention his daughter, Victoria?'

'Queenie, you mean... Yes. He was fond of her, in a way. She was at school, he told me, when he left his first wife. He saw Queenie twice, I think, after that. Went across an' met her. Then, she took up with a fellah Fred didn't like and when her dad said so, she told him, leck, that she was goin' to marry the fellah what-ever her dad said... Fred sort o' lost interest after that. He never saw her again.'

'He seems to have talked freely to you, John. You were together a lot?'

'Two or three days a week, sometimes, Superintendent. Fred loved it down here. The place got in his bones, he said. Specially the Calf. Whenever the weather was fit, he'd want to row across. He'd got a permit to go any time. It belongs to the Manx National Trust, you know. Bird sanctuary... We'd take a case of beer. Not that I like the drink much, but Fred had a thirst for it at times. I'd drop him offen, an' then go on an' do a bit o' fish'n or get a crab or two. Then, pick him up in the everin' and bring him back in time for his bus to Douglas.'

'What about winter?'

'He'd still come... The weather's nice here even in winter. Some days is calm and sunny. Quite frequent, it would be fit to cross the

Sound. Fred got terrible interested in the birds. He'd sit for hours watchin' the puffins or the jinny-divers... cormorants, you know.'

For seven years, on and off, Fred Boycott had been coming there, idling the hours away, watching the birds, sailing in Costain's boat, loafing about Calf Island, enjoying the warm laziness of summer days, and even in winter, seeking the company of this comfortable discreet Manxman, to whom he seemed to have told the story of his past life. Costain, like all Manxmen, was a good listener. *Traa dy Liooar*. Time enough. Give Uncle Fred time and he'd tell everything.

'And whilst you've been bedridden, John, has Fred been coming down here as usual?'

'Naw. Me bein' in bed seemed to upset his programme, leck. He'd call once a fortnight, about. He had all his letters addressed to him here. He didn't want them nosin' in his affairs at the boarding-house. Bring me somethin' to read an' smoke. Generous, he was. I told him he ought to get another boatman when he wanted to take a trip over the Sound, but he jest said he'd have to see about it. We seemed to know all about one another, he said, and talkin' to me was like talkin' to himself. "You get betther, John," he sez. "Then we'll teck out the boat agen." He seemed ready to wait till I was up an' about.'

'Meanwhile, do you know what he did with the time he once spent with you?'

'Naw... He never said.'

Uncle Fred, with all the time on his hands, might have got into mischief one way or another. There was no telling. Perhaps, with the old boatman to talk to and keep him company, he'd still have been alive. As it was...

Littlejohn looked round the room again, and then at the view through the open window. His eyes slowly moved to where the sun was gently sinking, and then to the stretch of horizon and sea beyond the great mass of Spanish Head, with the Calf right ahead. A place without vice or malice, where Fred had come and gone like one of the family. Conversation was pleasant and would probably drag on idly, and Uncle Fred would tell them, bit by bit, as though talking to himself, how he'd become a beachcomber, a loafer, who had, under the spell of the Isle of Man and its courteous, kindly folk, cast off from his unhappy past altogether, and started afresh. *Traa dy Liooar*. Plenty of time. All the time in the world and nobody to bother him. A life as harmless and serene as the lives of these people of Cregneish among whom he spent so much of it. Endless days in the sun and air, with the smack of the sea and the faint scents of ling and fuchsia on the breeze.

And then... Costain had become bedridden, Uncle Fred's restlessness had returned, and trouble had started... Was that it?

'What about money? How did Fred live?'

Again Costain shuffled uneasily in bed and the dog protested.

'Fred's dead and gone and there's no harm in telling us now, John. Did he get it dishonestly in some way?'

'Course not... Honest as the day, was Fred.'

He pointed to the top drawer of the washstand.

'There's a key in the top drawer there. Will you please, reverend, teck it and open the top drawer of the dresser in the nex' room? An' bring the parcel in the right corner, tied up with a bit o' string.'

The Archdeacon was soon back with the little parcel, wrapped up in brown paper.

'Please open it, master.'

A Post Office bank-book in the name of Fred Snowball; some Savings Certificates; an old Army Paybook in the name of Frederick M. Boycott; the birth certificate of Fred Mandeville Boycott, of Upton Byers, Sussex; a few share certificates which tallied with the small holdings Littlejohn had already noted on the old copy of the *Financial Times;* and a government annuity of £300 a year. Finally, in a separate envelope, a will leaving all Fred Snowball had in the world to John and Mary Costain... And he'd trusted everything to his two friends in the little cottage at Cregneish, probably to avoid the Trimbles' nosing into his affairs.

Fred Boycott must have been in a hurry to flee from his women in the past. First, he'd left a quarter of a million behind him, just to get away from the wife he couldn't stand any longer. And then, he'd got himself tangled with another. And from her, he'd bolted with just the clothes he'd stood up in and capital enough to bring him in about £400 a year. Five hundred in the Post Office, four hundred in Savings Certificates, and a few paltry shareholdings... And he'd found happiness at last. The busy world left behind. Eating, drinking, dozing, loafing.

'Did he marry the second woman?'

'How could he? He'd got a wife already.'

'He might have gone through a form of marriage and fled finally as a bigamist.'

'Naw. He never spoke of that. Just that he lived with the second woman till he couldn't stand it any longer. Then he jest tuck enough to live on and left her with the rest.'

'Well, that seems to be all, John, and thank you for what you've told us. We'd better be going now. Time's getting on.'

'You'll come again, sir. An' you, too, Archdeacon, and Mr Knell. If I think of anythin' else, I'll save it and tell you next time.'

The day was drawing in and the blue of the sea darkening as they left and made for the car. Another fine day tomorrow. A red sunset over Bradda and the faint chill of approaching night in the warm air. Nobody spoke. It seemed a pity to break the evening calm. Even the men gathered in small knots here and there in the village were silent, smoking and watching everything.

It was the same on the way home. As though the holiday crowds had somehow been cowed into quietness by the beauty of the dying day. Port St Mary looked homely and peaceful. People strolling along the main street and waterfront... No noise, no hurry. Cars glided past and, out at sea, a few boats and a couple of yachts with sails spread, were heading for port.

On the road back to Grenaby, the vast spread of lonely inland country was deserted. A few late birds singing, an odd rabbit running along the grass verge, a farm dog trotting off on some business of his own, a cat sitting rigid in a hedge watching a mousehole.

Back in the village again, Littlejohn knew he understood Uncle Fred perfectly. Time stood still. A faint breath of wind in the tree-tops, like a caress. No noise save that of the river rushing under the old stone bridge and on its course to the green tunnel of over-hanging branches where the local spirits haunted and gambolled, even at high noon, because they couldn't wait for the night. The hot evening air was heavy with the scents of old roses and wood-smoke. Joe Jenn, a bankrupt wool-merchant from Yorkshire, who'd settled there and run to seed, hanging over the gate, smoking his pipe, with his old coat and trousers drawn over his nightshirt. Just like Uncle Fred, except that Fred had always been meticulous about washing and shaving every day and was more fastidious in his dress.

At the vicarage, Maggie Keegin, the housekeeper, was waiting on the doorstep, looking annoyed.

'Telephone again!' she said to Knell. 'It's always telephones, murders, and upsets whenever you're hauntin' this place.'

The police-station at Douglas, ringing up Knell on the off-chance he was at the vicarage.

A Mr and Mrs Valentine-Rudd had been at the police-station asking for the officer in charge of the Fred Boycott case. At the mention of the name Snook, the lady had grown very annoyed. Uncle Fred had been her father and his name was Boycott.

Queenie had arrived!

6
QUEENIE

It was too much to ask Littlejohn to go all the way back to Douglas again that night, so, an appointment was made for him to meet the Valentine-Rudds at Douglas police-station at ten o'clock next morning. Knell, therefore, went home, looking like a man whose work was never done, and the Superintendent and the Archdeacon ate a good meal together, drank some of Mr Kinrade's special port, talked a lot, and went to bed respectably early. Maggie Keggin suggested the telephone be taken from the hook, but they didn't go so far, and were not disturbed.

Littlejohn was at Douglas promptly next morning. The Valentine-Rudds had not arrived at the police-station and didn't turn up until ten-thirty. When he saw them, Littlejohn understood why they were late. They were the type who took hours to dress and get ready for going out. Always late, always rushing about at the last minute, always apologizing for not being on time, always blaming one another for the delay.

A taxi halted in front of the police-station and an excited couple scrambled out of it. Knell watched them with a cold eye. He didn't give them time to hang about in the vestibule, but strode to the door and flung it open. Then he paused, as though something had taken his breath away.

Queenie and her husband were the most elegant couple who'd entered Douglas police-station for many a long day. They looked to have stepped out of an advertisement for clothes-hire or West-end tailoring and couture. The types you see strolling in the Bois de Boulogne or along the Corisette at Cannes... Film stars on location taking an hour off.

They were both sunburned, and if it was artificially done it was a good job. She was medium built, dark, slim, and handsome, and she wore a cream linen costume, with a red handbag and lipstick and nail-varnish to match it. She was carrying a daily paper, folded in her hand, and before she spoke she partly opened it and pointed to the photograph of Uncle Fred as though it were some kind of passport.

'May I speak to the officer in charge of the matter of Mr Frederick Boycott?'

She was perfectly self-assured, but made an initial feint of nervousness to secure Knell's sympathy.

'Come inside, please.'

Littlejohn looked at the newcomers and thought of Uncle Fred. It was laughable! First his wife; now this pair. All dressed up to the nines and trying to impress. Whilst Uncle Fred had spent his time pottering about in an old boat with John Costain, wearing old trousers and a pair of soiled white shoes. And now and then he'd have a little binge and come home to his seedy digs disreputable and smelling of drink. Another world...

The pair of them made straight for Littlejohn.

'You are the officer in charge?'

'No. Inspector Knell has the case in hand.'

They both seemed surprised and obviously wondered who Littlejohn might be. Queenie looked at her husband and blinked. She had long eyelashes, probably stuck on for effect. He took it as a sign to assume control and pulled out his card and passed it to Knell.

W. VALENTINE-RUDD
Objets d'art
17 CANK STREET, NEW BOND STREET, WI

Knell passed the card to Littlejohn. *Objets d'art!* It might cover anything.

'You're an antique dealer, Mr Rudd?'

'Valentine-Rudd... Yes. Mainly French. I have an office in Paris... Rue de la Paix.'

A tall, heavy, dark, and hairy man, swarthy-skinned and a bit insolent in manner. Uncle Fred hadn't taken to him. No wonder! He wore a fine merino suit of light grey, almost white, with a navy blue shirt and a red silk scarf knotted inside it. There was a slight trace of scent on the air around him. He gave you a faint impression of having some middle-East in his make-up. Living apparently on his wife and his wits.

'My wife was Mr Boycott's only daughter.'

He seemed to turn instinctively to Littlejohn, which pleased Knell, who was completely at sea with such people.

'So I gather.'

'How did you know?'

'Mrs Valentine-Rudd's mother has already told us.'

The young woman – she looked about thirty, but might have been less – blinked again.

'She is staying in Douglas? We... we are not on friendly terms with her.'

'She said so.'

A pause. It was obvious the Valentine-Rudds had rehearsed this scene, but it wasn't quite going according to plan. Rudd tried to bring it back on the lines again.

'You will allow us to see the body of my wife's father? She used to be very fond of him.'

He had a purring, insinuating voice, too sleek and far-back to be sincere, and Littlejohn waited for some kind of proposition to be made.

'We wanted to make quite sure it *is* Mr Boycott. From what we've read we're both very surprised.'

'Perhaps Inspector Knell will let you see it. It's in the mortuary.'

Mrs Rudd recoiled slightly and dabbed her mouth with a small handkerchief.

'Come this way.'

Knell had begun to enjoy himself. He would show them poor Uncle Fred's remains and the clothes he'd worn. Then they'd know he'd forgotten them and the world they lived in.

Littlejohn filled his pipe and waited for them to return. They were soon back. Rudd was wiping his hands on his handkerchief as though cleaning off some kind of contamination.

'It's my father.'

No tears; not even a trace of sorrow on the made-up face which might have been a mask. The eyes, however, were troubled, as though the calm of Uncle Fred had impressed her.

'He looks peaceful... He's even smiling.'

Nobody replied.

'He and I were very good friends when we were at home. I never got on with mother very well. My father didn't want me to marry, however. He was possessive about me. He was bored with mother... I must say it, then you'll understand. He found some sort of compensation in my company... We went about together... Then I met Willy... My husband. Dad didn't want me to marry... Not anyone, he didn't... And when I married, he didn't come to the wedding. I never saw him afterwards.'

No wonder! Uncle Fred was the type who would see through Willy in no time at all!

'Did your father settle anything on you before he went away for good?'

'I don't know what you mean, Mr... Mr...'

'Superintendent Littlejohn, madam.'

Willy almost jumped out of his skin.

'Not from Scotland Yard?'

'Yes, sir.'

'Oh!'

There was a wealth of meaning in the single word!

'I mean, Mrs Valentine-Rudd, did your father, being fond of you, assign some of his money to you?'

'Why do you want to know?'

'I want to know everything about the late Mr Boycott. This is a case of murder, Mrs Valentine-Rudd.'

'Well... I was at school when he went away... I was at Cheltenham. He wrote to me and asked me to meet him. He came to Cheltenham... He said he had left my mother. She'd grown apart from him.'

'What did he mean by that?'

Another flutter of the eyelashes and a sidelong look at her husband, who was peering through the window, his attention divided between the conversation indoors, and the pretty girls going past on their ways to the beach.

'She got to bossing him around. He was a quiet man with quiet easy ways, and all he wanted was his garden and his books and to go to Brighton and sail his boat.'

'He had a boat, then?'

'Yes. A fine motor-boat.'

She opened her bag and plunged her painted nails in it, fishing out at length a dog-eared snapshot which she handed to Littlejohn. Her husband turned and almost sneered.

'That's the only photo I ever had of him. I thought I'd bring it along in case... Identification, you know.'

Yes, it was Uncle Fred. Just recognizable. Only this time,

elegantly dressed in flannels, blazer, and yachting-cap. Facing the camera with the same sad, rather quizzical smile. Comparing the photograph with the one in the daily papers, you would hardly say he'd come down in the world. He was neat and serene even now in the morgue. Only at the time of his death, he'd given up... turned idler... let the rest of the world go by.

'In other words they lived in two different worlds.'

'Yes. She was keen on the county people, managing the affairs of the village, filling the house with types she thought *were* somebody. Dad preferred to be quiet.'

That was it. The first symptoms of the chronic complaint which, in the end, had fastened on him like a mortal disease... He'd wanted to be quiet, loaf about in old things, sail his boat... just give up and do as he liked.

'She nagged him nearly silly. So much so, that he'd grow queer and contrary, just to spite her. Once, when she was holding a garden party, he said he wasn't coming, and she had such a row with him that he gave in at last. And then, just as things were at their height, he appeared in old clothes and wheeled a barrow of manure across the main lawn... I thought mother would have died. All the people thought he was the gardener until...'

Rudd had had enough. He turned and bared his gleaming teeth as though getting ready to bite his wife.

'My dear Queenie! They don't want to hear all that... '

She gave him a queer look, and Littlejohn could see she was afraid of him. Rudd, the half-caste-looking Rudd, somehow had her under his influence to the extent of squeezing all the fun out of her. Uncle Fred had once been fond of Queenie. Probably they'd had good times together, laughed, perhaps joked about her mother and her domineering ways.

'I was saying... He came to Cheltenham and told me he was leaving home because they couldn't agree. I didn't blame him. He said, if ever I wanted anything, I must write to him.'

'Where?'

'Care of the G.P.O. at Leicester. He was living somewhere in the country nearby. I learned he was living with another woman, later. From then on, he sent me money about every month. Then, when I left school, he came and met me in London. I introduced him to Willy... He said I was too young to marry and got very awkward. We quarrelled... I never saw him again, but I wrote just once to tell him we were married. He sent me a wedding present without even a letter of good wishes.'

'What was it?'

She looked again at her husband, but he was still busy at the window.

'Five thousand pounds in bearer bonds.'

'I see.'

Rudd suddenly turned round. It was his turn now.

'Could we see his home... or wherever he lived?'

'He lived at a cheap boarding-house just off the promenade.'

Queenie's false lashes opened wide.

'Why... I thought...'

'He hadn't very much money, you know. He left most of his fortune with your mother, and he seems to have had to provide for the other woman you just mentioned. That, on top of your bearer bonds. It didn't leave much.'

'How much?'

Rudd almost hissed it.

'A few thousands... Next to nothing to live on.'

'But there was the money he left behind. I believe it was quite a fortune.'

'I suppose so. Mrs Boycott supervised that, of course.'

'But now that he's dead, the estate can be squared-up. My wife was his only child... There must be a will somewhere.'

And then it dawned on Littlejohn. The will Uncle Fred had lodged with the Costains. It left all he had in the world to the pair of them! Suppose the fortune in his wife's hands were thrown into the general estate. The Costains might get that, too. The Superintendent smiled grimly. There'd be a rare fight. Lawyers, doctors trying to prove Uncle Fred was off his head when he made his last will... Interminable litigation...

'I said there must be a will somewhere.'

'I dare say. That will come later. He's not buried yet.'

'Perhaps it's among his papers in his rooms.'

'There's nothing there.'

A cunning look crossed the swarthy face of Rudd.

'All the same, I'd like my wife to look around. Just to see where her father spent his last years. You want to see them, don't you, Queenie, dear?'

'I'd like that, Willy.'

'I suppose mother's been already.'

'Oh, yes. She was there almost as soon as she arrived.'

'When was that?'

'Yesterday afternoon.'

Willy made petulant gestures.

'I'll bet she was. Well, we're wasting time. We're leaving on the last plane today. My business doesn't run itself, you know. We'd a job to get a room for last night. Just got in at a place on the promenade. No bath in the room, no proper service... awful dump.'

Littlejohn could imagine the pair of them arriving elegantly and inquiring for a room with a bath in the high season. The hotel people would wonder whatever was coming, to begin with, and then when Rudd started trying to push them around, they'd be ready to show him the door.

'We have to call there. Inspector Knell and I will take you. It's a place called *Sea Vista*.'

Rudd screwed up his nose and wiped it with his scented handkerchief. He screwed it up a lot more when they pulled up at the seedy boarding-house where Uncle Fred had pottered his last days away.

Trimble let them in. He was in his shirt-sleeves again and wore an old pair of white shoes which were nearly black. He smelled of spirits.

'This is Mr Snook's daughter.'

He had to explain about Snook and Snowball to the agonized Queenie.

'I thought so. You don't look like 'im at all, but I could tell you because you take after your mother.'

Rudd took over.

'Show us his room, my man. We're in a hurry.'

Trimble barred the way at once, which wasn't a difficult thing to do. He simply stopped the gap between the stairs and the bamboo hall-stand with his flabby bulk.

''ere. None o' that. My man, indeed! This is my 'otel and I'll trouble you to keep a civil tongue in yer 'ead. I please myself who I show my rooms to.'

Littlejohn tapped him on the shoulder.

'Let's get it over, Trimble, and then we won't hold you up.'

'Seein' that it's you, Superintendent... But I won't be insulted in my own 'ouse... This way.'

Mrs Trimble must have been out on her usual morning stroll, but Maria appeared from the kitchen, carrying plates to the dining-room. Rudd's eyes fell on her and almost gobbled her up. Their looks met and she smiled faintly at him. Mrs Rudd didn't seem to notice. She was used to it. One day, like her father, she'd probably get fed up, too, and clear out for good. If she'd any money... If... now, she was trying to make up to Trimble for Rudd's rudeness.

'You'll understand I haven't seen him for years and naturally when we read about it in the paper, we were both completely knocked out. You must excuse us if we're both upset.'

'Of course. I understand. I get a bit touchy at times.'

'Did he ever speak of me?'

'I can't say he did. He must 'ave mentioned it casual, perhaps, one time. I'd always the impression he'd got a daughter.'

'Did he talk much to you?'

'Now and then. He was quite a sociable chap.'

'What did he talk about?'

'Oh... weather, pictures he'd seen at the cinema, Douglas in general, the Isle of Man and 'ow fond 'e was of it. Knew quite a bit about the Island... 'istory and customs. Liked to talk to the old Manx people he met.'

'He was happy?'

'In 'is way, yes. Content with just potterin' about, and now and then, he'd vanish for a day or two and come back... well... I used to say he'd been off for 'is little spree.'

'I'm glad he was happy. Did he seem poor... or...'

Her husband was now on her heels and she turned the conversation into channels which would suit him.

'I never found 'im flush with money. But never hard up. Just enough. When he came back from his little spree, like, he'd have a pocketful of the ready again, and pay his bills for his digs... 'ere we are.'

Rudd was almost holding his nose with disgust. But Queenie was still interested in her father. She continued to question Trimble.

'Did he ever have any visitors?'

'Never. Not here, at least.'

'Where else could he have visitors?'

'Well... as I said before, he'd sometimes take off. That always seemed to me as when 'e was short of money. Where 'e got his money from, I can't say.'

Littlejohn didn't say anything about the Costains. No use letting a crowd loose on the modest pair at Cregneish. Knell looked across at him and he almost imperceptibly shook his head.

Rudd wasn't interested in the social life of Uncle Fred.

'Did you ever see any papers about?'

'Eh? Wot papers?'

'Everybody has private papers... Bank books, investments, letters, official documents.'

'I never saw any. I wasn't in the 'abit of riflin' his drawers or snoopin' among his private effecks. In any case, the police won't allow any lookin' in his drawers or trunks. That is so, isn't it, Mr Knell?'

'That's right.'

'I suppose Mrs Boycott's been here already... I guess she's given his private affairs a good once-over.'

'Didn't I say nobody 'ad? If you don't believe me, ask the police... '

Queenie and her husband wandered round the room; she presumably trying to get a picture in her mind about her father's last days, he sizing up the place, valuing the contents.

Trimble took Littlejohn aside and started to whine.

'I wish you'd get all this settled an' over. We want to let this room. It's not good enough bein' strung up like this in the middle of the 'igh season. My wife and me 'ave 'ad to go up in the attic again. A boarder's turned up who'd booked Finnegan's room, and with you keepin' Finnegan here, we've 'ad to let 'im 'ave ours.'

'It won't be for long.'

'This new lodger's a bit of a trial, too. Religious sort of chap. Insists on sayin' grace before meals and he asked Vincent – that's the young chap 'oo plays the accordion – if he'd been saved. Asked 'im to play a few hymn tunes on his instrument. Very embarrassin' on top of wot we've gone through.'

The Rudds had had enough and were anxious to be getting away.

'We're catching the evening plane back to the mainland.'

Good job the Archdeacon wasn't there. He'd quickly have corrected Rudd. England isn't the mainland to a Manxman! Across the water, or the adjacent island, yes. But mainland...

'I'm going to call on Mrs Boycott, too. Whether she likes it or not, there are one or two business matters to settle.'

'You're not going to start an argument with mother, Willy? I wouldn't like that. After all these years as strangers.'

'I won't leave this place till I've seen her. I insist. Can any of you tell me where Mrs Boycott is living?'

'Fort Anne Hotel. On the way up to Douglas Head.'

Knell gave the address with relish. You could see him enjoying in anticipation the shemozzle when the rival parties met.

'It's really through her mother that my wife became estranged from her family. Now that her father's dead, we've got to settle about her birthright. It's only fair...'

Nobody seemed interested, and the little procession made its way downstairs again. This tramping up and down to Uncle Fred's room was becoming a kind of rite. On the trail down they met a large, big-headed, solemn man on his way up. He wore a black suit and a white dicky and a black tie. He looked ready to ask Rudd if *he'd* been saved, too, and then changed his mind. Perhaps he mistook him for a Mohammedan.

'I think I'll stay here a bit on my own, Knell.'

Knell looked surprised.

'I'd just like to potter about and get a bit more of the atmosphere. You take these people away with you, and I'll call after and let you know if I find anything fresh.'

'Just as you say, sir. What do I do with them?'

'Anything, old chap, as long as you take them away from here.'

Knell shepherded his charges off the premises and down the shabby path to the car. Queenie, tottering on her high heels, kept turning to look at the place, as though still thinking of her father's comings and goings there. Rudd, with his fancy suit, with its draped jacket and padded shoulders, embodied contempt, lit a cigarette, and wiped his hands on his handkerchief again, as though cleaning off *Sea Vista* and everything connected with it.

Littlejohn turned back with Trimble.

'That's a dirty little swine, if you ask me. The sort who makes you need to keep an eye on the spoons. For two pins, I'd 'ave shown 'im the door as soon as he came in. Did you want to see me about anythin', Super?'

'Would you mind if I had another look round the place? I'm trying to find out all I can about Fred's existence. For example, what happened here in the winter? Fred came down to a room on the first floor. Did he dine all alone in that large dining-room?'

'Oh, no. He kipped in with us in the kitchen. We all ate together... Snook, me, the missus, and Susie. That's the little girl you've seen knockin' about. Twenty, she is, and we've 'ad her five years. Doesn't look 'er age, I admit, but she's too good to let go in the winter.'

'What about the other girl – Maria, is she called?'

'She came at the beginnin' of the season. That is, as a regular, I mean. Durin' the winter, the wife took her on two days a week to keep the rooms tidy. She's Eyetalian.'

'Did she come here from Italy?'

'Oh, no. Matter of fact, born in London. Her father's an Eyetalian. Interned 'ere as an enemy h'alien in the war and liked the place and stopped on as a farm worker. Brought his family over.'

'Could I see the kitchen?'

Littlejohn didn't quite know why he asked it, but somehow, he wanted to see another of Uncle Fred's haunts.

'Yes. They're just gettin' dinner ready, but you can see it for what good it'll do.'

They went along the corridor, past the bamboo hatstand and the Trimbles' little office to a door at the end of the passage. A gust of cooking cabbage, roast beef, and steam met them.

Maria and Susie were busy watching a large gas stove with boiling pans on the top and meat sizzling inside. They turned and looked at Littlejohn. Maria gave him a lazy, challenging stare, the kind she seemed to give every man she met. Susie, wearing a long soiled overall, was sulky and looked as if she resented the intrusion. She had a pale face and large dark eyes with shadows under them. Hardly an orphan of the storm at close quarters! Quite good-looking, in fact. With her hair tidied and her face washed, she'd be very attractive.

Littlejohn looked round. The place was neat and clean in spite of the activities going on. A sash window overlooking the yard; black and white check curtains to liven it up a bit. A red tiled floor; cupboards for dishes on one side; along the length of the other, a Welsh dresser with blue plates on the shelves. A few chairs, a whitewood table, with a plastic top coloured black and white like a chessboard. A large gas-stove in an alcove where once there might have been a kitchen range. Over the alcove, a shelf with brass candlesticks and a couple of old china dogs on it, with a noisily ticking alarm-clock in the middle.

The world of the kitchens. And here Uncle Fred joined the family when the visitors had all gone home and the Island had settled down for its winter sleep. Littlejohn could imagine it all. The room, a bit dingy in the winter days. The party sitting round the chessboard table eating a meal. Uncle Fred didn't talk much. The conversation would drag on. Idle, desultory comments meaning little. Perhaps a word or two about a film one of them had seen, the weather, the chances of the coming high season on the basis of the daily postal bookings which came in for next summer... All meaningless, like the lives of those who dragged out the days there, with the noisy little clock ticking the minutes away. Uncle Fred, who'd first arrived on the Island spick and span, wearing his yachting cap and smart clothes, and then, after he'd given most of his money to Queenie, could only afford a place like *Sea Vista,* in his old suit, panama, and dirty rubber shoes. An ex-pantomime principal-boy, bored to death with the stale, endless days... A superannuated acrobat... Susie, with her pale classic face, straight nose, and big eyes... Now and then, Maria, arriving for odd days, waking the men up with her challenging body and her predatory eyes. And Uncle Fred had preferred it to his family and his estates in Sussex. He'd thrown them all overboard and had drifted aimlessly and peacefully along there.

'Where were all of you when Mr Snook met his death?'

They all looked up as though Littlejohn had fired a revolver in the place.

Trimble, of course, protested he'd answered that one before. He was in the house. No time for carnivals. After what he'd seen on his travels, he'd no interest in local events. Now, in Nice or Monte Carlo... those were the days...

Maria, of course, was out at the carnival.

'What! A false nose? Not for me! My own is nice enough, eh?'

She spoke Cockney; evidently born and bred in London. Susie wasn't at the carnival. The boys had wanted to take her with them. Maria taunted her.

'Every new batch of young men make a pass at Susie. Don't they...? Week after week, day after day, they all want to take her out, and she's too proud to have any of them. Isn't that it, Susie?'

The girl made no answer, but opened the oven door and released a blast of stifling, meat-smelling air which took all their breaths away.

The door suddenly flew open and Mrs Trimble stood on the threshold. Fresh and tempting as ever, with her cheeks flushed from her walk on the promenade, and growing more pink as she found what was going on.

'Good morning, Superintendent... There's a call on the phone for you. A Mr Valentine-Rudd, whoever he might be... And as for you...'

She indicated Trimble and the two girls with a sweep of her hand.

'They're all in, waiting for their meal. Get it dished up. It's late.'

Roast beef and two veg, and a large currant pudding boiling in the pan, with rice pudding for those who were unlucky when the boiled one gave out. They started to scurry around, and Littlejohn went to the telephone, which stood on the bamboo hallstand under somebody's overcoat.

'I've talked matters over with Mrs Boycott, Superintendent.

We've quite a lot in common. She says she'd like me to stay over here to see to things. She seems to want to be reconciled to my wife. After all, we've nothing to hide, nothing to reproach ourselves with. I can't hear you... Speak up... You'll call...? When...? I can't hear you.'

The lodgers were having to wait for their dinner and to keep them in good temper, Vincent, the accordionist, was at it again.

I left my heart
In the blue-grass country,
Where my buddy
Stole my baby
From me.

Uncle Fred's signature-tune, and Littlejohn was getting fed up with it. He hung up the telephone and went out.

At the end of the road he found himself back again in the holiday world. The blue sea, calm and still, the hot air, the shining asphalt, the shops, the horse-trams, cars gliding along the promenade... Everybody indoors for lunch and the place peaceful and clean. White sails in the bay, a man passing by in a panama hat. It might have been the south of France.

Littlejohn felt suddenly worn out and ready for his lunch as well. He turned in at one of the hotels on the promenade and made for the bar.

'Give me a Pernod.'

He poured the water on the greenish-yellow liquid which turned cloudy, and as he drank it, the bite of aniseed brought back memories.

Yes, it might easily have been the south of France.

7
SUSIE

'And now for some work... '

Littlejohn had dined alone in an hotel on the promenade and felt a lot better for it. The holiday feeling was still there, of course, and his conscience kept goading him not only to help Knell to solve the mystery of Uncle Fred, but also to find some way of allowing the Archdeacon to give him a hand with the investigation. The Reverend Caesar Kinrade was now an enthusiastic amateur detective, but it was certainly *infra dig* to trail him around on inquiries involving seedy boarders in third-rate diggings and people like Trimble and Valentine-Rudd.

'And now for some work... '

Littlejohn said it to himself as though excusing his languor to an unseen companion.

Not that Knell and his satellites hadn't done any work. In fact, they'd enlisted the whole police force of the Isle of Man, trying to find out anything fresh about the murdered man. It had been an almost door-to-door inquiry, like an invasion of vacuum-cleaner salesmen or an army of insurance agents. 'Did you know Fred Snook?' It sounded like an old music-hall song.

For example, they'd got to know from the Trimbles and everyone who'd seen Uncle Fred on the day he died, what he had been doing all the time.

8.0 a.m. Got up and ate his breakfast.

9.0 Pottered about in his room and in the boardinghouse, chatting to fellow lodgers.

10.0 Went out and spent two hours on the promenade. Seen speaking to nobody.

12.0 Back at home. Had a wash and then went in kitchen and talked to the two girls, Maria and Susie.

1.0 Lunch. Stayed snoozing and talking until 2.30, according to Trimble.

2.30 Nobody saw him again until he appeared on the promenade just before 3.0.

3.0 Dead.

Knell, sitting in his office brooding over the schedule, grew more and more angry.

'Had his breakfast! Had his lunch! Dead!'

He made as if to tear up the paper into little pieces and then paused and put it in a drawer.

'Fat lot of use that is!'

He might have made it hot for some of his hard-pressed subordinates if Littlejohn hadn't arrived just in time. The Superintendent smiled as he read Knell's time-table.

'Not much to go on, eh, sir?'

'No...'

'I've just put down a list of likely suspects and it looks just as ridiculous...'

Another long sheet of foolscap in Knell's neat hand.

*The Trimbles.....*They might have been after his money.

*The Costains.....*Beneficiaries under Uncle Fred's will.

*Mrs Boycott.....*Anxious to get the estate to herself.

*The Rudds.....*ditto.

*Fellow Lodgers.....*A quarrel about something, or might have been blackmail (e.g. Finnegan staying with woman not his wife).

*Others.....*Mrs Trimble, Maria, Susie (love affair?). Crowds on promenade (robbery, Teddy boys, or mistake for somebody else).

'It all looks so silly when you put it down on paper, sir. The Trimbles don't look like murderers, the Costains certainly aren't, Mrs Boycott and the Rudds are hardly likely to have run the risk of killing him in full view of everybody, and the lodgers... well...'

'Did you ask them all the routine questions, Knell?'

'Yes. They all said he seemed a decent chap, a bit reserved, didn't mix much, and didn't seem to have an enemy in the world. Only Mrs Nessle, the star boarder, had anything much to say. She seemed upset...'

Knell fished in a file of papers and took out a sheet bearing Mrs Nessle's observations in reply to police questions.

'I seem to have known Mr Snook all my life. I have been coming here on and off for the past fifteen years and have known Mr Snook since he started to live here, it must be five years ago.

When he first arrived, he was quite a dandy; wore very good clothes and often a yachting-cap and blazer. His fortunes must have declined, for he got shabby as time passed, although he never complained. He never talked about his affairs or of the past. He was a well-educated man with a great charm of manner.'

'Our man who questioned her said Mrs Nessle sobbed a time or two. She must have been a bit sweet on the old chap.'

Old chap, indeed! Mrs Boycott had said Uncle Fred was about sixty-one. The age at which many men get tender, start to spruce-up in a forlorn last grasp at departed youth, sometimes grow unpleasantly avuncular towards good-looking girls, and boast and throw their money about to compensate for the virility and charm of younger rivals...

Littlejohn suddenly remembered that Rudd was now installed in Mrs Boycott's hotel.

'You might ring up Fort Anne, Knell, and tell Mr Rudd we're calling to see him right away.'

The afternoon sun was hot and bright as they made their way to the hotel, which stood on the flank of Douglas Head facing the river and bay. The quaysides were crowded with trippers, looking in the antique shops like magpies after bright souvenirs and trinkets, and the Head Road was thick with lightly-clad holiday-makers, all in merry mood. There was a minstrel show outside the large hotel right on the peak of the Head, and a huge audience was roaring at the cracks and sallies and singing the choruses of popular songs.

I left my heart,
In the blue-grass country...

This time accompanied on a banjo!

The hall-porter met them in the porch of Fort Anne.

'Mr Valentine-Rudd, gentlemen? This way, please.'

Rudd was doing the heavy. He'd booked a suite and had gone to the extent of hiring a typist from an agency in town.

He shook hands with the detectives, asked them to sit down for a minute, offered them cigars, and asked them what they'd take to drink.

'I'm very busy... Got to get some letters away by the next post. Just take a letter, Miss Kissack...'

Mrs Boycott entered with Queenie in the middle of it all. She was completely transformed. Rudd had turned on the charm and won her over. She shook hands with the newcomers, too. Queenie looked bewildered and followed suit as though she'd never seen them before.

'I've decided to stay here, gentlemen, until this sad affair is cleared up. The sympathy and kindness of my daughter and son-in-law have touched me. I don't know what I'd have done without Willy.'

It was 'Willy' and 'Mother' now between the pair of them.

'I'd no idea there was so much to do. As sole legatee and representative of my late husband, I find the work overwhelming.'

She paused for breath and smiled at Queenie and Rudd, who was dictating with a flourish just to show off.

'Furthermore, as the deceased's affairs were subject to the control of the Court of Protection, I think it best for you to send a representative over to the Isle of Man at once... Got that, Miss Kissack? Get on with it right away and I'll sign it.'

The girl bustled into an adjoining room and a typewriter began to click.

Rudd looked sleek and important. He'd changed his clothes to something more businesslike; a black suit, polka-dot tie, and every hair brushed in its place. Mrs Boycott and Queenie were in deep black as well. It looked as if Uncle Fred was being mourned with a vengeance now! Littlejohn felt a growing disgust. Mrs Boycott had cut off Queenie with a shilling when she'd married Rudd. And Uncle Fred, when Queenie had appealed to him, had stumped up the money he could ill afford and descended from his yachting cap and blazer to his old clothes and settled down to a drab existence at *Sea Vista*. It was the last resort of one who'd grown tired of everything. Family, excitement, money, perhaps even of life itself...

The telephone bell rang. Rudd snatched the instrument brusquely.

'Oh... Mr Crellin... I'll sell the yacht. Yes... I know it's dilapidated. It's been in the river basin for seven years. He couldn't persuade himself to part with it and just kept it neat and tidy. But he couldn't afford to run it. Think it over. We won't refuse any reasonable offer.'

Littlejohn remembered the little craft he'd seen tied up at the old quay. Half unconsciously, he'd wondered whom she belonged to and why she'd got in such a state. Rusty, paint flaking off, brass gone verdigris... The *Queenie*. He even recollected the name, now. And for Queenie, his daughter, who'd probably in days long gone spent happy hours aboard her, Uncle Fred had given up another joy, sacrificed the money which would have kept his little boat trim and in commission, and gone to strain at Costain's rowing-boat across Calf Sound.

'Well, Superintendent...'

Rudd ignored Knell; he was too small fry now that Mrs Boycott's fortune was in the offing.

'You're sure you won't smoke... or take a drink? Very well. I understand. On duty, I guess. Well, I'm on duty, too. Too much for a helpless woman to cope with. Isn't that so, Mother?'

Mrs Boycott smiled proudly at him and turned to Littlejohn.

'My late husband led a wild life. I don't want to speak ill of the dead, but he almost ruined us. If I hadn't managed to rescue his business, we'd all have been on the street.'

She gulped for air.

'His business, Mrs Boycott? I gathered your late husband was a man of leisure.'

'In a sense, yes. He had formerly been a mining engineer in South Africa and he made a fortune there. His wealth needed careful handling... Investments, tax problems, his estate management... He'd started to neglect everything before he left home. He would absent himself for weeks at a time and spend money like water. Meanwhile, all his affairs, his letters, his accounts, were standing idle. Of course, he had secretaries and accountants to deal with technical matters, but they needed a firm hand to retain control.'

She almost sobbed to regain her breath.

'He drank a lot. And, I must tell you – because you will surely need to know in the course of your investigations – I must tell you that there were other women involved. I admit I denied it the other day. I was embarrassed and didn't know you were so kindly and understanding. I dislike to say it, but I had to put inquiry agents to work. He would disappear and turn up at Monte Carlo or the Canary Islands spending his means and living a life of debauchery; yes, debauchery... It's no use, Victoria. You may sob if you like. But it's true... You were too young to be told the truth, and I had it all to bear alone.'

Queenie, now dignified by her baptismal name, ran to the next room, weeping and gurgling. Rudd thought he'd better explain.

'My wife's a bit overcome by events. We always have scenes like this whenever emergencies or troubles arise.'

Mrs Boycott nodded.

'She was always a difficult child. It's a good thing she married someone who could control her and who has a sense of proportion.'

'I overheard something about the Court of Protection, Mrs Boycott.'

'Yes. When I felt I could stand no more, and when all my late husband's fortune was in grave danger, I put matters in the hands of my lawyers. They appealed to the Court of Protection to grant me the right to take over his affairs and control them. Mr Boycott could have lodged an appeal and fought the matter. I fully expected it. But he didn't. He offered no resistance at all. I was given certain powers over his estate. Although I say it myself, I did my duty. I saved the ship!'

Rudd thought it time to put in his oar.

'In a way, Mrs Boycott's hands were tied through her husband being alive and lying low. She could have doubled the capital if she'd had a free hand. That's so, isn't it, Mother?'

'Yes. I did all I could.'

The telephone again. Rudd snatched at it.

'Yes... Oh... Is that you, Scarffe? Yes... you'll attend to the funeral entirely. Mrs Boycott wants the best and will pay for everything. A first-class funeral. What? The Borough cemetery, of course. Yes, I know he wanted to be cremated and his ashes thrown on the Calf of Man, but he can't be. There's no crematorium, for a start, and he was a bit queer in his mind. A coffin with silver ornaments... He was Church of England, so get an appropriate clergyman... Very good...'

Littlejohn stood looking through the window with the rigmarole sounding in his ears. Down below was the road to Douglas Head, with fishermen, dogs, and strollers passing to and fro. The river entering the harbour and slowly joining the sea. Swans. A cormorant fishing from a buoy. The channel steamer, *Manxman,* tied up at the nearest pier and, beyond it, the *King Orry* ready for off.

The dock basin, harbour lights, the harbourmaster's office. Cargo boats moored near the large marine warehouses, and behind, the vast stretch of bay to Onchan Head, with gentle hills sweeping to the sea. Villas on the hill-sides, crowds on the promenade like a lot of white ants.

It was like a poster advertising the Island. And somewhere, in the mass of buildings, boarding houses, hotels, and shops, clustered between the hills and the sea, was *Sea Vista,* last refuge of

Uncle Fred, who according to these people, had led a life that didn't bear mentioning.

Everything was shining in a haze of heat. Dockers unloading a neat little Diesel cargo boat, shouting at one another, throwing boxes and crates about. Easy-going, cheerful men, working at a leisurely pace. The world going on as though nothing had happened to Uncle Fred and he didn't matter at all.

Another visitor, now. Littlejohn nodded to Knell and they took up their hats.

'Don't go. I want you to meet Mr Boycott's lawyer. Then you'll hear for yourselves how he left his money. Show Mr Squeen in.'

The lawyer entered smiling, walking sideways, like a crab. Rudd introduced him. A small, stocky chap, who looked fond of the good things of life. Red face, pneumatic-looking paunch, flushed nose, affable smile, and soft white hands which he kept rubbing together. He wore a formal black jacket and striped trousers.

'Mr Squeen, of Squeen, Berk, Raby & Squeen, advocates.'

'Glad to meet you, Superintendent. Hullo, Knell.'

'These two gentlemen were just leaving. I thought they might like to hear about the will, Mr Squeen.'

The lawyer put on a pair of half-moon spectacles and looked at some papers which he took from his bag.

'Briefly, his will was left at my office. He made it three years ago. It was executed under the name of Snowball. Fred Snowball. An alias he assumed, presumably to hide his identity. It seemed he was known by the nickname of Snook at his boarding-house. He appeared to have a mania for outlandish names. Well... we'll soon sort that out.'

'What did I tell you?' shouted Mrs Boycott, panting. 'He was mad! Quite mad!'

'All he had went to some people called Costain, who live at Cregneish, in the south of the Island,' continued Squeen, as though she hadn't spoken at all.

There were skeletons in the closet, however. Mrs Boycott and Rudd looked too complacent to be suffering much.

'It's a strange affair, though. The Costains will only benefit by about two thousand pounds. The loose cash, shall we say. By a deed executed nine years ago, Mr Boycott assigned all his English assets to his wife and daughter in equal parts... '

Mrs Boycott erupted again.

'Monstrous! He made over all he'd got to me, and he didn't even let me know. I thought he might return at any time and commence litigation to recover his rights. It was not fair!'

'It's all right now, Mother. Your troubles are at an end.'

Mrs Boycott broke down and sobbed in self pity.

Littlejohn was still looking through the window. A little ferry boat was crossing the harbour, crowded with trippers, from Douglas Head to the pier and promenade. A violinist aboard was playing a plaintive air. Borodin's *Serenade*... It floated sentimentally across the still water and lingered on the quiet of the afternoon. It seemed an appropriate accompaniment. Not to Mrs Boycott's distress, but to the hopeless sadness of Uncle Fred's last days.

'So, that's how it stands. The Costains won't get a fortune, after all, but they're lucky to get what's coming to them.'

Lucky in more ways than one! What would the simple, God-fearing fisherman and his wife in their thatched cottage down at Cregneish do with Uncle Fred's quarter million...? Probably go mad and fall foul of all the bloodsuckers, spongers, and rogues who heard about it. Yes, they were lucky...

'We must go now.'

Littlejohn was sick of it all, and was glad to get outside and breathe pure air again.

'I've had enough for one day, Knell. I'd better get back to Grenaby. The Archdeacon will wonder wherever I've got to. Let me know if anything turns up.'

They were standing by the swing-bridge which leads across the river to the promenade. And then, something did turn up.

A girl emerged from the crowds on the seafront and hurried down the street leading to the bridge, but instead of crossing, turned right along the old quay. Littlejohn got a good view of her, but she didn't see him. She was intent on her errand, looked straight ahead, noticing nobody, nervous and preoccupied. It was Susie, the maid from *Sea Vista*.

Littlejohn had to look again before he recognized her and then he stepped back out of sight and drew Knell with him.

Susie had her hair neatly brushed back and gathered in a pony-tail at the crown of her head. A navy-blue flaired linen skirt, a thin, white woollen jumper with a fashionable square low-cut neck. She was quite transformed in her smart get-up, with fine nylon stockings and high-heeled shoes. Her little breasts showed prominently under her jumper and her figure, usually hidden under a grubby overall, was sleek and attractive. Several of the men tried to catch her eye or whistled as she passed, but she didn't seem to see or hear them. The anaemic shadows under her eyes made them seem larger and more impressive. As they stood watching her, she disappeared into one of the jeweller's shops on the quayside.

There was no point in following Susie inside the shop. Littlejohn and Knell waited. It was a quarter of an hour before the girl reappeared, looking flustered, and made off along the quayside in the direction of the upper town. They called at the jeweller's.

A place set out to attract holidaymakers with money to spend on souvenirs and jimcrack odds and ends. Rings, bangles, pottery bearing the Three Legs of Man... 'A Present from the Isle of Man...' But in cases in the background of the shop, there were better things. Articles in silver and silver plate, most of them period stuff and valuable. China, too. Dresden, Staffordshire salt-glaze figures, carved ivories... The jeweller, a small thin man with a bald head and a pair of spectacles on the end of his nose, looked up expectantly, recognized Knell, and lost heart.

'Afternoon, Inspector.'

'Good day to you, Mr Bernstein.'

'What can I do for you?'

'The girl who's just been in. Can you tell me her business?'

'No business. She was offering me a diamond ring for sale. The sort her type don't come honestly by. She said it was her own, but I wasn't going to take the risk.'

'What was it worth?'

'A five-stone dress ring. Very good stones, too. In a normal deal, I might have given her eighty or even a hundred for it.'

'And sold it for twice as much?'

'Now, now, Mister Knell, be fair. I might have it on my hands a long time. Those kind of rings don't sell every day. People haven't the money. The setting was an old one, too.'

'Thank you, Mr Bernstein.'

'No trouble, I hope.'

'No trouble. Good day.'

Knell looked at Littlejohn, waiting for orders.

'Do we go to Whaley Road again and see Susie on the premises, sir?'

'Yes, I think so, Knell. It looks as if the ring might have been the last of Uncle Fred's finery.'

At *Sea Vista,* high tea was again in course of preparation. Most of the boarders were indoors waiting hungrily, and, in the lounge, some flashy hit-and-miss pianist was playing the piano, a tinkling instrument, out of tune.

Yes, sir, that's my baby...

Mrs Nessle was just entering the dining-room, where, as star lodger, she was installed at a small table of her own at the window. She paused.

'Good afternoon, Superintendent. I haven't had the pleasure of speaking with you. I hope the case is going well and that you'll soon find out who... who killed poor Mr Snook.'

Was she fifty or sixty? Difficult to give her an age. She was fat, but not overdone. Her figure had a plump firmness and she carried herself with erect dignity. She was well dressed, too, in a rather old-fashioned style; grey tweed costume, brogues, and some expensive pieces of jewellery, if it was the real stuff. She spoke well. She was well made-up and her hair was hennaed.

'We're doing our best, Mrs Nessle. He was a friend of yours?'

'A very good one. I'm a widow on my own. I have been coming here even longer than Mr Snook. I am always promising myself I'll find a little house and live here for good, and get the benefit of the lower income-tax rate, but I just can't make the break with the mainland. I have relatives and associations there. My husband, who died fifteen years ago, was a merchant in Manchester... Mr Snook had a flair for stock exchange business and helped me a lot with my little bit of money. I shall miss him.'

She wiped her eyes and gulped.

'Afternoon, ma.'

Greenhalgh pushed his way past her, putting an arm round her shoulder as he did so. She jumped.

'Good afternoon.' And the look she gave him would have withered anybody less case-hardened.

'I must be getting to my tea, Superintendent. I suppose you wonder why I tolerate such awful people as Mr Greenhalgh there. I have always had my own room and they have looked after me well, here. It is better in the off-season... But now that Mr Snook is no more, I may have to make a change. It is getting more and more intolerable.'

She sailed into the dining-room and left them to Trimble, who appeared from the kitchen.

'What's *she* want? Might think this place was the Savoy, London, with 'er airs and graces.'

'She was just passing the time of day. May we have a word with Susie, if she's in?'

'What's up? Not been misbehavin', 'as she?'

Trimble blew a blast of whisky in Littlejohn's face. His wife must have been out again, for he seemed in charge of the premises.

'No. We're going to interview everybody who had contact with Mr Snook, in course of time. Is she free?'

'Bit awkward, just at tea-time, but it's been 'er afternoon off, and Maria and me 'ave done all the needful. She's in 'er room, I think. Probably fancyin' herself in front of the lookin'glass. Got a bit above 'erself of late, 'as Susie.'

'Could we use your private room under the stairs?'

'Of course. Treat the place as if it was your own. I don't mind. In fact, I couldn't care less...'

Trimble was a bit drunk and truculent. More boarders had arrived and, as the police wouldn't let Finnegan and his paramour leave, he'd had to find them digs elsewhere.

Susie was coming down the stairs clad in her overall. She was transformed into the maid-of-all-work again, except that her face was still made-up and her hair tidy.

'They want you...'

Trimble thumbed in the direction of the private office. Susie looked alarmed, but followed Littlejohn and Knell without a question.

'We won't keep you long, Susie. I want to ask you just one question. Where did you get the ring you've been trying to sell to Bernstein?'

A sulky look crossed the girl's face. Not the look of somebody guilty, but of resentment at interference in her private life. The large dark eyes opened wider in their shadowy settings.

'It's mine. I don't see what it's got to do with anybody.'

'It is a very valuable ring. The kind a girl like you doesn't usually possess. Now come along, Susie. Just answer my question if you don't want to get in trouble. Please show me the ring.'

She took it from a fine chain round her neck and placed it in Littlejohn's palm. It was warm from the heat of her body. Five fine large stones, which, even to inexpert eyes, were magnificent diamonds, worth many hundred pounds.

They all stood there, with the cheap clock, which might have been won at a shooting-gallery, ticking the minutes away. An atmosphere of indifference and laziness seemed to permeate the whole of *Sea Vista*. Mrs Trimble out most of the time; Trimble tippling in the kitchen during her absence; the staff getting on with their work in an indolent, lackadaisical way. And Susie, with hundreds of pounds hanging round her neck, dreaming what she'd do with it.

'It belonged to Mr Snook, didn't it?'

The girl started and flushed.

'It was mine. I can prove it. I've got a letter. I was selling it before the police searched me and my things and took it away and perhaps accused me of stealing it.'

'You'd better get the letter and show it to me.'

She left in no hurry and without a word. Knell looked at Littlejohn and shrugged his shoulders.

'A rum affair, sir.'

Susie was back, carrying a little imitation leather handbag from which she drew a sheet of cheap note paper.

DEAR SUSIE,

This letter is just to prove that the five-stone diamond ring I gave you is yours. If anybody questions you, show them this and say I gave it to you.

Yours sincerely,
F. SNOOK

'Well, Susie? Why did he give it to you?'

Littlejohn folded the note and handed it back to the girl.

'You won't believe me if I tell you.'

'All the same, you'd better.'

'I came here five years ago, when I was fifteen. My dad was drowned at sea and my mother had to get me what job she could.'

She spoke in a sulky monotonous voice, resenting every word. But funnily enough, she spoke accurately, carefully, without much trace of local or any other accent.

'Mr Snook was living here. I called him Uncle Fred, like the rest. I looked after him... No more than I'd done for anybody else at first. Then, later, he started to give me little presents, as he called them. They were really tips. He seemed to get fond of me. Nothing wrong. He was as decent as they make them, was Uncle Fred. Not like a lot who come here, mauling you and making suggestions, and asking where your bedroom is... He was a decent, good sort. He was a gentleman. One who'd been rich and known better things and had come down in the world.'

Once started, Susie went on and on in the same toneless voice, as though she was privately grieving for Uncle Fred, and wanted to talk about him to someone.

'He used to ask me what I was going to do with my life. He was that way. Interested and a bit sad, if you get my meaning. I didn't know. I told him so. I'd to earn my living and I'd no qualifications for any other job. So, he what he called took me in hand. He'd been a real gentleman at some time in his life. Not that he wasn't always, but you get what I mean. Well educated, knew good things, well mannered. He bought me clothes and women's good-class papers and taught me how to make myself what he called presentable... Make-up, how to walk properly, and talk... He used to correct what I said and when he'd the time, he taught me a bit of English, too. He gave me books. I can show you them. They're in my room. Grammar and stories. Jane Austen and Dickens. He made me read them and asked me questions. I must have been a poor pupil, but I did learn a lot. I liked it, too. I wanted to make something of myself. I don't want to be in this dump all my life with men eyeing me up and down and pawing me about, and the women looking as if they could scratch my eyes out.'

'What about the ring, Susie?'

'I'm coming to it. Uncle Fred said that if I could only use a typewriter and get used to simple book-keeping, I might get a job as a receptionist or something in a good hotel. He'd suggested at first I might become a hospital nurse, but I could never stand the sight of blood. I said I'd like it. It would be a definite step up and I'd meet nicer people there. He said it was no use trying to do anything here with the Trimbles bullying and keeping me working all the hours God sends. So, we'd arranged at the end of the season I should give notice and take on a job as maid with some private people Uncle Fred knew, some old maiden ladies, who'd let me have evenings off to go to night-school for lessons in typing and such...'

Full of her dreams of bettering herself, Susie grew a bit excited, her cheeks flushed and her large eyes glowed.

'I don't know whether he expected something happening, but he said in case he wasn't here when I needed the money, I was to take a ring he'd got. "I can't leave you anything in my will. It wouldn't seem right and people would mistake the motive." That's how he put it. The ring was all he'd got. It had been his mother's, he said, and he'd hung on to it as a keepsake. I didn't want to take it, but he said "If I'm gone by the time you need the money, I won't want this any more and I'd rather you have it and sell it and do some good to yourself than have my family take it." He gave it to me this spring and the letter just in case of trouble. That's all there is to it. Do I keep the ring? Or am I going to be had up for stealing it? Because if I am...'

'That's all right, Susie. You can keep the ring. But get a friend or someone like Inspector Knell here, to have it put in a safe place for you and, when you need to, help you sell it. Otherwise, you'll be cheated. Did anyone else know about you and Uncle Fred and the lessons he was giving you?'

Littlejohn could imagine it! Uncle Fred, once a family man with a daughter of his own, teaching Susie how to behave like a lady; put powder and lipstick on properly instead of merely daubing herself like the rest of her kind. Giving her instructions on how to carry herself with dignity, instead of shambling about in Trimble's kitchen; teaching her to speak grammatically and without local accent. Making a lady of her, like the ones he'd once lived among and left behind. In other words, she'd become the lonely old man's darling, and he was anxious to raise her to something like his own lost level.

'Mr and Mrs Trimble knew that Uncle Fred took an interest in me. They used to call me his darling and say he was my godfather... And other things, I bet, when our backs were turned. But he was a good lodger, you see. Income in the off-season. They had to keep on the right side of him. And he could talk... use words right. If Mr Trimble ever started hinting or arguing, Uncle Fred would set about him and wipe the floor with him.'

'So you're going to carry on and do what Uncle Fred wanted you to do?'

'Of course. Now that he's gone, I can't stand this place another day. I won't leave them in the lurch right in the middle of the season, but I'm off as soon as the visitors stop coming.'

She was still a bit childish and unsophisticated for her age, but, standing there defending herself, she assumed a kind of dignity which Uncle Fred had given her. He'd taught her to despise the life and ways of *Sea Vista,* resist its easy-going manners and morality, and protect herself from its type of easy virtue which led to vulgar sophistication and a poor finish when the end came.

'Right, Susie, you can go now.'

'Thank you. Good afternoon.'

She hesitated and then took the ring off the little chain round her neck again. She held it out to Knell with a pathetic trusting gesture.

'Will you mind it for me, as he says...?'

Knell hesitated and then smiled and put the ring in his waistcoat pocket.

'Right, Susie, I will.'

A polite farewell and a dignified exit! Just as Uncle Fred had taught her!

Uncle Fred had been quite a man. Littlejohn was beginning to feel as if he'd known him all his life.

8
TRIMBLE VANISHES

Trimble was hanging about in the hall, waiting for them. In the dining-room, sounds of high tea in progress. Chatter, rattling plates, laughter now and then...

'Everythin' all right? She told you all you wanted to know?'

Trimble would have asked what it had all been about, only he daren't. Instead, he stood there sweating and breathing heavily.

'All the boarders behaving themselves, Mr Trimble?'

Trimble looked as though his capacity to handle them was somehow in doubt.

'Meanin' what?'

'The police told them that none had to leave here without their consent.'

'Don't I know it! When are we goin' to be able to call the place our own again?'

'None of them has tried to leave or got restive?'

'No. That is, except Finnegan. You know that, and why 'e's in such a 'ell of an 'urry to get away. *Missis* Finnegan's not 'is wife. She's given 'im the bird and is sleepin' out next door. He keeps threatenin' to leave if the police don't give 'im the word soon.'

'He'd better not try.'

All the ports, the daily boats, and 'planes were carefully watched and the police were even on the *qui vive* about private craft and small harbours, of which there were many. Impossible to check everyone who left from the pier or airport, but any of Trimble's little lot would stand a poor chance.

'Oh, I want a word with you. How much longer am I going to be kept here? I've told you before, my business is going to pot while I'm penned up on this island. When can I go?'

It was Finnegan himself. He'd emerged from his solitary room and descended upon them unheard. He didn't seem interested in high tea.

'We hope to let you all go before long, sir. Meanwhile, please be patient.'

'Patient! You've got a nerve, I must say! Patient... Do you think I killed old Snook? Because, if you do, you've another think coming. Never saw him before in my life. Once I get away, I'll never want to see the Isle of Man again! Unless I get the OK tomorrow, I'm going to see a lawyer. Habeas corpus runs here, I believe, as well as on the mainland.'

Trimble, since Mr Finnegan's act of treachery, wasn't prepared to have much truck with him.

'Go and get yer tea. It's goin' cold. And as for patience, wot about me? Me, as has to put up with the likes of you. Why, if I'd me own way, I'd chuck you and your luggage in the middle of the road... Patience!'

Mr Finnegan didn't seem disposed to argue with Trimble. He looked all in. His flashy grey suit was creased and soiled and his linen was seedy and over-worn. There were large bags under his eyes as though he'd been drunk and sleepless since his girl had denounced and walked out on him. He strolled in the dining-room for his share in the cold meat and pickles, and flung a last taunt over his shoulder as he vanished.

'You... you bloomin' rabbit! You couldn't throw a rice pudding in the street.'

'That's wot I've to put, up with. I wish you'd hurry up, gents, and get this job finished.'

They left him still lamenting and returned to the police-station. Knell made a routine report after examining the rapidly growing file on Uncle Fred.

Alibis of all the lodgers had been checked. Nothing suspicious. He handed over a list of all of them with notes added.

Room 1. Mrs Nessle. Regular boarder, comes several times a year for a week or two at a time. Knew Snook well. Lives Manchester.

Room 2. Mr and Mrs Finnegan. Not married. Mrs F. has now left room and is lodging next door. Finnegan a business consultant. Finnegan lives Seymour Mews, London sw1.

Room 3. Mr and Mrs Mullineaux. Honeymooners. Middle-aged. Keep to themselves. Address: Chez-nous, 12 Cypress Grove, Birmingham, 12.

Room 4. Greenhalgh family. Three children. 'Pontypool', Wisden Road, Hyde, Cheshire.

Room 5. Fred Snook.

Room 6. The Trimbles.

Room 7. Miss Arrowbrook. School teacher recovering from operation. Home address: c/o Mrs Benfield, 11 Deanery Lane, Birkenhead.

Room 8. Four young men.

Vincent Farrer (21).

Sid Horseley (20).

Jack Fletcher (21).

Sam Hollinrake (22).
all of Atherton, Lancs. Party on holiday.

All boarders and Mrs Trimble out at the carnival at time of murder. Checked.

Littlejohn looked lazily over the list. He wasn't at all interested. Under Knell's eager scrutiny, which suggested that some oracle was being consulted, he felt conscience-stricken, but he just couldn't bring his mind back to dreary routine.

Outside, the holiday crowds were milling about. A little red sports car passed brimming over with girls in beach pyjamas and young men – one with a handlebar moustache – clad in thin open shirts and flannels. An elderly man, dressed up like a young blood, strolling past with a girl on either arm. He was obviously intoxicated by the proximity of their supple, half-clad bodies and was swanking and showing off as they laughed at each other behind his back.

'Have you checked up the list with the mainland police, Knell? I mean, have you telephoned to see that the addresses are all as stated?'

'Not yet, sir. I didn't think there'd be any suspects among that lot. None of them would follow and kill Uncle Fred in cold blood, would they?'

Littlejohn thought again. His mind just wouldn't stay put on routine. The atmosphere of jolly crowds and holidaymakers enjoying themselves seemed almost solid and tangible and seeped even inside the police-station, giving everything an unreal, dreamlike touch.

'Who's the police surgeon? Who did the autopsy?'

Knell shuffled the file and produced the report.

The usual routine stuff. Nature of wound. Cause of death. General condition of the body and description of the victim... Certified by J. Rees Whatmore, M.B. M. R.C.S.

'Can you get Whatmore on the phone?'

No sooner said than done. The doctor was on the other end of the line. He sounded to have the holiday feeling, too.

'Superintendent Littlejohn here, sir. I'm just helping my friend Inspector Knell on the Snook case. You did the post-mortem.'

'Yes. Anything wrong?'

'No, doctor. But I just need your opinion. Snook died on the promenade. He might have been stabbed in the crowd.'

'That's right. No doubt about it, is there?'

'That's what I wanted to ask you. Could Snook have been stabbed at his home – the boarding-house, I mean, and have *walked* to the promenade and died there?'

An eloquent pause. Whatmore hadn't thought of that!

'Look here, Superintendent... That's a very serious technical question. I assumed from the start that he'd been stabbed by someone in the crowd.'

'But you examined the damaged heart, doctor, didn't you? Would you care to think it over?'

'That wouldn't do much good. My official report wasn't extensive. Just the bald facts... I... er... yes, I'd say he might not have died right away. The wound hadn't penetrated or damaged the actual *machinery* of the heart... the valves or even the great veins or artery. It entered the muscle... the fleshy part, and he wouldn't have died in a flash, so to speak. There had been internal bleeding. A hopeless case, of course. But a powerful and determined man might have dragged himself along for some distance, bleeding to death, you understand.'

'Dragged himself from Whaley Road to the promenade, held himself up for a little while against the railings, and then dropped dead?'

'Perhaps a man full of vitality and determination... yes... But I'd like to think about it and telephone my old professor of pathology at London... I can let you have a considered opinion then.'

'Very good, doctor. Sorry to trouble you. But it would be a great help.'

The oracle was working now, and Knell's eyes almost shot out of his head.

'You don't mean, sir, Uncle Fred was killed at *Sea Vista...*? There was nobody there, except Trimble and Susie.'

'Are you sure? Easy to say you were out, but be skulking in your room. With all that crowd, nobody could give a real alibi unless they were shoulder to shoulder all the time.'

'Had we better go over the alibis again?'

'The alibis? Oh, yes. I'd check them again, if I were you.'

Alibis... And there, right opposite was a poster baking in the sun.

VILLA MARINA
SID MARTINI AND HIS BAND
EVERY NIGHT AT 8.0
GRAND GALA EVERY FRIDAY

Everybody strolling about half-clad and Littlejohn in the heavy tweed suit he'd worn in Dublin. He could just manage a long cool iced beer or another *Pernod* with little blocks of ice floating on the top.

'By the way, Knell... Mrs. Boycott mentioned having her husband followed by a private detective. You remember? Everybody was talking at once and it quite slipped past us. You ought to get the name of the agency. Uncle Fred's light of love, the girl he went away with when he left Mrs Boycott and his extensive estate and his yacht... The girl hasn't shown up, you know. She hasn't seen Uncle Fred's picture in the paper, or if she has, she hasn't recognized him or is lying low. The private detective might give us some line on her.'

Knell was already asking for Mrs Boycott's hotel. Rudd was

soon on the other end. No doubt about it. You could hear his self-opinionated voice all over the room.

A pause whilst Rudd made inquiries.

'Warren & Hanby...'

It sounded like a firm of patent-medicine manufacturers or a couple of knockabout comedians, but Littlejohn knew them. Run by a man called Gravell... Wilfred Gravell, ex-policeman, supplementing his pension.

'12b Bedford Street, Strand, WC2?'

Knell recited it all again.

'You might get Scotland Yard. Ask for Sergeant Cromwell, if he's in...'

Yes. Cromwell was in. Waiting to be called to the Law Courts to swear away a pair of forgers for two or three years. At the sound of his voice, Littlejohn felt a bit homesick.

'Having a good holiday, sir?'

Holiday! *Sid Martini... Gala Night Every Friday...* Unofficial assistant to dear old Knell, finding out who killed Uncle Fred, and clad in a heavy tweed suit with the sun absolutely frying everything to a cinder!

'Fine, old chap. Wish you were here.'

Littlejohn told Cromwell what he wanted.

'Are you on a case, sir? I thought...'

'Nothing much. The local police are quite capable of handling it... An old man stabbed on the promenade. The Inspector in charge is an old friend and we're trying to clear it up in double quick time and then he can take a bit of a holiday and show me the sights.'

Knell was coughing with mirth, trying to stifle his cries in his handkerchief. He envied the man at the other end of the line, the object of such affectionate banter.

'I really must go now... I don't know what the Archdeacon will be thinking.'

Littlejohn felt like getting up and running out like mad before yet another telephone call sent them back to Mrs Boycott or *Sea Vista* again. This sort of thing had just got to stop! It wasn't the way to conduct a case at all. Disjointed, running here and there, and gathering facts without any coherence. The smart young detectives in Dublin had been right. Littlejohn was growing into an old buffer, a period piece, respected, but carrying on like a horse-tram in these days of planes and quick little diesels.

'I'll run you out to Grenaby.'

Over the old road and back down the little lane to dear Grenaby again. Littlejohn's spirits rose as they got nearer, and then, there they were. He might never have left it. It took hold of him and he felt himself again.

Knell left him at the gate. No use going in the vicarage and getting another slaughtering from Maggie Keggin.

The parson had written his sermons for Sunday and now the rest of the week was his own.

They ate a late tea and Littlejohn tried to sort out his thoughts and give the Archdeacon a clear account of how the case was progressing. He could sift out the useless from the useful, but there wasn't a trace of a scent which might lead to a suspect, someone who had, in his heart, such a shocking and powerful motive, that he would risk killing Uncle Fred in front of a crowd, or, if he'd stabbed his victim and left him to bleed to death, was so demented as to risk Uncle Fred's gasping out his name before death took hold of him.

'If Snook wasn't killed outright, Littlejohn, he must have been shielding someone. On his last dying walk to the sea, he could have stopped a hundred people and told them who had stabbed him. Instead, he died without a word.'

'I'd thought of that, parson. But it's either the hot sun or the holiday feeling... The picture won't take shape.'

'You need a change. Come, and I'll take you out to dinner with friends who are dying to meet you. The Creers, of *Claghyn Baney*... the White Stones. It's a farm...'

It *was* a farm, a fine one, between Glen Maye and Peel, with great fertile fields rolling down to the sea and, in the middle of them, a large white farmhouse, a small mansion, in fact, surrounded by a ring of tall trees. There was a beggars' house, *Yn Shemmyr*, the chamber, where, in old times, wayfarers and vagrants found food and shelter for the night. The homestead was, according to those who knew, infested by fairies, *Themselves*, as they were anonymously called. 'Little fellahs, singing with happiness...' Now and then, the Water Bull, the *Tarroo Ushtey*, stamped and roared around the fields in the dead of night, when all the doors were locked, and sported with the civilized cows, which, in due course, bore his monstrous calves.

All this the Archdeacon told Littlejohn as they drove across the hills towards the red sunset over Peel. They passed on their way, old places, crofters' cottages, the *tholtans*, decaying as they stood, but never pulled down, because they are the homes of spirits who once were happy there... Fuchsias of forsaken gardens... Old roads, green and overgrown, but still plain to be seen and hard from the footsteps of travellers long gone, trailed away into the wilderness which once was fertile, and lost themselves in dead ends.

The Creers were typical Manx patricians, courteous, kindly, reserved, slow-moving, loyal. Because of the Archdeacon, Littlejohn was received among them as a friend right away. An elderly man and his wife, and two young men and a girl of the next generation. A graceful house, full of fine Regency furniture, handed down from generation to generation and polished to the consistency of bright glass by a long succession of housewives. Genuine and gracious hospitality and good manners survived there; very different from the modern back-slapping alcoholic *bonhomie* of the busier world in Douglas and over the water.

Littlejohn ate a great meal and, round the fire, as the chill of the dead day blew from over the sea, they entertained him with tales of ghosts and fairies and monsters of all kinds; the sort of stories men told round winter fires when they had to provide their own diversions and their neighbours were far distant. As he smoked his pipe, his mind wandered away from *Claghyn Baney* and back to *Sea Vista*. Ridiculous! But there it was...

Uncle Fred had been murdered. And, as likely as not, it had happened at the boarding-house and he'd walked out and died on the promenade. Died without telling who'd stabbed him.

Mr Creer was telling a tale of how his grandfather had found himself accompanied one dark night in Glen Maye, by a phosphorescent stranger and had said to himself, 'Good God, who's this?' At the name of the deity, the phosphorescent one had fizzled out and gone.

Yes, but if he'd been stabbed at Sea Vista, *anybody there might have done it. Easy to lose one's companions in the carnival, sneak back, and... All the alibis were useless.*

Mr Creer was fully in his stride. A friend of his had sworn he'd seen five fairies sitting on a gate as he went at dusk once to be seeing to the cattle. This friend was a Mormon and they called him Dipper. Well, the fairies wouldn't let him close the gate and get indoors again. 'Give us another swing on the gate, Dipper,' they kept saying, and Dipper afraid not to, lest he annoy them and they set the place on fire or else dry up the cows...

All the alibis were upset, except, of course, the lad with the accordion and his three pals who were always together; and perhaps the honeymooners, who were a pair of scared rabbits; and the Greenhalghs, minding the kids all the time...

'My grandmother, who came from Scroundal, near Ballaugh, said herself she'd seen the fairies riding on the grindstone of the mill there. A great place for themselves, was Scroundal...' Mrs Creer was saying, not to be outdone.

Unless Mrs Boycott or the Rudds had nipped across by plane, stabbed Uncle Fred and then hurried back, that left Trimble and his three women, Mrs Nessle, Finnegan and his girl, Miss Arrowbrook, who was an invalid, and... nobody else...

The Creer boys were telling their own story. Mermaids used to be seen by the fishermen down at Dalby, a few fields away. They might have been seals, of course, but the old man with the long white hair who used to be seen fishing there in a little coracle wasn't a seal. He used to sing a song as he fished. The fishermen had noted the tune and somebody had written it down. The *Arrane Ghelby,* it was called, the Dalby Song... One of the boys played it on the piano, a plaintive air, like a lament.

Had Trimble been connected with Uncle Fred in the past? Or Mrs Trimble? Or, now that the scene of the crime might easily have been Sea Vista, *could it have been an impulsive act of jealousy involving Mrs Trimble, Maria, or even little Susie? Uncle Fred had been fond of the women; he liked a pretty face and a nice figure...*

Time to go, and another run over the hills back to Grenaby. At that time of the year, it never went quite dark at night and they drove over deserted roads with the peaks and the gentle lines of the curving hills etched against the skyline. Quite a night for meeting some of Mr Creer's collection of little people, black dogs known as Moddhey Dhoos, phantom pigs, goblins, and Manx counterparts of Old Mother Shipton.

Back at the parsonage, the Archdeacon let them in with his key. Voices in the kitchen. Knell and Maggie Keggin hobnobbing like old friends before the fire. Knell was eating a large hunk of game pie. An unsolved mystery was how the pair of them had buried the hatchet and become close friends.

Knell rose a bit sheepishly, trying hard to gobble down his savoury mouthful.

'Sorry to turn up again at this hour.'

The clock had just struck midnight!

'But I felt it would do me good to get away for a run in the country.'

'And a liberal portion of Maggie's excellent pie?'

'Aw... that was quite a surprise... but when I got back after seeing you home, sir, I found things had been happening at *Sea Vista*. In the first place, Trimble's disappeared.'

'Well, well... So things are warming up.'

'He's not gone by boat, because the last one had sailed when he was last seen. He's not flown over, either, because we've enquired. We've doubled the watch on the 'planes and boats.'

'How did it happen, Knell?'

'Just after we left, Trimble went out. Said it was on an errand. He'd a parcel like a boot-box under his arm and he said he wanted to post it. Susie offered to go, but he said he'd go himself. We looked all over the place but, so far, there's no clue where he's gone. His wife got home about six and when she found he wasn't back by eight, she 'phoned us.'

'We can't do anything until morning, now... You'll be sure he doesn't slip past at the pier or airport.'

'Trust us. There's another thing, too. Finnegan's woman is missing. She went off with her suitcase this morning in a taxi... Hasn't been seen since. She must have got fed up with all the fuss and especially with Finnegan.'

'All the same, she mustn't get away, yet.'

'No. There's the usual look-out for her, too.'

'What about the taxi? Did you trace him?'

'Yes. Kelly, the owner of the boarding-house next door to *Sea Vista,* phoned for him at Mrs Finnegan's request. A chap called Shimmin. We got in touch with him. He just took her to the electric railway station at Derby Castle, the end of the promenade, and she got on the tram there.'

'Who reported it?'

'Mrs Trimble. Kelly had told her. She mentioned it casually when she phoned about Trimble. I wonder if the pair of them's bolted together.'

'That *would* be funny. Any idea where she might be?'

'None, as yet, sir. We're following things up.'

Things were bucking up at last. Trimble, indeed! At least, it gave them something concrete to bite on and Littlejohn was glad of it.

As for Finnegan's woman, if she'd run away with Trimble, she hadn't much taste. At any rate, it had freed the air at *Sea Vista* and Finnegan himself of the aroma of scandal which had been hanging round there. Not that it wasn't more or less there all the time.

Knell's back tyre was flat when he returned to his car at around one o'clock. He changed the wheel with Littlejohn's help.

'The little people must have been playin' a trick on me,' he said as he rubbed his soiled hands on an old rag and got ready for off.

Littlejohn laughed, and then he looked at Knell's face in the glow of the dashboard light. It was dead serious. Knell must have meant it, after all!

9

FINNEGAN BOLTS

Trimble had vanished without a trace!

The guests at *Sea Vista* didn't seem to mind that very much. It meant that Mrs Trimble had more to do, but she was a much more appetizing ornament about the place than her husband, half-washed, unshaved, in his shirt-sleeves all the time.

The thing that upset the lodgers, however, was that Trimble had embezzled the four pounds he'd collected from them for Uncle Fred's wreath. 'It's worse than rifling the kid's money-box,' said Greenhalgh, who might have done the same thing himself at some time in his life.

When Littlejohn and the Archdeacon arrived in Douglas the morning after Trimble's disappearance, they found poor Knell up to the neck in work. It was only nine o'clock and he recited what he'd done already.

The whole of the police force on the Island had been warned to be on the look-out for Trimble, who, Knell now firmly suspected, had killed Uncle Fred himself out of jealousy. Door-to-door inquiries had been instituted again. This time a new theme song: Do you know Ferdinand Trimble...? Watches on the boats, planes, and ports large and small had been redoubled. 'We've even called in the Loyal Manx special constabulary... '

Scotland Yard had already been on the telephone and Cromwell had left a message of affection for Littlejohn. They'd checked up on Finnegan at Seymour Mews, London, SW1. There were three workshops there and three houses occupied by the owners of the workshops. A man who manufactured tailors' dummies; another who made shrouds; and a third who engraved armorial bearings and monograms on cutlery... None of them had ever heard of Finnegan!

As for Warren & Hanby, Mr Wilfred Gravell was doing a stretch in gaol for blackmail, and it would take Cromwell a bit longer to get hold of the required information. He would see that it was soon forthcoming, however.

All the addresses of the other lodgers at *Sea Vista* had been checked by telephone with the police across the water and were authentic. The mainland police went even further in one or two cases. Mrs Mullineaux owned a flourishing second-hand furniture store in Birmingham and her name had been Cleve until she'd married her shop assistant a week or two ago. Greenhalgh had been a bookie and now was an undischarged bankrupt trading in his wife's name. The late Mr Nessle, described as a merchant, had been a rather shady moneylender.

'You've done a good day's work already, Knell. I'm proud of you,' chuckled the Archdeacon, and Knell was obviously pleased with the compliment, although, in his usual modest way, he tried to make light of it.

'But it leads us nowhere, sir, does it?'

And he looked at Littlejohn to make sure he was right.

'Of course it leads us somewhere, Knell. It proves Finnegan is a fake, for one thing. It's all right his trying to hide his identity when he plays Don Juan, but he's lied to the police, now, and that's quite a different matter. You won't have called on' him yet?'

'Well, no, sir... Hardly had time.'

'Shall we go on the usual route march to *Sea Vista* again?'

'I'd be glad if you would. Mind if I stay behind and deal with all this routine stuff?'

'Of course. You'll be here, too, when Cromwell rings up with the news he gets from Gravell.'

This time, the parson and Littlejohn walked along the promenade to the boarding-house. It was early in the day and the sun hadn't yet reached its full strength. A fresh little breeze blew in from the sea and people were walking briskly to keep away the chill. The promenade was full of visitors and many of them were setting up deck-chairs on the beach for the morning bask. The tide was going out and a mob of children, parents, and dogs were following the waves as they receded, like a little army occupying the deserted positions of a retreating conqueror. A few swimmers were already rollicking in the water, boatmen were rowing parties out to explore Conister Rock in the middle of the bay. The Salvation Army were holding morning service near a small breakwater and their cornets sounded along the promenade and far out to sea.

'Why did Uncle Fred, who seemed to like peace and quiet, settle down in Douglas with the Trimbles, in a boardinghouse which got crowded out every summer, and where they turned him out of his own room and shoved him on another floor higher up for three months of every year? He made the excuse to Costain that he liked it; said that although Cregneish was his heart's delight, he wanted company... crowds... And all the time, I don't believe he did want crowds.'

The Archdeacon nodded his head.

'I've been thinking about that, too. Could it have been that he had some financial interest in the boarding-house and wanted to keep an eye on it? Mrs Trimble likes playing the lady, you must remember, and would rather stroll about the promenade than work in the house. Trimble is a shiftless tippler... If Boycott had put money in it, he would naturally want to protect his investment.'

'That's true, sir, and I must follow it up. There's one other hypothesis... Uncle Fred was reputed to be fond of the women. It might be a silly piece of scandal. On the other hand, might he have been interested in, say, Mrs Trimble? Or more than a little fond of young Susie? Hence, he'd want to be about the place most of the time.'

The Archdeacon's clear blue eyes searched Littlejohn's.

'Do you believe that? Knowing Boycott as well as we do... and I must confess I feel I've known him for years, now... knowing him as we do, can you honestly say you believe it? Is it in character with the man you call Uncle Fred?'

'Not exactly. I'm not suggesting some sordid affair between him and one of Trimble's three women. But he had adopted Susie, if what she says is true.'

'My suggestion that Boycott was somehow prevailed upon to invest in *Sea Vista* is more feasible. Don't you agree?'

'Yes.'

Horse-trams clopping along full of delighted passengers; whole families carrying buckets and spades, little fishing-nets, beach balls, toy yachts, trudging purposefully to the foreshore for a morning's earnest work; charabancs filling up for all-day trips round the Island; women knitting and their husbands reading the morning papers in the sunshine on seats facing the sea.

A tall, flabby, shabbily-dressed young man took a snapshot of the Superintendent and the Archdeacon, and passed a card to Littlejohn. *Flic Studios...*

'Just a minute... '

The hungry-looking photographer turned in his stride and smiled. He looked tubercular and wore a heavy overcoat in spite of the weather.

'They'll be ready at five this evening. The address is on the card, sir.'

'Are you the young fellow who photographed the man who was murdered here the other day?'

The smile broadened.

'Sure. Did me quite a bit of good. For a couple of days people seemed to take a morbid delight in having themselves snapped by the camera which took the murdered man. It's dying down a bit now, but I did have my little hour of notoriety. You'll find your picture's a good one. The bishop especially... He'll come out fine. He's a good type for camera work.'

'You seem interested in your job.'

'I used to be a film cameraman... Been in Hollywood. But my health broke down.'

As he talked, he kept snapping likely passers-by and handing them his card.

'Did you notice anything peculiar about the old man when you took his picture?'

'Such as...?'

'His appearance... His looks. Did he seem ill?'

'He certainly did. He was as white as a sheet... even grey...' and he just managed to totter to the rails and hold himself up. I've felt that way myself many a time. I made a mistake when I snapped him. One gets that way. Doing it automatically, if you get what I mean. He wasn't fit to photograph and not the sort who'd come to the shop to claim his picture even if it did turn out good. I ought to have asked what ailed him, but the procession was moving towards us and I was eager to be getting on with the job.'

'Was he wearing a raincoat when you met him?'

'Yes; loosely over his shoulders. I remember wondering why, in such weather. Then I thought he might be one of those pessimists who always think it's going to rain sooner or later...'

Littlejohn rubbed his chin. The raincoat had disappeared. In the mob of revellers which had suddenly surrounded Uncle Fred, it could easily have slipped off or even have been dragged from his shoulders. And perhaps it had been trodden under foot, kicked in the sea and carried away by the tide, or picked up by someone...

'Is this your own business?'

'No. I can't afford the set-up. I just rent a bedroom in town and spend my days in the open air. I get a percentage of pictures sold.'

'Had any breakfast?'

The young man bridled.

'Of course.'

'A bun and a glass of milk?'

'You police?'

'Yes.'

'I thought so. Superintendent Littlejohn?'

'Yes.'

'Glad I've met you. Well, if that old chap hadn't been stabbed when I took his picture, he was precious near dying of something else... '

'You didn't see any traces of blood on him. He'd been stabbed in the back.'

'No. As I told you, he'd a raincoat draped across his shoulders which hid his back. But his eyes were a bit glazed and he looked as if he didn't quite know where he was. He saw me when I put up my camera and looked as if he resented it. He seemed to want to be left alone. But I'd snapped him before I reacted to him, you see.'

'Did the police pay you for the snapshot?'

'I got nothing for it. Probably the boss drew something.'

'Here's a couple of pounds. Now, now... no silly pride. You've helped us no end by what you did. If you hadn't taken that picture, we might never have known Snook's identity.'

'All right, then. If it's pay for honest work, sir. Damned decent of you.'

'*You* did *us* a service. One more question. Was there anyone else in the vicinity when the dead man appeared on the promenade?'

'I didn't see a soul. The carnival was starting farther along the prom, and everybody rushed there like a flock of sheep. This part was absolutely empty except for the old man and me. He didn't seem interested. I doubt if he even knew what was going on around him. I couldn't rush. My breathing's bad and I stayed waiting for the crowd to come this way and then I could get busy.'

'Snook arrived on the promenade from Broadway, I believe. The road leading from here to the upper town?'

'Yes. He was all on his own. Nobody bothered with him and he didn't bother with anyone. In fact, when I saw him come out of Broadway, I thought he looked tight. He staggered a bit and sort of held himself loosely, like a drunk... '

'There was nobody following him?'

'No. And nobody came near him while I was here.'

'Thank you.'

'Thank *you,* sir. I'll be seeing you. My name's Bannister. You'll always find me somewhere about here if I can be of any more use.'

But he never was. Two days later, Bannister died like Uncle Fred, quietly, almost apologetically, in the middle of a carnival. Crowds, an ambulance, women fainting... Only Bannister had no claim to fame. He died of a sudden haemorrhage. Natural causes; no fuss – or even a little paragraph in the newspapers... Nobody claimed him, and only the Rev. Caesar Kinrade, Littlejohn, and two grave-diggers attended his funeral. He did, however, finish up with the benediction of an Archdeacon over what was left of him.

Sea Vista seemed short of something without Trimble there to act as guide, to whine and complain, and to limp about in the now familiar processions up to Uncle Fred's room and then down again, after the manner of the famous Duke of York.

Susie answered the door and led them to the little office under the stairs where Mrs Trimble was doing some bookkeeping, as though nothing unusual had happened.

'I thought I'd better let the police know, although Trimble's done this before... Vanished for a day or two and then come home again looking like nothing on earth. He's a bit temperamental and I guess he's gone off on a spree somewhere.'

She gave them seats and asked them if they'd take anything to drink.

'No, thanks... We won't keep you long, Mrs Trimble. I just wanted to ask if there was any reason why your husband should suddenly take it into his head to bolt.'

'I've already answered that one, Superintendent. I think he's suddenly got all temperamental and gone off for a spree.'

'But where? Has he friends he can stay with or has he been in the habit of going off to some specific place for his sprees?'

'Sorry, I can't help you there. When he's been off before, I've never been able to get out of him where he went.'

'You know, of course, Mrs Trimble, I was here yesterday when you were out, and interviewed Susie, the maid. Your husband wasn't present at the interview, but seemed a bit anxious and put-out that it should occur at all. Why should he feel like that?'

She bit her lip and her face grew hard and set.

'I really don't know. Would it be asking too much to inquire what she told you? I mean, did my husband overhear any of the conversation which might have upset him?'

'I can't see why. She told me of the interest Fred Snook took in her well-being and how he tried to help her better herself.'

Mrs Trimble's face was now positively sour. She seemed to be turning over words carefully in her mind before speaking.

'I didn't like the way things were developing between Mr Snook and Susie. She's little more than a kid and he was sixty... I don't like old men's darlings. It's not natural. I'm sure my husband felt the same.'

Littlejohn lit his pipe.

'But that has hardly anything to do with Mr Trimble's vanishing, has it? Do you think he might have been upset, or even afraid of something he thought Susie told me, and felt he couldn't face interrogation?'

She tried to smile, but it seemed she was too angry to do it.

'Whatever should Trimble have to fear about Susie? You don't think Mr Snook and he were keen on the same girl... Susie... do you, and one killed the other on account of her? It sounds like grand opera! I can assure you that nothing of that sort was going on. I'm just as much in the dark as you are about who killed Uncle Fred, but I'm sure Trimble didn't do it. He hasn't the guts.'

'Suppose we have another word with Susie.'

'It's all the same to me. I'll get her. Want to speak to her alone?'

'No... It might be helpful if you stay.'

Mrs Trimble left to get the girl. The Archdeacon had been listening and saying nothing. Now he spoke.

'Do you think that's right, Littlejohn? Trimble hadn't the guts? He struck me as being one who might do anything if he lost his temper. The flabby sort who go off half-cock and commit acts of folly they afterwards regret.'

'He struck me as being the same.'

Mrs Trimble was back, pushed Susie through the door, and stood with her back to it as though the girl might try to run away. Susie was sulky again and gave Mrs Trimble an eloquent, scorching look which boded no good for the peace of *Sea Vista* when the two women were left alone.

'Come here, Susie, please. Now tell me, after you and I spoke together yesterday, did Mr Trimble ask you what it was all about?'

'Yes. I told him it was confidential.'

Mrs Trimble drew in her breath with a hiss.

'You saucy little madam. That was no way to talk to your boss.'

'Boss, did you say? You know as well as I do, who's the boss here.'

'Please... Don't let's get down to quarrelling among ourselves, Susie. You told Mr Trimble what you and I said was confidential. What then?'

'He asked me a lot of questions, trying to get at it that way. He stood between me and the door, to keep me there till I'd told him.'

'What kind of questions?'

'He wanted to know if you asked about him, or Mrs Trimble.'

'Was that all?'

'He tried to get to know if you'd asked me what sort of relations existed between him and Uncle Fred, and then he said did you ask about Uncle Fred and Mrs Trimble.'

Mrs Trimble crossed the room like a tigress and Littlejohn had to stand between her and Susie to prevent an open quarrel, if not violence.

'It's no use you trying to frighten me... I'm only telling the truth and you can ask Mr Trimble when he comes back... If he ever does.'

'What do you mean by that, Susie?'

'I think he was frightened that you'd asked me and got out of me something that would make you suspect him or Mrs Trimble... And when I wouldn't tell him, he cleared off and hid himself out of the way.'

Mrs Trimble made another effort to get at Susie, but Littlejohn was in the way again.

'You little liar! After all we've done for you. Brought you up and looked after you like our own. Well... as soon as you leave this room, you can pack your bag and get out... I won't have you in the place another hour... You hear?'

'I hear. And I wouldn't stay if you begged me on your knees. If it hadn't been for...'

She paused. Mrs Trimble finished it for her.

'If it hadn't been for Old Snook... Go on, say it. Always playing up to him. That's what you were. Always playing up to him. Don't try to tell me you didn't set your cap at him, you little liar... Out for all you could get...'

'That will do, the pair of you. You'd better go, Susie.'

'She'd better have her bag packed next time I see her, or I'll throw her out.'

'Get along, Susie.'

'I'm going... Wild horses wouldn't stop me after this. You owe me a month's pay, and I want extra instead of notice. You can't sack me without notice.'

Littlejohn took her gently by the arm and piloted her into the passage. The house was quiet. All the guests out in the fresh air, which was a good job. Upstairs someone was using a vacuum cleaner...

Mrs Trimble was so upset she could hardly speak. She crossed to a cupboard and helped herself to a glass of what looked like gin.

'You'll excuse the language and my temper, reverend... I didn't intend to let go like that in front of you. But the things I've put up with from that girl. It's all over now. She'll have to go.'

Littlejohn sat down again opposite Mrs Trimble, whose colour was returning as the gin did its work.

'Is all this true? Uncle Fred's interest in Susie wasn't entirely paternal?'

'Of course it wasn't. She played up to him. I must say, that when she's dressed up, she's quite good-looking, if you like them that way. Uncle Fred was smitten on her. Any woman of the world could see it going on before our eyes.'

She paused, took another drink, and raised a warning finger.

'Now, don't get me wrong. Uncle Fred was as decent as the day and I won't have a wrong thing said about him. He was too much of a gentleman to try anything on with her. But she used to put on that air of dewy innocence with him. He fell for it. She wouldn't let any of the young boarders here take her out, even to the pictures, in case Uncle Fred might think she was flighty. He fell for it, as I said. And him a man of the world. They get that way sometimes. Heaven knows how much she got out of him. I threatened to send her packing a time or two before, but Uncle Fred went off the deep-end about it and we were so fond of him here that we let him have his own way. Well, there's nobody now to take her side and she's on her way out.'

'Isn't Mr Trimble likely to object if he returns?'

Another pause. The large eyes opened wide.

'You're not suggesting... ? Surely, you don't think my husband...?'

Then she laughed. A vulgar, self-confident, noisy laugh.

'Ferdy! Ferdy setting his cap at Susie? I'd have liked to see him do it! He knows better than try tricks with me... You'll forgive the unpleasant turn the conversation's taken, reverend, I'm sure, but I'm trying to help all I can.'

Mrs Trimble seemed at least to have been brought up with a great respect for the Church and the cloth of its clergy. The Archdeacon nodded gravely, but his blue eyes twinkled.

There was no window in the room and it had never been intended to hold three people. The air was heavy and soaked with kitchen smells. Littlejohn was anxious to be off.

'Just another couple of questions and then we'll leave you to your own affairs, Mrs Trimble... Did you know Mr Snook before he came here and asked for lodgings?'

He eyed her keenly. She hesitated and then made up her mind.

'No. He just turned up one day and seemed to settle down. We liked him, and he liked us.'

'Did he ever help you financially? I mean, did you ever borrow from him or did he invest money here in the business?'

Another pause. She seemed to be wondering just how much Littlejohn knew.

'I think I ought to tell you, Mrs Trimble, that his private papers are at our disposal. They may contain references to his investments.'

'I hope you're not suggesting that I'd tell lies to you. No. We didn't owe him any money. We make ends meet quite nicely in the season. Sometimes, he had lent us a hundred or so, just before the new season started... When we wanted to do some decorating or such like... We always paid him back from profits in the summer.'

'Good. Can you tell me then, why he should settle down in a town like Douglas, crowded to such an extent in the season that he had to move up to the top floor from his usual quarters? He was a man who liked the country and quietness, as far as I can gather... What held him to your place, Mrs Trimble?'

For the first time, she looked distressed. Tears rose in her eyes and she couldn't speak. Then she recovered and dabbed her eyes dry.

'He liked us. He said so. After all, we always made him feel at home. He was one of the family. That's what kept him here.'

It might have been true. Perhaps the inertia of the Trimbles' establishment had got in Uncle Fred's blood. The kind of place where they didn't care what you wore or when you came in or went out. He'd done just as he wished and nobody had bothered. Gone to Cregneish, stayed away for a day or two, returned smelling of drink... No fuss, no questions asked. Life started again just where it had left off. It seemed to be the same with Trimble now. He'd made off somewhere leaving no message, no excuse. And here was his wife, quite unperturbed, quite indifferent, carrying on as if he'd just crossed the road for a drink and would soon be back. And when he returned, if he did, he'd probably just take up again as though he'd never been away.

'Any news of the lady who came here with Finnegan? I believe she's run away, too.'

Mrs Trimble's good humour was back again. She'd just finished her second drink.

'You're not suggesting that Ferdy and Finnegan's woman have bolted together, are you? That *would* be funny. Just all that was needed to make a comic opera of it.'

She laughed harshly again. Now that the gin had loosened her up a bit, she looked like a real third-rate theatrical trouper. But funnily enough, she never lost her freshness. All her anger at Susie, all her mirth at Ferdinand and his ways, all her apparent fondness for Fred and her memories of him, all the gin she'd consumed... She emerged from it all just as, long ago, she'd probably left the footlights and arrived in the wings as fresh and neat as when she went on at her first cue.

'Has anyone any idea where Finnegan's friend went?'

'None, as far as I know. She was staying with the Kellys next door. After she broke with Finnegan, she wouldn't stay here... As a matter of fact, it was a bit funny.'

More hearty laughter.

'You see, after the police discovered they weren't married, she came all over virtuous... They'd been occupying the same room and she suddenly said she wanted a room of her own. A woman of her type, too... You'll excuse me, reverend, but the Superintendent asked me. We hadn't a room to spare, so I asked the Kellys and she went there.'

'I see. Perhaps we can get some clue, some idea, if we call on the Kellys.'

There was a tap on the door and without waiting, a stranger opened it... or at least, she was a stranger to Littlejohn.

'Oh, excuse me. I didn't know you'd visitors.'

'What is it, Mrs Brew?'

A little wisp of a woman with her hair untidy and a streak of soot across one cheek. The daily help. She spotted the Archdeacon, smiled at him, and bobbed a half curtsey to him.

'I just wanted to say that there's nobody in Mr Finnegan's room.'

'He's usually out at this time of morning, isn't he?'

'Yes, but his bags has gone... He's packed up... Done a moonlight, as likely as not... Come an' see for yourself, Mrs Trimble.'

Mrs Trimble was quickly out and back again.

'It's true. He's packed up and off. Though I must say he's left money for his bill on the dressing-table.'

'I'd better use the phone, Mrs Trimble.'

Littlejohn broke the news to Knell, who lamented bitterly.

'It never rains but it pours, sir. What are we going to do now?

Pass the word along the line about him as well as Trimble, Mrs Finnegan and Fred Snook? It's getting more than we can manage.'

'Don't worry, old chap. The more the merrier, you know. They'll all come home to roost. They'll have to, if they can't get off the Island.'

'We'll see to that.'

Finnegan had thoroughly spring-cleaned his room. Not a scrap of paper, a letter, nor even a cigarette end to give any idea of what he'd been doing or where he'd gone.

'He ate his breakfast with the rest, as usual. He never was one for talking to others. Him and his woman had a little table of their own and except for passing the time of day as they came and went to meals, they never mixed. He must have been ready packed... or else he got his luggage away in the night and then came down for breakfast before following it... As Mrs Brew said, he must have done a moonlight with his bags.'

Next door was a more palatable place. The Kellys were cheerful busy people, the house was clean and modern, and there was more air and space in the rooms and hall. Mrs Finnegan's room had been left untouched on police orders.

'I hope you'll let us clean it and get it ready today, sir. There's more arrivals on the incoming boat and we'll want the room.'

A chubby cheerful fellow, this time, and obviously prospering at his business. There was a good carpet on the stairs and the room he showed them was carpeted, too, and furnished decently. The house was called *Rossendale,* a souvenir of its first owner, a man from Lancashire, presumably nostalgic for the place he came from, who'd ended by going bust and returning to Rossendale in double-quick time.

Littlejohn looked round the room. Finnegan's light of love hadn't been quite as tidy as her partner. She'd left powder sprinkled over the dressing-table, hair combings in the washbowl, cigarette ends and charred paper in the hearth, which held a gasfire.

'What a mess she's left. Can we clean the place up now, Superintendent?'

'I'll just take a look round first and then you can get on with it, Mr Kelly.'

There was nothing much to guide them where Finnegan's woman had gone. Odds and ends of rubbish, a pair of nylon stockings hung out to dry and forgotten, a box of chocolates with a few left in it. Indications of self-indulgence and untidiness all over the place. There was ash in the fireplace as though the woman had been at pains to burn letters. Littlejohn turned it over with his forefinger and it all fell away to dust.

'Are you wondering where she's gone to?' asked Mr Kelly who had been standing watching quietly.

'Yes. Do *you* know?'

'Not for certain, but there was a woman from next door came in with her when she moved her things to here. A Mrs Nessle, I think I heard her called. I came up to see that the room was satisfactory and I just heard the tag-end of a conversation. Mrs Nessle was saying... "I was always charmed with Agneash... so quiet..." I wondered...'

The Archdeacon was on it like a shot.

'Of course. You remember, don't you, that Knell told us the lady in question took a taxi to the Manx Electric Railway terminus and got a tram there? That railway goes to the north of the Island along the coast and passes Laxey, the stop for Agneash, which is quite near it. It's a mining village in the hills there and, incidentally, I should think a wonderful hide-out. Shall we go and try?'

'No harm in taking a chance, sir. It will at least be a pleasant outing. Thank you, Mr Kelly. And you can get on with the cleaning of the room now if you want to let it to someone else.'

Littlejohn telephoned Knell again, just to cheer him up and let him know they were on a promising trail.

'No news of Trimble?'

'No, sir. All the men on the beats have been told to ask about strangers or suspicious circumstances. We're doing our best, but it looks like being a long hard grind.'

'Cheer up, Knell. You can't do more than your best, can you?'

'That's right, sir.'

Littlejohn left the phone-box and was silent for a while as they made their way to the tram terminus at Derby Castle, where a police car was to meet them to take them to Laxey.

'I've just been wondering, parson... Is there any spot on the Island where there's no constable on the beat? Knell says all his men on patrol are combing the place. If you wanted to hide out of the way of a roving bobby, where would you go?'

The Archdeacon didn't hesitate for a minute.

'To the Calf of Man,' he said.

'The Calf... Why didn't I think of that before? I've never been there.'

'There's a warden on the island, of course, who's really in charge of the bird sanctuary. But one could easily get on and off without his knowing. It's a large stretch, no police, no telephone, very few visitors and they don't stay there long. There's plenty of cover and one could hide there indefinitely, provided one had food.'

'Yes. I wonder if Trimble thought of that. He must have been there with Uncle Fred on one of his fishing trips, I'm sure. He said they went together sometimes.'

Another port of call. Uncle Fred seemed to have started a trail all over the Isle of Man!

The breeze had died away and now the sun was shining fiercely and the heat was sizzling again. Horse-trams, some people in a landau jog-trotting along the seafront, the beach cram-jammed full of people sunning themselves in deckchairs... A bowling-green surrounded by little tables at which customers were drinking beer, whilst their companions leisurely rolled the woods about on the cool green turf... Littlejohn mopped his forehead and lit a cigarette. It was too hot for a pipe.

A busy little tout standing by his charabanc accosted them.

'Afternoon tour of the Island, gents?'

Littlejohn smiled blandly at him.

'We've booked already, thank you. With Uncle Fred...'

'Oo the 'ell's Uncle Fred? Never 'eard of 'im.'

'I wish I hadn't.'

The tout's mouth fell open and his beery eyes followed the strange pair out of sight. A bishop... And another chap blethering about his Uncle Fred. He finally shrugged his shoulders and decided they'd escaped from somewhere...

It takes all sorts of people to make the strange colourful world of the Isle of Man in the golden summer-time.

10

AGNEASH

'This is absolutely breathtaking...'

Once or twice, Littlejohn, captivated by the beauty of the scenery, almost drove the police car in the ditch.

The main road from Douglas to Laxey runs a magnificent course all the way. It hardly ever leaves the sight of the sea. It may take a brief twist inland for a spell, but never for long. To the left, little fields, a patchwork of many colours from dead earth to flaming gorse, climb gradually upwards to meet the gentle Manx hills; to the right, the rocky coast and blue ocean...

Now and then, a car-load of trippers, passing on the electric railway, shouted encouragement, stimulated by the sign POLICE and feeling immune from traffic laws and regulations.

'They actually had the temerity to talk of pulling up that nice little electric railway and selling it for scrap, because it didn't pay dividends. Dividends, indeed! Look at those happy faces, which will be happier when they've seen all the beauty of the journey. They've only just started to enjoy themselves and will be drawing dividends for life when they remember it in the future. Monstrous! Luckily, wisdom has prevailed. It's been saved and nationalized!'

Littlejohn had never seen the Archdeacon looking so annoyed before...

They turned the corner from Garwick and climbed to find the whole stretch of Laxey Bay spread before them. From the hill top, the sea, calm and blue; Lonan new church on its hill; Old Laxey village below, hugging the shore. A tiny port, with a small steamer tied up, a thin wisp of smoke rising from its funnel, discharging wheat for the flour mills.

The main village lay at the end of a wide luxurious glen, the river running through, and modern villas on the hillsides. A little shopping centre, the terminus of the Snaefell mountain railway, a pub or two...

An old mining village, with rich underground lodes of lead and silver, now much improved by the clearing away of old Laxey 'deads', the heaps of slag once piled along the river banks from the workings. In the background, the famous Laxey Wheel, the *Lady Isabella,* once the pump to clear the underground waters, now painted up and spruce for the pleasure of visitors and slowly turning for the sheer fun of it.

Directed by parson, Littlejohn turned left at the mountain railway station and after skirting the river for a spell, they began to climb and entered Agneash Glen, a tributary of the main Laxey stream. A fine rising run, with everywhere signs of past mining enterprises; old mills, forlorn shafts, neglected mansions and cottages which had housed masters and men. Trees and bushes running riot and overgrowing the abandoned remnants of dead endeavours.

An old man was descending the road and the Archdeacon suggested they'd better stop and question him. Littlejohn was puzzled at first.

'The grapevine... I think that is the term professionally used,' said the parson. Littlejohn put on the brakes.

The wayfarer was a small, aged, thick-set man, with pale blue eyes, a craggy lined face burned by the sun, and a large sprawling moustache across his upper lip. He wore old clothes and a cloth cap. When he saw the parson his eyes lit up.

'Good morning, Jacky Dan Kennish.'

'Good day to ye, Master Kinrade, and how are ye at all?'

Jacky Dan Kennish had a *Traa dy Liooar* look in his eyes. Time enough! Littlejohn knew they were in for a session. Gossip... hours and hours of it! A real Manx *cooish*...

The Archdeacon introduced Littlejohn.

'How are you, Mr Kennish?'

'Aw... middlin', middlin'... It's a grand day.'

They talked and talked, first through the open windows of the car, and then all three of them sitting on the bank of the sod-hedge. Littlejohn smoked his pipe. He didn't care. The sun was hot; he removed his jacket. The holiday feeling... The winding road with its fringes decked in wild flowers, climbing up to the little village of Agneash. Beyond, Snaefell, with the crowded trains of the mountain railway crawling to the summit. Cars tearing along the mountain road at the top of the valley, with another deserted mine and the headwaters of the Laxey and Agneash streams flowing down to the sea. Below them, the main Douglas–Ramsey coast road, with people looking like little insects, and red buses passing to and fro... *Traa dy Liooar*... All the time in the world. Littlejohn thoroughly understood Uncle Fred. Let the rest of the world go by...

The Archdeacon and Jacky Dan Kennish had dismissed the crops and fishing, and the holiday traffic as well. They were all middlin'... Now they were talking about happenings of fifty years ago. Littlejohn lit another pipe. A great languor took hold of him, encouraged by the gentle drone of the lilting Manx voices, halting with regular courtesy, so that both participants should have a fair share of the *cooish*.

Fred Snook had been murdered... It was no ordinary murder. As likely as not, some woman was involved. It couldn't have been for his money. A crime of that kind would have been carefully planned.

Certainly not a matter of inexpert stabbing and leaving the victim to stagger to where the crowds were gathering and where he could tell the first person he met who'd done it.

The parson and his ancient friend were now discussing the mines with the confidence of experts. The prices of lead and silver had made the local industry tempting again and a company from 'over' had been busy prospecting.

'Aw, till the mines closed in 1921, millions and millions of pounds of ore was taken from the Laxey mines for the benefit of folks across the wather, master.'

'But they brought work and wages.'

'Aw, a good job when the Manx goviment bought out the rights in '49... Betther for us all...'

An argument was boiling up. Down below the red bus which Mr Kennish intended to catch to see his daughter at the Dhoon, came and went, and two more, as well.

Fred Snook and his women... Mrs Trimble, Susie, perhaps Maria and... who was the other woman; the one he'd gone to when he left his wife...? Leicester... that was it. Why hadn't the Leicester woman put in an appearance? Wilfred Gravell, Mrs Boycott's 'private-eye' might be able to tell them something... Littlejohn wished that Cromwell would hurry and send more news from gaol.

The two Manxmen had now got round to the general state of business and prosperity of the Laxey neighbourhood.

'I see there's a boat tied up at the quay, Jacky Dan.'

'Aw... '

Talk of fishing and seafaring in general. Littlejohn lit another pipe.

'My son-in-law, Caesar, was halpin' with the unloadin'... Said a fellah from across was enquirin' about crossin' back to Liverpool on the *Camlork*. It seems, accordin' to him, that he's fond o' taking' passages on coasters. Hasn't no time for the big luxury boats and liners, leck. Caesar said he didn' look leck a seafarin' man... However, you never know.'

Littlejohn looked up.

'What happened, Mr Kennish?'

'The skipper wouldn' teck him, of course. The *Camlork* hasn' any accommodation for passengers, for one thing... Another is that, accordin' to Quine, the police constable, they're powerful again' anybody leavin' the Islan' by any other way than the proper boat from Douglas or the airy-planes.'

'Where is the man, now?'

'I couldn' tell ye... I wasn' there when all that was goin' on.'

'Any holidaymakers staying at Agneash, Mr Kennish?'

'Aw... it's not favoured much by the likes... Too far from the rest o' the world, an' no buses or sech.'

'So they don't take in boarders?'

'Naw... Mrs Quilliam, Claram Cottage, has a young woman stayin' there. Not the usual sort for the lecks o' Agneash... Fancy piece, I'd call her. Come up by taxi yesterday, passed me on my road down. Not seen her about since... Seems to be stoppin' indoors, leck. Perhaps she made a mistake an' not bein' the counthry sort, prefers to stop inside... She'll soon be on her way, in that case.'

Jacky Dan suddenly became aware of the flight of time, drew a large silver watch from his trousers pocket, and consulted it solemnly.

'Aw, man! Hal' pass twelve and me here still newsin'. Ye put the jerrude on me, parson... Ye make me ferget. An' me daughter Jinny's expectin' me at noon... Good day to the both of ye. Good to be puttin' a sight on ye, Archdeac'n.'

He stumped off down hill at a steady pace as though he'd still time enough!

Claram Cottage stood at the top of the uphill road, a little beyond the centre of the hamlet which was marked by a chapel and a slight thickening in the houses. The highway ceased nearby and a cart-track made its way over rough ground to the old Snaefell mine. A white house, once thatched, but now slated and looking self-conscious in its new head-gear. A small garden with a fuchsia bush or two in full bloom. Faces appeared at windows and over garden hedges. Very unusual for the Archdeacon of Man to appear in Agneash. There must be something unusual afoot! The news flew from back-door to back-door and soon an unseen audience was watching the drama going on at Mrs Quilliam's. The excitement even seemed to rise like a vapour to Creggyn Agneash, the rocks which overhang the village, for two faces appeared, peeping round, like spectators in a theatre balcony.

Littlejohn himself felt the tension of the local atmosphere. Agneash, known for some unearthly reason as 'the City' by some of its aged inhabitants, is infested by ghosts and fairies, and there is even talk of people being 'sperrited away'.

The odd things a man finds there,
The hid things, the lost things,
They tease him, they tempt him to ponder,
They set his thoughts straying...

Walter Gill's lines might have applied to Littlejohn, for the 'hid things' suddenly materialized and, as the car drew up, Mr Finnegan and his woman emerged from the back door of the cottage and started running in the direction of the cart-track to the mine. They were carrying three suitcases between them.

It was just incredible! A charming little village, neat houses, peace and quiet... Bees buzzing round and sheep munching on the hillsides. A strange delicious scent on the air, perhaps honey-suckle or fuchsia. Littlejohn could have settled down on the soft grass of the hillside and taken a nap... And suddenly, this grotesque pantomime had started.

Finnegan and his companion were like two rabbits suddenly scared from a burrow by a ferret. They didn't know where to run. The main road was blocked by the car, so they took to the open. What they hoped to do that way, heaven alone knew. All they wanted to do was to bolt! Finnegan was wearing his natty grey suit and the hat to match. He was panting already and his eyes were popping with fear. His woman was in an even worse plight. She wore a light-grey costume and the peroxide blonde of her hair shone in the sunlight. She was buxom, almost luscious, and between her high heels and her tight skirt was having a poor time. Finnegan was a yard or so ahead and she tottered and staggered after him, trying to say something and too short of breath to get it out.

Littlejohn fished in his hip pocket and took out his police-whistle. He carried it as a kind of talisman and rarely used it. He looked distastefully at it and blew it. The fleeting couple stopped dead like a pair of gun dogs.

'Come back.'

They paused for a minute and then Finnegan went all to pieces. He seemed to shrink in his flashy suit and slowly turned, almost collapsing under his two suitcases and dragging his feet. He ignored his woman, who followed as well, and slowly came and faced up to the Superintendent.

The window curtains of the clustered cottages fluttered like little banners and the two spectators on the Creggyn emerged fully and leaned with their backs against the rocks waiting for the next act. In one or two houses the time signal preceding the one o'clock news sounded in vain. Local affairs had grown more important than the antics of the noisy world across the water.

'What do you think *you're* doing?'

Finnegan was too breathless to reply. He merely shrugged his shoulders to indicate he didn't quite know himself.

'You ought to be ashamed of yourself.'

'That's what I told him, but he thought if we could manage to get to the mountain road without being seen, we might thumb a lift into Douglas.'

'And what then?'

It was too much to watch from behind window curtains and

little knots of people were now starting to gather at front garden gates.

'Can we talk indoors?'

Finnegan pointed to Claram Cottage and just managed to pant out his request. Mrs Quilliam was standing at the front door and, judging from the look on her face, she was going to be very unpleasant about everything. Then she saw the Archdeacon.

'Aw, Masther Kinrade, and what are they doin' mixin' you up in these indaycent carryin's-on? It's a shame... Come indoors, an' welcome... But I won't have any of the others... Sech goings-on.'

The parson introduced Littlejohn. Mrs Quilliam did not smile. She let it be known that only on account of his friendship with the Archdeacon would she tolerate him at all. Scotland Yard and its affairs were quite unknown to her. Its fame and reputation had not yet reached 'the city', where there was never any crime and where the police only appeared perhaps once in a dozen years to help off to the workhouse some poor soul who couldn't manage for herself. As for constabulary efforts to trace odd ones 'sperrited' away by Themselves, the fairies... Well... It seemed that with the flabby, frightened Mr Finnegan and his woman, crime had, for the first time in recorded history, raised its head in Agneash.

'You'll be doing us a public service, Mrs Quilliam, if you allow us the use of your front room for a little while. We just want to question these two people.'

Mrs Quilliam gave way at last under the compelling eye of the Archdeacon.

'But it'll have to be made plain in the papers and in the Deemster's Court that it was done against my wishes.'

Littlejohn took Mrs Quilliam aside and had a word or two with her.

'Tell me, please, Mrs Quilliam, how did the lady come to stay with you? Who gave her your address?'

Mrs Quilliam's lips tightened. She was beginning to like Littlejohn, but the nature of the business in hand precluded any smiles or relaxation. She folded her hands across her ample bosom.

'Some years since, a woman of the name of Mrs Nessle used to come an' stay here in the summer. A nervous, botherin' sort, who said the rest an' quiet did her a lot of good. It was her who gave the address, and when Miss Crawley came along, sayin' Mrs Nessle had recommended me, leck, I thought no more about it, though with her dyed hair an' scent an' her fancy ways, I didn't teck very much to her. I did it to oblige Mrs Nessle. I was sure Agneash wasn't to Miss Crawley's likin' and expected her makin' off any time.'

'What about Finnegan, the man... ? When did he arrive?'

'Early this mornin'. Came here an' asked for Miss Crawley. I disliked him right away. He was up to no good. A friend, he called himself. Said he'd a message for Miss Crawley. I kep' him at the door and sent her to him. She came back cryin'. She said he'd brought her newses that would make her have to leave right away and cross by the afternoon boat to Liverpool. Could I give them a cup of tea... ? I said yes out of pity for her, so I let him in.'

'Had he any luggage with him?'

'Yes... two cases. He came by taxi. At first, I thought he'd got it in mind to ask me to put him up... On no account would I have done that. My late husban' and me has alwis been respected in Agneash and nobody's goin' to take my good name away.'

'What were they doing when we arrived?'

'She was packin' her things. I wasn't havin' him upstairs with her. Sit in the parlour, I told him, and wait... They must have seen your motor-car comin' up the hill. Next thing was, he was up the stairs and in her room. Shameful! That's why I forbid him the house jest now... They was out of the back door an' off before I'd gathered myself together.'

She led him in the front room where the rest of the party were waiting. A crowded little place with some beautiful bits of furniture in it... A lot of photographs on the walls, including a prominent one of Captain John James Quilliam, master of the barque *Purt-ny-Hinshey*, who had gone down with it off King William's Bank... Souvenirs and the like under glass shades, stuff which at some time in the past had had its moments of splendour... Hangings, antimacassar, cloths... all dust collectors, but the place was spotless.

'I was just makin' a cup of tea... You'll take some, Archdeacon?'

'If the rest may join in.'

'If you say so, pazon, but I must say...'

'Go on with you, Mrs Quilliam. Never let it be said that you weren't Manx in your hospitality.'

She went to attend to things without more ado. Littlejohn got to work on Finnegan at once.

'You'll kindly stay here, Mr Finnegan, with the Archdeacon, whilst I have a word with Miss Crawley in private... We'll take a stroll down the road, if you please, Miss Crawley.'

Finnegan was past protesting; he just acquiesced. Miss Crawley, astonished but obedient, tottered after Littlejohn on her high heels.

The gossips in the village were surprised to see what went on. Littlejohn and Miss Crawley walking to the chapel, and then back to Claram Cottage. Then back and forth again. Four times, talking all the while. The nosey-parkers, those locally known as 'skeets', suffered much by not being able to overhear it all.

'What made you come all this way?'

'I was very distressed about the commotion at *Sea Vista*. I wanted to get away to somewhere quiet. Mrs Nessle was the only one I ever spoke more than a couple of words to. She gave me this address.'

'After the police had told you to remain where you were?'

'I thought it didn't concern me. I was almost off my head with shame and fear. I just had to run away and hide. I'm sorry.'

She took out a small handkerchief and dabbed her eyes. She looked between thirty and forty, and without her make-up and peroxide she'd probably show her age. All the same, she improved a little for knowing. She spoke well, lacked the vulgarity one assumed on first seeing her, and seemed genuinely put out by the situation in which she'd been thrust.

'Your name is...?'

'Elsie Crawley.'

'You and Mr Finnegan have been posing as man and wife in Douglas.'

'I... I...'

'Please tell me the truth, Miss Crawley. We've had enough trouble with the pair of you. Now...'

'Yes. I... I...'

And she started to weep, great sobs of frustration or annoyance at being unable to excuse herself or find a proper tale to justify her behaviour. Littlejohn let her calm down and, as she couldn't make do with her postage-stamp of a handkerchief, he passed her his own. She covered it with tears, mascara and lipstick and handed it back without a word. The 'skeets' rolled their eyes and hugged themselves at this heavy touch of melodrama.

'Mr Finnegan is married?'

'Yes. He doesn't get on with his wife. She doesn't understand him.'

The old, old story. Littlejohn simply couldn't take it seriously. Murder and sordid intrigues seemed to belong to another world. The road winding down between its flowery hedges; the rolling fields and hills. In the distance, the sea, incredibly blue, with ships passing on the skyline and the coaster still unloading at the pier. Sheep watching them as they munched the grass and two smiling pigs rooting and grunting nearby. And now, the antics of Finnegan and his woman spoiling it all. His eyes wandered down the little street to where the knots of inquisitive women were standing, and they pretended to be talking together and not heeding him at all. He and his companion strolled back to the chapel and then round again.

'He has some children?'

'Two... Both working... When his wife divorces him, we're going to be married.'

'When did he promise that?'

'When he asked me to come away with him. He says he won't go back to his wife. They're unhappy together.'

'I thought you broke apart after the death of Mr Snook.'

'Not exactly. We separated. It didn't seem decent in the circumstances.'

Well, well. She seemed to have a hit-or-miss kind of morality. Uncle Fred mattered; Mrs Finnegan didn't.

'How long have you known him?'

'Quite a time. He was my music teacher.'

Littlejohn felt the need of something to support him. The sun must be getting at him. Or he was just dreaming and would soon wake up. Music teacher! Finnegan! What next?

'Are you a singer, then?'

'Yes. Only in my spare time. My real job's a receptionist to an osteopath.'

'Where?'

'In Leicester.'

'You live in Leicester?'

'Yes.'

'Does Finnegan?'

'Yes.'

Leicester! The place where Uncle Fred, Fred Snowball, had lived with his second woman! Littlejohn felt the first faint stirrings of the old feeling which always came when a vital point had been reached in a case.

'Let's go inside, Miss Crawley.'

Finnegan was sitting where they'd left him, talking to the parson, looking more at home and reconciled to his fate. Mrs Quilliam was just entering with a large tray covered in cups and saucers and plates of soda cake.

'We'd better eat as we talk, Mr Finnegan. We must hurry back.'

Fear crept in the little flabby man's pop-eyes.

'Are you taking us with you... to... to...? Does it mean jail?'

'No. You're going back to *Sea Vista* and Miss Crawley to *Rossendale*. It's going to be all decent and correct, but no more running away. You understand? No more bolting.'

'I promise.'

'Your name is...?'

'Oswald Finnegan.'

'Your address? And it's *not* in London. I want the real one now.'

'*Bosworth*, Abbey Vale, Leicester.'

'That's better. Occupation? *Not* business-consultant, please.'

'Traveller for a hosiery works.'

'A musician?'

Finnegan glanced hastily across at Miss Crawley, who gave him a look of apology.

'Yes. I play the organ and teach music in my spare time. It's to supplement my income.'

'You knew the late Fred Snook? The man recently murdered at *Sea Vista*?'

'I met him at the diggings, that's all.'

'Are you sure? Did you ever know Fred Snowball?'

Finnegan was just drinking. His face flushed scarlet and he coughed and spewed a mouthful of tea down his light grey suit.

'You obviously did. He once lived in Leicester. You met him there?'

Finnegan behaved like a trapped animal. He looked at the door as though about to bolt, and then at the window as though contemplating taking a dive through it.

'Come on, Mr Finnegan. The truth, this time.'

'I met him there once or twice, casually. I was quite surprised when I found him at *Sea Vista*. It was a big shock.'

'Why a shock?'

'He'd changed so much. He used to be such a dandy... splashing his money about. The best only good enough... He'd got tumble-down as though he'd hit hard times.'

'You seem to know a lot about him.'

'Only the difference between him in Leicester and when I met him in Douglas.'

'Did he recognize you?'

'He may have done. He didn't let on if he did.'

Finnegan licked his dry lips and took a deep swig of his tea. He wasn't eating anything. He just couldn't face it.

'How did you meet him in Leicester?'

'I don't quite recollect. I must have seen him about the place.'

'And remembered him all that time afterwards and he so changed. Come, come, Mr Finnegan. That won't do.'

Finnegan showed a bit of spirit for the first time.

'Why keep on needling me? I'm trying to do my best. I'm telling the truth. Why don't you believe me?'

'I want the whole truth, that's all.'

'He was quite a prominent man in Leicester. The sort you don't easily forget.'

And Uncle Fred had changed his name when he ran away from his wife, just because he didn't want to attract attention!

'But I know, Mr Finnegan, that he tried to keep out of the limelight during his Leicester days. How do you reconcile that with your story?'

'Don't ask me. I knew him when I saw him. I can't say more however much you question me.'

'Think it over. Then let me know. Because I'm sure you've either forgotten something, or else you're hiding information. Well... let's get along to Douglas. We'll take you with us in the car. By the way, why did you run away from *Sea Vista* and follow Miss Crawley here?'

'We were both embarrassed by the fuss. We had to give our names to the police and then Trimble started to be offensive... I mean...'

Finnegan swallowed awkwardly.

'I quite understand. It was awkward in view of your having passed off the lady as your wife. I know all the details. You've caused us a lot of trouble.'

'I'm sorry.'

He drew Littlejohn still farther aside.

'I hope you won't make too much fuss about it. I don't want a lot of publicity.'

'You don't intend to get a divorce and marry Miss Crawley?'

Finnegan looked annoyed. He flushed and his eyes protruded.

'Why, no. Who's told you that? I've some children I'm fond of...'

'You ought to have thought about that before... Was it you who tried to book a passage on the little steamer tied up at the jetty in Laxey?'

'I was desperate. I should have been home long since.'

If the trip to Agneash hadn't been so pleasant, Littlejohn might have said a lot more.

Miss Crawley returned from the kitchen where she had been settling accounts with Mrs Quilliam, whom they now thanked and bade good-bye.

'If it hadn't been for you, Archdeacon, none of the others would have crossed my doorstep.'

'Not even Superintendent Littlejohn?'

'Aw... he's a nice enough fellah, if only he hadn't been from the police... '

They got in the car again, with Finnegan and his woman, now silent in each other's presence, in the rear. Back down the twisting, flowery road to the valley, and the spectators on the hill-side silently watched them vanish out of sight.

11

THE CALF OF MAN

They dropped Finnegan and Miss Crawley at the door of *Sea Vista*. Then, there was more bother. Mrs Trimble wouldn't let him have the double room on his own. He and his woman were at last found an attic apiece, one in *Sea Vista* and the other in *Rossendale,* next door. Their dormer windows were side by side and, had he wished, Finnegan might have taken a bit of romantic risk and clambered from one to the other. But he didn't feel like frivolities. He'd had enough.

At the police-station, Knell was still waiting for news from Cromwell. Littlejohn added another burden to poor Knell's back. The Leicester police must now be contacted and Finnegan and Miss Crawley checked. Had they, to the knowledge of the police there, ever been connected with Fred Snook, Snowball, or Boycott, and had Uncle Fred ever crossed the path of the Leicester constabulary? Also, Mrs Finnegan might be discreetly... very discreetly... questioned about her husband's movements and where he was supposed to be at present.

'And now, Knell, have you time to come with us to the Calf of Man?'

Knell looked at Littlejohn as though he'd gone mad. He must

have regarded the suggestion as a temptation to shirk his work and go on a little binge by way of a change.

'You needn't look so surprised, old man. We had the idea that as he'd been there fishing with Uncle Fred and there isn't a bobby on patrol within miles, Trimble might have hidden himself on the Calf.'

Knell looked relieved.

'Yes, of course, sir. The very spot. Just let me give some instructions and then we'll be off right away.'

The same old pleasant road to Port St Mary, Littlejohn was beginning to know like the palm of his hand. In fact, just as well as he knew the way to and from Uncle Fred's room at *Sea Vista*!

Knell led them down to the harbour at Port St Mary to find a boat. A spot with some character about it. Old whitewashed fishermen's cottages, a little harbour with a stone jetty, with fishing and pleasure craft with coloured sails tied up to it. A few herring boats... An extensive view of Carrick Bay and the sea beyond, with the towers of Castletown shining in the sun on the skyline.

'Comin' to look into the stealin' of Charlie Bridson's boat, Mr Knell? I wouldn't have thought they'd send down an Inspector for that.'

The owner of a trim little motor-launch, and burned by the sun, salted by the sea. A thatch of stiff hair under a peaked cap and a large moustache hiding almost all the bottom part of his face. Clear blue eyes and a smiling care free look.

The Archdeacon, who had been standing apart while the bargain was struck, came forward to listen.

William Kinley was a fisherman, joiner and lifeboatman all in one. He did a roaring trade with his boat in the summertime. Now, all his customers were having tea and he was disposed for a yarn. He liked Archdeacon Kinrade, who'd rowed side by side with him in the Port St Mary lifeboat through more than one storm in the past. The boys were never very keen on taking a dog-collar with them in the boat, but Parson Kinrade... he was different. Kinley began to gossip about the past.

'Not now, William, please. Later. What's this about Bridson's boat?'

'Aw... he keeps it down at the Sound, ye know, tied up there for the fishin' an' crabbin', leck. This mornin', he went down for it, but it wasn't there...'

'You've been over to the Calf with a party today?'

'Aw, aye... I took two lots across.'

'You didn't see Bridson's boat while you were there?'

'Naw. Never put a sight on her at all. Why would I? Even if someborry had rowed over in it, I wouldn't have seen it. We landed our party at the Burrow, Master Kinrade.'

'I ought to have known.'

The Archdeacon introduced Littlejohn to William Kinley and then explained that the Calf had two little ports; Cow Harbour on the Sound facing Cregneish, and South Harbour, or the Burrow, on the east side. Port St Mary boats used the Burrow; those from Port Erin, the other, when currents permitted.

'You've not heard from Port Erin that they've seen the boat at the Sound?'

'Naw... They haven't been on the Calf today. All booked for fishin' trips.'

'You'd better take us over, right away then, William.'

William was disposed to continue the little *cooish* a bit longer, but they bore him off by sheer weight of numbers.

Far out to sea from Port St Mary, with a full view of the rocky splendour of the Mull coast, and then a right turn round Spanish Head. A scene which silenced them all and almost made them sit open-mouthed... A magnificent expanse of blue-green water, like a picture on a postcard and, straight ahead, the Calf of Man, lazily stretched, like a great sea monster sunning itself, between them and the horizon. The little island of Kitterland and the toothed rock of Thousla rising between it and the mainland of Man, with its tall cliffs, caves, headlands, and then the gently sloping hinterland, green and fresh, rising to the Mull Hills.

The criss-cross of tides and currents of the half-mile Sound between the Calf and the mainland rocked the boat even on the calmest sea. Kinley took a pair of binoculars from under his seat and scanned the coast around Cow Harbour.

'There she is...'

They passed round the glasses to confirm it.

Bridson's little boat, barely large enough for two big men, was tied up under the rocks near the jetty there.

'Someborry's tried to hide 'er where she can't be seen. There'll be terrible throuble when Bridson hears of this.'

Kinley's rugged face and calm eyes lit up at the thought of the coming row. Whoever had taken the boat had better look out. Bridson loved her more than wife and children. She was his little darling.

The Burrow itself was a huge grotesque rock, which, from certain aspects, looked like a fabulous horse rising from the sea. It was pierced by a fissure known as The Eye, and Kinley skirted it, gently drawing up his boat at a small jetty with a stony cove behind it. They climbed out...

Due south-east, the Chicken Rock topped by its lighthouse, all serene and still like a backcloth for a nautical musical comedy. Beyond, a large liner steaming west. The path from the coast hugged the beach for a short way and then turned inland, where first signs of life began to appear.

'About five miles in circumference with about a thousand acres, sir,' said Knell, taking Littlejohn in hand like a professional guide. A stream appeared and then a ruined mill. Then, a deep sheltered valley with cultivated fields rising to the warden's house. Encircling the valley, rough ground rising to just over 400 feet.

'We'd better see the warden first. He might have seen someone prowling about.'

Knell led the way and they climbed the slope to the farmhouse. Littlejohn and the Archdeacon made up the rear.

'A courtier named Bushell lived here around 1630, seeking peace and solitude. About a century ago, a man named Carey, a lawyer from London, arrived and founded a colony even large enough to run a tavern. One and another has owned it since. Now it's National Trust property and there's just a warden and his family... I've heard old men on the mainland talk of the good times they had here in the old days. Carey built the present house and they farm between a hundred and a hundred and fifty acres. Rather awkward... have to swim the cattle over... No telephone... They flash an emergency message to the lighthouse, which passes it on over the short-wave radio... What is the matter, Littlejohn?'

The sun was still shining and hot and everything was pleasant. No wonder one of the owners of the Calf had said he'd rather live there than in heaven! But, somehow, Littlejohn felt uneasy. As though a dark cloud had passed across his spirit. The parson's talk seemed to fade in and out of his consciousness.

'Do you feel the same as I do, Littlejohn? As though something unholy had been going on here?'

The penetrating blue eyes searched his own and Littlejohn didn't need to say a word.

The warden received them courteously. He occupied the strong, squat house at the head of the valley which ran through the centre of the island. A small garden, a neat forecourt, all sheltered from the elements by the rising ground. *Parva Domus Magna Quies, 1878,* on the stone over the door. Small house, great peace... It was here that Uncle Fred had often found refuge.

'You remember Fred Snook, Warden?'

'The one who was murdered? Yes. He came often with Costain from across at Cregneish.'

'Anyone else ever come with him?'

'Yes. A little stoutish man who used to limp and puff as he climbed the slope from the harbour. Trimble...'

'Have you seen him lately?'

'Yes. He was here, officially, with Snook, about a fortnight ago. I mean, it's usual to call at the house and get a ticket permitting one to land. He may have put in since without paying.'

'Is that easy?'

'Quite. If I didn't happen to see him rowing across he might easily help himself to the freedom of the island for quite a time.'

'Perhaps we'd better take a look round.'

The ground rose to the west behind the house, and after climbing for five minutes, they came in view of the two deserted lighthouses overlooking the Stack rock with an uninterrupted view of the sea across to Ireland. Strongly constructed, the old buildings were now rapidly falling in, as though vandals had been loose among them. Lead stripped from the gutters, timbers smashed, roofs leaking, copings caving in. The first lighthouse had a fairly watertight room or two in its living quarters. It was there they found signs of recent habitation. Old food papers, a half-consumed packet of sandwiches, fag-ends and spent matches, and, more surprising, a half-empty bottle of whisky. As though an intruder had been suddenly alarmed and hurriedly left.

Knell got quite excited.

'Somebody's been camping here,' he said as though he'd made a great deduction.

The three of them stood in the doorway looking out. Not a soul in sight. The second lighthouse, on higher ground, was even more derelict and desolate. A small motor-boat crossing the intervening water to the Chicken Rock lighthouse, rising gracefully from its reef against which the waves were lapping gently. To the west some herring boats making their way out from Peel.

'Let's take a look around.'

The upper light was on wilder ground. Hooded crows and jackdaws circled round as the trio approached it. Nothing there. The rough turf rose beyond to a high eminence overlooking savage cliffs with gulls eternally launching themselves into the air and guillemots perching and diving from ledges. A few sea-parrots, puffins, performed little antics around their nesting-holes, the deserted burrows of rabbits decimated and cleared by disease.

The Archdeacon opened his mouth to tell them something or other about the birds or the island itself, and then closed it again. None of them seemed interested... Trimble, the flabby failure, was more important now than the majesty of the scenery or the beauty of declining day, with the sun beginning to cast a bridge of gold to the west of Chicken Rock.

'But the green boat was there, stolen, and then hidden along the rocks on the Sound... Somebody must have done that.'

Knell sounded to be arguing with an unseen opponent.

They stood there on almost the highest spot of the islet and looked all around them. One side of the Mull peninsula was visible, and Bradda Head and the western coast beyond. The sunlit mainland in the background. They could even see vehicles and little people moving in what looked like another world. A fulmar launched itself into space and made a wide sweeping arc before landing on the sea. Littlejohn half unconsciously followed its flight... And then he saw the body.

It lay spreadeagled on one of the jagged rocks half-way down the tremendous cliffs almost below where they were standing. They could plainly make out the form of a man, but could only guess who it might be. It was impossible to approach any nearer. The ground between themselves and the edge of the precipice was covered in dry shrivelled turf, slippery as ice and with no chance of a foothold. To lose one's balance would mean a running jump into space and certain death.

They all stood dumbfounded for a moment.

'Is it Trimble?'

'I can't make out, Knell. We'll have to get some help. You might run back and find the warden and Mr Kinley.'

Knell was glad of something active to do and scrambled off and away by the shortest route.

'Did he fall from here, I wonder?'

'Or higher up, parson. Shall we go and look?'

Up the slope above them was firmer ground, a little slippery plateau of grass riddled by rabbit-holes. A puffin opened its mouth at them in silent rebuke and waddled away. At the entrance of one of the burrows lay a small green object. Littlejohn picked it up. It was a numbered ticket.

THE MANX MUSEUM AND NATIONAL TRUST
PERMIT TO LAND ON THE CALF OF MAN

and a brief list of conditions.

No responsibility for the holder whilst on the Island...

Poor Trimble! Nobody responsible for him! But...

'Didn't the warden say he hadn't issued a ticket to Trimble for over a fortnight?'

'Yes, Littlejohn.'

'Then someone else has been here recently. If this ticket was issued today, it may be that Trimble was followed and perhaps murdered.'

'Isn't that rather jumping to conclusions? He may have fallen over. It's very dangerous ground here. If he's been drinking... and the whisky we found might easily have been a part of the cargo he brought with him... he might have staggered to his death.'

'That's true. We must get at the body as soon as we can. The earth is too hard and slippery even to bear impressions of foot-marks or a scuffle.'

'In other words, we get deeper and deeper. Whoever could have followed Trimble if what you say is true?'

They stood there, waiting for help. Utter silence and desolation, except for the birds busy about their own affairs and swooping and crying over the body of the man sprawling among their nests and territory.

Knell and his companions appeared almost at the double. Kinley was the first to speak.

'We'll have to get ropes and someone will have to go down for him. Who is he?'

'It might be Trimble, the man we're searching for.'

'Well, we can't get at him from the sea... The coast there's too rocky even to land with a little row-boat.'

'I've got ropes at the house. They'll be long enough.'

The warden turned to go.

'Just a minute, sir. This ticket...'

Littlejohn handed over the little piece of green cardboard. 'When was it issued?'

'Today... The number's recent. Where did you get it?'

'Just down the burrow there.'

'But Trimble didn't take a ticket.'

'I know.'

Another puzzled silence punctuated by the sad cries of the gulls.

'Didn't you say, Mr Kinley, that only your boat had brought visitors over today?'

'Aye. Two lots of 'em.'

'How many?'

'Five one trip and six the next.'

'By arrangement? I mean, were they booked beforehand?'

'Naw. Not ezzackly... A party of three booked one trip and two the other. Then the rest jes' drifted along, leck, as usual. Folk in the village recommend 'em to me.'

'Would you know them again if you saw them?'

'Aye, I reckon I would. I've a good memory and bein' with them most of the trip, I get to know them.'

'Anybody special, or peculiar with you today?'

'Naw, couldn't say they was. Both parties about even, men and women.'

'Any of them just on their own?'

'Two fellahs on the first trip, an' a man an' a woman on the next.'

'Were these isolated trippers young or elderly?'

Kinley pushed his cap to the back of his head and scratched his bald forehead.

'First lot... An elderly fellah, might have been a docthor or some eddicated sort o' chap. Asked a lot of questions, leck. The other was a young 'un... dressed like a hiker.'

'And the second?'

'The fellah might have been a writer or sech... Sort who like to put a chap like me in their books. Askin' for stories and yarns, leck. He didn't go far. Stayed with me most of the time, askin' about the boat and storms, and how it was here in winter when gales blow up. Terrible smoker... Lit one cigarette from the stump of the other.'

'The woman?'

'One o' the usuals... Middle-aged an' on her own. A bit stand-offish. Didn't mix or talk with the rest. Listened to what I said to 'em and was busy puttin' it all down in a li'l book.'

'What was she like?'

'Medium build... dark hair, sun-glasses all the time. I didn't see much of her face. City sort, because she was made-up... powdered heavy an' red lips.'

'Dark, did you say? Very dark?'

'Almost black, her hair was.'

'Long, or cut short?'

'Longish and a bit rough, or wild, leck, as though it had been blown about, as doubtless it had.'

'What did she wear?'

'No hat. A scarf... She put it on when we got away from land. A sort o' long light-coloured coat. Almost white, it was. That's all I can remember... An' here's the warden.'

Knell insisted on going down. He'd been used to that kind of thing from boyhood, he said, when he'd climbed the rocks for gulls' eggs. The warden had brought a pair of rubber-soled pumps and Knell managed to get his feet in them, although they were a bit small. Ordinary shoes were no use on the slippery turf and rocks which led down to the body. They tied him to the rope and slowly paid it out as he slid down from foothold to foothold with remarkable dexterity. He had stripped off his coat, and his white shirt showed clearly against the black background of the cliff. Finally, he reached the body.

Knell gingerly scrambled about for a bit and then took hold of the figure, examined the face, and waved back to the men above. Then, he called between his cupped hands.

'Trimble... Trimble...'

The rocks echoed the call.

'Trimble... Trimble... Trimble...'

As though they were calling poor old Trimble home.

Knell pointed to the body again and cupped his hands a second time.

'Dead... Dead...'

'Dead... Dead... Dead...'

He knotted the body to the second line and, as the four men at the top hauled gently, guided and thrust it onwards until he appeared again with his grisly companion over the cliff edge.

They laid Trimble on the turf and Littlejohn patted Knell on the back.

'A good job of work, old chap.'

'All in the day's work, sir.'

Trimble wasn't a pleasant sight. He'd been dead for some hours, but there was still a faint reek of whisky about him. He had caught the projecting rock with the full weight of his body, which was crushed and broken. He had bled from the mouth and his hands were torn. But it was the expression of utter terror in the face, the open mouth, the staring eyes, which turned them all up. The Archdeacon knelt and closed the eyes and tied up the stiff gaping jaws with his handkerchief. He even stroked back the thin ruffled remnants of hair and made it look decent. Finally, they found an old shutter in the wreckage of the lighthouse and carried the corpse, covered by Knell's jacket, down to Kinley's boat.

'I think you'd better come to Douglas with us, Mr Kinley. There are one or two matters there to square up.'

'That's all right, Superintendent. I'll come along.'

Poor old Trimble, the failure, the man who'd run away from trouble and stumbled into worse, was driven off in an ambulance and the rest followed in the police-car. They stopped at the police-station and waited for a brief preliminary examination by the surgeon.

'He obviously died from the fall. There are no stab wounds or bullets involved. His head isn't even damaged. He must have slipped and shot through the air, and then literally spiked himself on the projecting rock. I guess the post-mortem will show some fearful internal injuries. He probably died between noon and when you found him. I can perhaps be more precise later.'

They hurried away to inform Mrs Trimble and took Kinley to *Sea Vista* with them. 'Home Sweet Home,' muttered Littlejohn to himself as the boarding-house came in sight. They never seemed to be away from the place.

Tea was long over and all the boarders were out enjoying the evening's pleasures. The streets were full of rowdy merrymakers. It was Thursday. Only one more day for those finishing holidays on Saturday. The melancholy feeling as the sands of freedom, pleasure and money-spending run out, was gnawing at most of them. They wished they could live on the Isle of Man in the summer sunshine for good, and that every day of the 365 was a holiday... To forget and cast out the thought of the daily grind again next week, they made more noise than ever.

I left my heart
In the blue-grass country...

There it was again, like a dirge for Trimble now.

Mrs Trimble collapsed when they brought in the news. Very different from her attitude of earlier in the day. They gave her brandy and Maria and Susie laid her on the couch. Susie was still there. After Littlejohn's departure following the row between the two women, Mrs Trimble had turned on Susie and abused her for thinking of leaving them in the lurch in the middle of high season. The pair of them weren't on speaking terms, but Susie remained. Now, Mrs Trimble was hysterical about her.

'Don't leave me, Susie. You're all I've got.'

They told her Trimble had had an accident on the Calf. There was no sense in making matters worse by full details. Finally, the two girls persuaded her to go to bed. She let them lead her upstairs, still clinging to the brandy bottle.

'It wasn't any of them women. I'm sure of it. I'd swear it.'

Kinley was emphatic that neither Mrs Trimble, Maria, nor Susie had been in his boat to the Calf that day. As for the other women, Miss Crawley had an alibi. She'd been at Agneash. Mrs Nessle was indoors, resting after a day in a charabanc.

'I never seen *her* before, either,' said Kinley.

Mrs Nessle was upset and shed a tear or two. She was definitely pro-Trimble.

'The poor man. I knew him when he was on the halls. Not personally, of course, but I saw him perform a lot. *Ferdinand of the Trapeze...* that was he. Then he fell in love with Mrs Trimble... Gracie Goodson, a second-rate vaudeville artiste, with pantomime, third-rate, thrown in at Christmas. I knew her, too.

My husband financed certain shows, you see. Did I tell you he was a businessman?'

'Yes, Mrs Nessle.'

'It was a tragedy... She ruined Ferdinand. He was very much in love with her and she treated him like dirt after they married. She was good-looking in a certain kind of way, and always had a lot of men around her. Ferdinand was terribly jealous... And one night, he fell from the trapeze... I always said it was her fault... As I said, a tragedy. Such a fine artist... Well... He's at the end of his troubles now... How did you say it happened?'

Littlejohn briefly mentioned a misplaced step in a dangerous part of the coast, and left it at that. Mrs Nessle broke into a flood of tears.

'Did they get on well together here?'

'He still thought the world of her, but she despised him and didn't hesitate to show it. You see, he felt dependent on her for so much and acted like a failure. I was very sorry for him. He ought to have risen up and beaten her. It would have done her good.'

'They both got on well with Mr Snook?'

'Yes, for the most part. Now and then, they've had words. Mr Snook was always fond of Mrs Trimble, and Ferdinand resented it on occasion. But it blew over. I often suspected there was something *between* Mr Snook and Mrs Trimble... At times they were very affectionate. I'm sure it was her fault. She tried to use her charms on every man that came her way. She was always like that right from the first days I knew her. Mr Snook was a very nice man... charming... I'm sure he was taken in by her. However, both men have gone now... It won't be the same here.'

More floods of tears. Bucketfuls now... Littlejohn joined the other three in the car.

At the police-station they planned to leave Knell and drive home at once, but a constable met them at the door. They could see him from afar, shading his eyes against the dying sun, like the father looking out for the prodigal son. Cromwell had been on the line. He had seen Wilfred Gravell in gaol and Wilfred had given him the benefit of his phenomenal memory.

'Easy! Great pleasure to be of 'elp. Don't forget to put in a good word for me in the proper quarter. I shadowed Boycott on his wife's behalf. He was knockin' about with a bit of stuff from Leicester. Name of Crawley...'

12
THE OTHER WOMAN

It couldn't be helped. They just had to see Miss Crawley before the day was out. Perhaps she was somewhere among the milling crowds entertaining themselves in the town, but they must, at least, try to find her.

Littlejohn was anxious about the Archdeacon. Since breakfast, albeit a substantial one, they'd had a cup of tea and a bun at Agneash and a couple of fresh crab sandwiches at Port St Mary. The parson must be *in extremis...*

'What! Leave you now just as the trail's becoming hot, Littlejohn...? Certainly not!'

So, they took the Archdeacon with them.

It was eight o'clock and still broad daylight, although the sun was setting behind the hills and etching their gentle curves along the skyline. Everybody seemed abroad. Singing, dancing, merrymaking, and those who were tired from the day's exertions were packing the cinemas and variety shows. People were sitting on the front steps of boarding-houses sentimentally enjoying the dying day, the pubs were full, and all the dark and secret places were occupied by canoodling couples. Littlejohn even dislodged a pair in a passionate embrace as he entered the vestibule of *Rossendale* to ring the bell.

Miss Crawley was indoors taking a cup of tea with the motherly Mrs Kelly. Miss Crawley had had a surfeit of gallivanting for one day. She had dismissed Mr Finnegan for the evening on a pretext of a bad headache, and he had rushed away for a pub-crawl to drown his sorrows. All Miss Crawley wanted was to go home... home to Leicester.

Littlejohn and Knell spoke to Miss Crawley whilst the parson gossiped with Mrs Kelly, who knew him well and, once started, was quite adequate for the task of talking him to death.

'You didn't tell us, Miss Crawley, that you already knew the late Mr Snook... perhaps as Mr Snowball... when you arrived at *Sea Vista*.'

She showed no signs of panic.

'What do you mean, Superintendent, I knew him before?'

In spite of her blonde dyed hair and the fact that she'd run away with a married man, there was something straightforward in Miss Crawley's make-up. An intelligent woman, too, by the looks of it. And the sort who didn't easily lose her self-possession.

'Let's sit down and talk sensibly, Miss Crawley. All this beating about the bush will do no good. We know that Mr Snook was, at one time in his life, associated with a certain Marion Crawley, of Leicester.'

'My name is Elsie.'

'Did you know Marion Crawley?'

There was a brief pause as Elsie Crawley tried to make up her mind what to do. Then:

'Yes. She was my sister.'

'*Was?*'

'She's dead. She died six years ago... Committed suicide. It was through Fred Snowball she did it.'

'Hadn't you better begin at the beginning, Miss Crawley, and tell us the whole story?'

'There's not much to tell, and it's all been told before, one way or another. Marion went off the rails with a married man. Just like I've done, only Marion was in love with the man; I'm not.'

Her mouth hardened and she took out a cigarette with an effort at nonchalance which didn't quite succeed.

'From the beginning, if you please,' said Littlejohn, giving her a light from his lighter.

'Marion met him while on holidays at Brighton. He had a yacht there and he picked her up one night in the bar of his hotel. It might sound a bit sordid to you, but it wasn't. I think they genuinely fell in love. Anyway, it wasn't very hard for him to capture her fancy. His yacht and his money and his taking ways. She fell for him and even broke off her engagement with another man nearer her own age. Snowball was old enough to be her father. Marion was a good-looking girl... very. But she was a bit flighty. She paid for it.'

'Snowball left his wife and lived with your sister?'

'Yes. There were mother, me, and Marion at home. Dad died years before. Nothing Mother or I said would make her change her mind. He'd promised to marry her as soon as his wife would divorce him. She never did. Mother wasn't in very good health, but that didn't count in the arguments. Marion wanted to be near her, though, so she and Snowball took a flat on the outskirts of Leicester and there they lived for two years. Then he walked out on her and she never saw him again. He just vanished into thin air.'

'Why?'

Another pause.

'Why *do* men walk out on women? They had a row, of course. He'd been getting tired of her for some time. At first, they were like a pair of love-birds. Thought the world of one another. Then, Marion started to nag him. I didn't blame her for it. Waiting there for a divorce that never came and more or less talked about by everybody. She'd no friends left. In other words, they'd messed up one another's lives and didn't know how to straighten things out. They should have gone far away where they weren't known, but Marion wouldn't. Mother was, by that time, bedridden, and Marion was always her favourite. I blamed Snowball for it all. He, as a man of the world, should have known how it would end. I believe he suggested they should call it a day and part, and Marion should go back to where she started. She wouldn't... So he went. Only unfortunately there was a baby on the way by then and he didn't know... or so Marion said.'

'Is the child alive?'

'Yes. I adopted her. I was left to bear it all in the end. Mother died and Marion put her head in the gas-oven. She tried to do away with the baby, too... Sealed up the kitchen the week after mother died and turned on the gas... We had a dog, though. It howled the place down and somebody broke in. They saved the baby. Marion died. I was out at work at the time. I've had to bring the child up.'

'Didn't Snowball provide for your sister?'

'He left a note saying good-bye, and two thousand pounds in bank-notes. Most of it was intact when Marion died and I used it for bringing Bertha up... Bertha's the child. The sweetest thing, and I'm as fond of her as if she was my own. But the money ran out a long time since. It's taken every penny I could earn to keep her and me and bring her up nicely.'

'Snowball never knew about this child?'

'How could he? She never told him and we didn't know where he was.'

Dusk was falling and outside the lights were going on. The windows were open and they could hear the steady heart of the town beating, a rhythmic throb as thousands of visitors circulated, talked, shouted and tramped the seafront and streets. Dim sounds of music somewhere, the shrill whistling of young men, and the answering shrieks, bordering on hysteria, of light-hearted girls. History repeating itself. Uncle Fred and Marion Crawley at Brighton, long ago; only their affair hadn't lasted for one evening, but for years and tragedy.

They sat in the dim light, the ends of their cigarettes glowing.

'How did you find him in the end?'

'A picture at the cinema... It was one of those funny coincidences you meet sometimes. It was last month. On the news reel. They showed the Manx Tynwald day... You know, the kind of fair where they read the laws.'

Littlejohn nodded. His old friend, the Archdeacon – now drinking tea with Mrs Kelly in her kitchen – read the laws in Manx and the First Deemster read them in English.

'Yes. And what happened?'

'It showed the official part and also the crowd at Tynwald fair. And believe it or not, there was Fred Snowball, large as life, one of the crowd. He didn't know they were taking him. That was obvious. He was busy talking to two men. And one of them was Ossy Finnegan.'

'Ah! I see.'

'Yes. Mr Finnegan used to come over here now and then travelling for men's socks. He came across Mr Snowball one day on the promenade. He didn't know, of course, that I wanted to see Snowball. I never made a song and dance about Marion's relations with him and, as for little Bertha, well... I just said I'd adopted her when her mother died.'

'You knew Finnegan at the time?'

'Yes. It was quite true. He did teach me singing.'

'Was he ever a business consultant, by the way?'

'Yes. He was a native of Leicester who went to London to a firm of business consultants. They failed and he came back and got another job.'

'And how did you come to be here at the time Snowball died?'

'Finnegan took a fancy to me and wouldn't leave me alone.

He'd suggested a time or two that we might spend a few days at the seaside together when he was on one of his tours. He's not a bad sort, really, but I wasn't having that. Him a married man with children...'

'It's not true, then, that you were going to be married if he could get a divorce?'

'No.'

'Why did you tell me it was?'

'I was in a panic and wanted to appear, at least, as decent as I could. I didn't want you to think I was a woman who would go away like that with the first man who suggested it.'

'I see.'

'I don't think you do, Superintendent. I didn't mean it to turn that way, at all. I don't think Mr Finnegan did at the time, either. He'd never have married me with Bertha. She's away on her holidays with a school-friend and her family just now.'

'Tell me exactly how and why Finnegan and you arrived at *Sea Vista* as man and wife.'

'I asked Finnegan who was the man I'd seen him with on the film. He said an old friend he once knew in Leicester. They used to meet at some angling club. They were both fond of fishing.'

'Finnegan pretended he merely knew Snowball by sight.'

'He told me you'd been asking questions. He was afraid that if he said he knew him well, you'd suspect he killed him.'

'Very well. How did you come to be here?'

'It was difficult asking a lot of questions about Snowball. Mr Finnegan got suspicious and asked what I was getting at. And then, as he'd always said he'd do anything for me and wanted me to regard him as my best friend, I was foolish enough to tell him the whole story. I played right into his hands. He wouldn't tell me where Snowball lived, but, he said, he'd take me and give me a holiday. And, he'd support me in talking things over with Snowball. In fact, he said he'd see he did the right thing by Bertha.'

'So you came as man and wife?'

'Yes. What else could I do? If I'd come alone, it would have been hunting for a needle in a haystack with all these people here. I didn't know Snowball's address.'

'And you were going to approach Snowball together?'

'Yes. We said we'd tell him about his daughter and ask him to help with her education. I can't afford to give her all she ought to have and she's a clever child.'

'But why come to the very boarding-house Snowball was living at? Why not find another and call on him here?'

'That's what I said to Mr Finnegan. But he said that, as I already knew, Snowball had a habit of bolting when trouble blew up, and if we were at *Sea Vista*, Finnegan could keep an eye on Snowball until he'd met his obligations.'

'What happened?'

'We arrived on Saturday and checked in as man and wife. Mr Finnegan had arranged to do a round of business here and I was on holidays. We were to stay till next Saturday. I wanted to see Mr Snowball right away and get it over. I thought I might make an excuse and go back home if we could settle matters soon. Instead, Mr Finnegan wanted to put it off for a day or two... Till a suitable occasion, as he expressed it. Before we saw him at all, Snowball had been killed. We were both in a terrible panic. If the police got to know why we were here and not married... well... it might have been awkward.'

'An understatement, Miss Crawley! Are you quite sure neither of you saw Snowball before he died?'

'What do you mean?'

'Can you assure me there was no interview, no quarrel, no violence between you or Finnegan and Fred Snowball?'

'Of course, I can. If you think either of us had anything to do with the murder, you're very much mistaken. Why should *we* want to murder him? Alive, he could have helped me; dead, he was no use at all.'

'That's quite logical. Well, thank you for answering the questions and please stay here until we say you may go.'

'I've to be back at work on Monday. I can't afford to lose my job.'

'You'll be able to go, Miss Crawley. If what you tell me is true you've done splendidly by your sister's child and when this is over, go back and forget it.'

Her self-control broke at last and they left her in tears.

After a pause to explain to the parson where they were going, Littlejohn and Knell returned once again to *Sea Vista*.

Mrs Trimble was nowhere about. In fact, she was in bed and the boarding-house was now in charge of a relief manageress, who did that kind of emergency work. Miss Archibald, known locally as Miss A. A tall, bony, sour-faced woman, who ruled other people's roosts with a rod of iron. She met the police at the door.

'You're making it awkward for everybody, you know. Here's poor Mrs Trimble prostrate with 'er grief, and the police never off the doorstep. It's not good enough. As if we hadn't enough worry...'

'Has Mr Finnegan come in, yet?'

'He's in the lounge.'

'Kindly tell him we want to see him, and I'd like the favour of the use of the small room we usually interview people in. The office under the stairs.'

'Don't be long, then. It's supper-time and I can't be bothered just now.'

Knell saw red.

'Look here, Miss A. I know you and you know me. If you don't stop obstructing the police in the discharge of their duties, it will be very serious for you.'

Not very convincing, but it convinced Miss A. She went in the lounge to find Finnegan. There were apparently quite a number of lodgers there, having a final cheerful hour before supper. As usual, the accordion was hard at it, and someone was busy on the piano playing a florid accompaniment.

I left my heart
In the blue-grass country...

It was a wonder someone didn't strangle the fellow! Certainly, Littlejohn remembered the sentimental refrain in his dreams. It was now the incidental music to the death of Uncle Fred. Hoarse voices, lubricated and sloppy from drink, were howling the chorus like dogs at the moon. The piano stopped, but the singing continued. The pianist must have been Finnegan! He emerged, bleary-eyed and unsteady.

'What again! At this time? Can't you leave me alone? You've done enough at me, haven't you?'

They took him by the arm and led him into the cubby-hole. He struggled and protested all the way. Littlejohn wasted no time. It was late and he was fed up.

'You arrived on Saturday, Finnegan. When did you see Snowball after that?'

'Didn't see him. He died before I could.'

'Don't tell me any more lies. You've told enough already. You'll answer properly here and now or else come with us and spend the night at the police-station.'

Finnegan went all to pieces. He started to snivel.

'Why can't you leave me alone? I'm that mixed-up, I don't know which way to turn. I want to go home an' you won't let me. I want to tell the truth and you won't let me again. What *do* you want?'

'When did you see Snowball?'

'Sunday, for just a minute, that's all.'

'You met him last Tynwald day. What did he say to you?'

'I don't remember. It's so long ago.'

'I'll tell you. He asked you not to tell anybody you'd seen him.

He said he wanted peace and quiet and to be left alone. He'd settled and was happy. Is that right?'

Finnegan bucked up. He smiled broadly in great relief.

'That's right. Egzackly right.'

'Then you brought Miss Crawley here. You insisted on staying under the same roof as Snowball. Why?'

'A good place, that's all. Recommend it.'

'Rubbish! You thought if you told him why you were here, he'd pack up and bolt, as he's done before when trouble followed him. So you came to keep an eye on him.'

Finnegan looked owlishly at Littlejohn.

'Right again, sir. I'd a juty to my frien', Miss Crawley. What we came 'ere for. To see zhustice done. Intended to get it done.'

'So you saw Snowball alone on Sunday without Miss Crawley knowing, and started to put on the screw. You told him why you were here. How much did you ask for?'

'I don't know what you're talkin' about.'

Littlejohn took him by the lapels of his coat and shook him till his teeth chattered.

'Lemme go. Here... leave me alone... I... I only asked him for a couple of thousand to educate little Bertha... A nice gel, Bertha...'

'And you intended to give her aunt a thousand or less... Don't bluff me. You came here to blackmail Snowball. And now you look like facing a murder charge.'

It sobered Finnegan at once. He staggered back, lost his balance, and sat down with a thud on the floor. Littlejohn stood over him.

'It was that, wasn't it?'

'I intended to pay over to Elsie all excep' my out-of-pockets.'

'Good of you. Get up! What did Snowball say?'

'He took it calm. He hadn't all that money on hand. But he'd see what he could do.'

'Are you sure you didn't have a row with him about it when he refused and told you to get out?'

'Damn sure. He was mos' polite. Surprised when he heard he'd got another daughter he didn't know about. Matter of fact, seemed quite moved.'

'So, to make sure he didn't bolt again, you kept an eye on him?'

'Right again.'

'Did you see him on Sunday morning for the first time?'

'Night. He'd gone out when we got up and I couldn't talk private over dinner. Now could I? So I went to his room when he came in after tea.'

'Did you see him again that night?'

'No. Monday. Just before dinner. About hal' past twelve. I say, can I go now? They'll be wondering... '

'Stay where you are. After lunch, you still kept an eye on him?'

'Yes. He went in the kitchen and brought out that bonny little girl, Susie. And they came and talked private in this room. I was in the lounge, readin'. Nobody knew I was in. I was keepin' an eye on Snook, you see. Not goin' to have him doin' another bunk.'

'Let's get this right... He'd lunch and then, a short time after, he'd a talk with Susie in here. What next?'

'Then the pair of 'em went upstairs. They thought nobody saw 'em. Yours truly saw it. So did Trimble, who was also keepin' an eye on them on the q.t. He went quietly up after 'em and stood for a minute, listenin' on the first landin'. Then, he came down again. I was peepin' through a crack in the half-open door of the lounge. Trimble looked mad with rage. Purple with it. Talk about committin' a murder. He looked ready for it. When the coast was clear, I nipped up to my own room to get ready to go out myself.'

'Then what happened?'

'Nothin' much. Snook, or Snowball, or whatever you like, and Susie was still up in her room. I started to wash and was runnin' water. But I heard Snook comin' down the stairs agen.'

'Trimble was nowhere about by then?'

'No. He'd vanished in the kitchen and I suppose, as usual, he started on the bottle agen. I've caught him a time or two. You see, with bein' lame, he didn't get out much and his missus didn't seem to want him with her. She always went out on her own.'

'What were you proposing to do when you went up for a wash?'

'I was at a bit of a loose end. I decided to go out to the carnival.'

'Where was Miss Crawley?'

'She went out on her own with Mrs Greenhalgh and the kids. She said she wanted a change.'

'Did anybody else see all this?'

'No. They'd all gone to the carnival.'

'Are you sure?'

'There was only Trimble, Susie and Snook in the place, as far as I knew.'

'What time was this?'

'I took my watch off to get a wash. It was three o'clock by it and it was ten minutes fast. Ten to three.'

'Obviously. Well?'

'I heard Snowball comin' down the stairs, put out me head, and saw him half-way down the last flight. It was gloomy, but I could see he'd got his hat on and no bag. So, I thought he's not likely to welsh on me without all his belongin's and just in a panama an' his suit... I went out a minute or two later and just saw 'im turnin' the corner on to the prom. I went the other way to the carnival. When I got back, they said he'd not been in... And he didn't come in to tea. I thought he'd done it on me. However, news came later; he was dead. And that's the ruddy lot, and can I go now? They'll be talkin' about all this among the lodgers.'

'Yes. You can go. But don't try to get away from here until I give permission.'

'How much longer? I've business to attend to.'

'I don't know yet. Miss Crawley will be leaving, alone, with my consent, on Saturday.'

'Well, of all the...'

'Be off with you, now. And don't forget...'

Finnegan shambled off sheepishly and they could hear a cheer to greet him from the lodgers as he joined them again.

After that, Littlejohn called it a day. They arrived at Grenaby just after eleven-thirty and the place seemed dearer to him than ever.

13

THE FUNERAL OF UNCLE FRED

Friday. A melancholy day in more ways than one. Not only was there the funeral of Uncle Fred to cast a blight upon it, but it was the last day of holidays for most of the visitors.

Littlejohn and the Archdeacon were at the police-station early. 'They can *all* go tomorrow, Knell,' Littlejohn had told his colleague concerning the visitors at *Sea Vista*. 'Get them to leave their addresses.'

'But I thought...'

Knell was baffled. Only last night Littlejohn had said nobody was to cross back to England without his special permission. Now, he was simply opening the cage door and letting all of them scatter like a lot of captive sparrows being freed. And they'd be as easy to catch, too, if they were wanted again.

'It will be all right, Knell.'

'You mean to say, sir, you know who did the crimes?'

'Almost, Knell... almost...'

The great sigh heaved by Knell was partly from relief and partly disgust. When Littlejohn and his companion had arrived, Knell had been reprimanding a very conscientious constable and it had upset him. P.C. Doyle had actually reported a chimney on fire at *Sea Vista* and wanted to make a case of it! In the very middle of a ticklish investigation of murder on the premises, Doyle had argued about a summons which would result in a fine of ten bob!

'But it's not right they should be let off, Inspector. The chimney was on fire and throwing out soot and an awful stink. The fire-brigade were there, too, when I arrived.'

'Don't keep arguing and giving cheek to me, Doyle. We've enough on at that house with two dead men on our hands without botherin' about chimneys on fire.'

'What's the matter, Knell? You look put-out.'

Littlejohn had arrived in the middle of it and Doyle had had the nerve to start airing his grievances in front of the Superintendent! And at a time when Knell was trying to impress him with the fact that the Manx police were just as efficient and on their toes as the mainland force. Littlejohn didn't need any convincing, but it was natural that Knell should put up a good show.

'There was smoke all along the promenade and people in their white dresses and shorts carryin' on somethin' awful. The fire-brigade was there... Someborry havin' a lark, I guess... They'd broken the glass on the fire-alarm, you see.'

'That will be enough, Doyle. The Superintendent's got a lot to do.'

'Let him go on, Knell. One of the chimneys at *Sea Vista* was on fire, you say? I thought they didn't have open fires at this time of year... I've not seen any burning when we've been there.'

'This was in one of the bedrooms... One occupied by four young fellahs... It isn't used, but it hasn't been bricked up. Mrs Trimble said it was stuffed up with paper to stop the soot fallin' down, and there was a piece of fancy paper in the grate to keep it neat, like. She said one of the young men must have thrown a fag-end... '

'Cigarette end!'

Knell was on tenterhooks.

'Cigarette end, then. Where was I? One of the young men must have set it alight by throwin' a lighted cigarette end in the paper in the grate. It set the paper up the chimney going and then the soot. The whole neighbourhood was chokin' with it. It smelled like a burnin' body instead of paper and soot.'

'Now don't be silly, Doyle,' exploded Knell. 'Who'd want to stuff a body up a chimney and try to burn it? Be your age.'

'Wait, Doyle. A body? What else might it smell like?'

Doyle was quite a bright constable. He replied almost right away to Littlejohn's question.

'Well, if it wasn't a body, it smelled like an old feather bed or a hair mattress bein' burned.'

'Did you go inside and look the place over?'

'Yes. There was Mrs Trimble with a brush and dustpan and a bucket, cleanin' up the grate and the room. She said she couldn't leave it like that with four young men sleeping in it.'

'What time was that?'

'Nineish, sir. They were all havin' their breakfasts at *Sea Vista* when the conflagration started.'

Doyle smiled with pleasure at the word. He liked it and gently muttered it to himself again. 'Conflagration...'

'What did the rubbish look like, Doyle? Soot?'

'Not exactly. As I said, the smell was like cloth burnin' or an old feather pillow. The rubbish looked a bit like old cloth, too. She must have been trying to beat out the sparks and set fire to the pillow, or somethin'.'

'She hurried away with the bucket when you arrived?'

'Not exactly hurried, sir. She sort of casually took it away and I suppose threw it in the dust-bin. Anyhow, she'd cleaned up the room spick and span. Of course, the chimney fire was out by then. But what I was sayin' to the Inspector, sir, is, that she oughtn't to get away with it, even if her husband has died. Other people don't... '

'Leave it with us then, Doyle. Thank you for your help.'

'Help, sir?'

'Yes.'

It was almost ten-thirty. Uncle Fred's funeral was at eleven. Trimble's inquest was at twelve. It would end like Uncle Fred's. Adjourned, with nothing new to help the police. It had been arranged to bury Trimble on the afternoon of the next day. They didn't want him hanging about with more lodgers, a houseful, in fact, arriving.

'Always go to the funeral of the victim, if you can. You might learn a lot.'

Knell had made a mental note of Littlejohn's advice.

The morning sun was hot as they left. And a little breeze had sprung up to make it more pleasant, a last bowl-up of good weather for those who were off by tomorrow's boat.

The promenade and streets were packed. Everybody looked easygoing and gay, as though trying to forget tomorrow and drain to the dregs the pleasures of the final day before returning to home and work. The shops were full of people buying souvenirs to take back with them, filling in labels on boxes of kippers to go away by the next post, taking photographs of holiday companions. Young couples indulging in holiday romances, embraced and held each other close in secluded spots, in the sad, bitter-sweet way of those who wish it could go on for ever, but know it will fade away with time.

Both Uncle Fred and Trimble were being buried from Scarffe's Funeral Parlour. To take the bodies to *Sea Vista* with the place full of holidaymakers would just be the last straw. Already, the lodgers there were busy packing up for off on the first boat Saturday. They packed with relish, as though they were going away for a holiday instead of home to work at the end of one. They'd all had enough, except the four boys sharing one room. They were quite carefree. They met Littlejohn on the front steps.

Four boys in their narrow-cut, black Edwardian trousers and coats of many colours. Blue, navy, beige, and autumn leaves, ornamented by embroideries done by their dancing-partners at home, and their initials on the pockets. Greasy black hair, all tonsured alike, combed back, parted, and feathered behind the ears. Half-washed and with impudent looks, they brushed past the police. Littlejohn realized that he hadn't seen them before. He'd heard the accordion player, of course... A murder or two in their digs didn't seem to have put them out in the least. You got the impression they might commit one or two killings themselves in the course of a night's spree.

The rest of the boarders were out, with the exception of Mrs Nessle, who was fully clothed in black, ready for Uncle Fred's funeral. Mrs Trimble was in her room, being ministered to by Maria and Susie, who were also draping her in black. 'You ought not to go,' they'd told her. 'You've enough trouble with your own husband lying dead and having to attend his inquest at twelve o'clock.' But she'd refused to be persuaded.

There were some wreaths in the lobby. Two exactly alike. One for Trimble, whose funeral wasn't until next day but when they'd all be scattered and far away, *From his sorrowing lodgers, with deepest sympathy*. The other for Uncle Fred. *From his sorrowing fellow-lodgers, with deepest sympathy. A good sport*. The last obituary comment arose out of the holiday feeling and a desire, suggested by Greenhalgh, to speak well of the dead man. Seeing that Trimble had already looted the lodgers' wreath-fund for Fred, they'd treated him magnanimously.

The blinds were drawn and Miss A., fully in charge, was prowling about in the half-light superintending the daily chores. Mrs Nessle, too, was wandering disconsolately about in the shadows. Littlejohn greeted her.

'You knew poor Trimble in his heyday as an acrobat?'

'Yes. Such a fine figure of a man, then. Almost heartbreaking to think what he came to and how he's ended.'

'His accident made a lot of difference to him?'

'Completely changed him. He wasn't like the same man. Lost

all his self-confidence and pride. It was only to be expected. He was a cripple for a long time and when an acrobat, or really a trapeze artist, falls, it is like an airman who crashes. He comes to earth and is never the same again.'

She struggled for a moment to find words.

'He was like an eagle that is shot down from the skies.'

She painted eagles and skies with a fat forefinger high in the air.

'He wasn't a man, but a wreck, after his tragedy. He took to drink and his wife merely tolerated him and went her own way. My heart bled for him. In his prime, he was *first-rate*. She, on the other hand, was decidedly third-rate.'

A taxi drew up to take Mrs Nessle away and she departed in a flurry of black clothes. The police returned to their waiting car as Mrs Trimble descended, assisted by Maria. Her face was pale and stony, but she was quite self-possessed. Another taxi picked her up and took her off. Littlejohn went back to the house.

'Susie. I want a word with you.'

'Won't it do later, sir! With all this bother and we've to get on with the dinner now.'

'Come in here a minute, please.'

The little cubby-hole under the stairs again and Susie, even paler than Mrs Trimble, standing before him, half afraid, half defiant.

'A short time before he went out and met his death, Mr Snook spoke to you and you both went upstairs to your room, Susie. Is that true?'

She looked completely nonplussed and flushed a deep red.

'Who told you that?'

'Never mind. It's true, isn't it?'

'There was nothing wrong in it. I'm not the sort you're thinking.'

'I'm not thinking anything. I'm asking you a question, Susie. Please give me a straight answer.'

'All right. We did go to my room.'

'What for?'

'He wanted the ring back. I'd left the ring hidden there, because Mr Greenhalgh saw the chain round my neck and tried to put his finger down my blouse to see what was at the end of it. He needed some ready money and he was going to sell it right away. He said it was worth five hundred pounds.'

'Why didn't you tell me all this before?'

She was afraid now and looked terribly alone and forlorn.

'I wasn't trying to deceive you, sir. I gave him the ring and he said he'd get some cash or something for me later in place of it. He talked of selling investments.'

'How did you come to have the ring again, then, when we talked together the other day?'

She wrung her hands.

'I know you won't believe me, but I'm telling God's truth. I picked it up on the stairs. He must have dropped it. We stayed in my room ten minutes, or a little more, arguing.'

'Loudly?'

'No. We were whispering... Perhaps a bit excited, but whispering. I told him to keep his voice down. I didn't want anybody to catch us both in my bedroom. It didn't seem right.'

'Why was he there so long?'

'I didn't want to give up the ring. It was lovely, as you know, and I'd never had anything like it before. It made me feel better... independent... almost a lady... And there he was, wanting it back. However, in the end, he said he'd sell some investments and buy it back for me, or another like it. But he wanted the money right away and investments would take a bit of time to get rid of. I said all right in the end.'

'And he left you with the ring in his hand?'

'Yes.'

'Did you follow him out?'

'No. I stayed in my room about ten minutes, bathing my eyes. I'd been crying. I didn't want anybody to know and ask questions.'

'Where did Mr Snook go, then?'

'I don't know. He closed the door quietly after him. I was crying, and I didn't hear his footsteps even.'

'There was nobody in the house?'

'Mr Trimble, down in the kitchen, when we came up to my room.'

'Where was the ring when you found it?'

'I went down about ten minutes or so after he'd taken it. There wasn't a soul about. And there was the ring at the foot of the stairs in the hall. As though he'd dropped it out of his pocket.'

'So you picked it up again?'

'Yes. I put it back round my neck on the chain he'd bought me for safety. I was going to ask him what he'd been doing to drop it. But he never came back.'

For the first time, Susie was moved. She screwed her face up in a horrible grimace and wept bitterly.

'Just one more question... Why didn't you tell me all this, Susie?'

'I wanted to keep the ring, sir. Suppose I'd said I gave it back. It wouldn't have been mine then, would it? It was no use saying he'd promised me money... And who would believe me if I said the ring was mine, really... a ring like that? They'd laugh at me. So I kept it and said nothing. I'd the letter he wrote about it, but that might have been about *any* ring... A poor little thing... So, I treated it as if he'd never asked for it back and I kept quiet about it.'

'Thank you, Susie. And now go and bathe your eyes again and don't worry any more. I'll see to things. You haven't anything else to tell me?'

'No, sir. You believe me, don't you? I swear it's true.'

'You didn't quarrel or come to blows with Uncle Fred, did you?'

She stood aghast.

'Never! I loved him too much.'

Well, well... Uncle Fred had a real mourner, after all, and someone was going to remember him with love and kindly thoughts. All his futile, wasted years at *Sea Vista* hadn't gone for nothing.

Knell eyed Littlejohn curiously as they started off to the cemetery.

'Any nearer, sir?'

'Yes. I'll tell you later, old man. We're going to be late. Sorry to hold up the party.'

The procession hadn't arrived at the cemetery when Littlejohn got there with Knell and the Archdeacon. They walked along the paths between the graves. Even there, it was pleasant. A profusion of flowers, the faint scent of them on the hot air. Birds were singing, and the gravediggers, throwing earth from a new grave, were whistling as they rhythmically shovelled it out. In the distance, below them, a magnificent view of the whole of the bay, with the calm blue sea and little pleasure boats buzzing and bobbing about and, far away, a little cargo-boat gliding in the direction of Douglas as though eager to be in port again.

Mrs Costain was standing half-hidden by a large white marble angel. She had come all the way from Cregneish for the sake of Uncle Fred, and held in her hand a large bunch of garden flowers, a little wilted, but beautiful in their simplicity.

'Come and join us, Mrs Costain.'

Littlejohn hurried to bring her. She smiled and looked a bit flustered, but was relieved to find friends.

'How is your husband?'

'Middlin', middlin'. A bit upset, all the same. He's wantin' to talk to you, Mr Littlejohn. You see, he saw Mr Trimble on the Calf the day he fell on the rocks and killed himself. He offen puts a sight on the Calf from his bed with his telescope. Spends hours lookin' out that way.'

'We'll take you home after all this, Mrs Costain, and then we can talk with him.'

The funeral entered the gates promptly at eleven-fifteen. Crowds of people, inspecting the T.T. course, which starts just outside the cemetery, stood to attention as Uncle Fred passed in the hearse, a vehicle which seemed out of place in the dazzling sunshine with the birds singing and the trippers looking so care-free and full of easy-going life.

There was a bit of a mix-up at first. Willy had intended it to be a quiet and private affair, merely attended by Mrs Boycott, Victoria and himself. But others had attached themselves to the cortege, at the funeral parlour, greatly to his annoyance. And then, to mend matters, on the busy highway a blue brewery lorry had cut in and divided the sheep from the goats. The Boycotts' two taxis in one half, behind the hearse; then three unofficial intruding cabs following the lorry.

'It's like a blasted circus,' hissed Willy, who, to make the family procession seem a bit larger and more dignified, had hired two fine cars, one for Mrs Boycott and Victoria and another for himself and his temporary hired secretary, a good-looking girl whose company he was beginning heartily to enjoy, and who carried a wreath.

The undertaker, sporting a top hat, climbed from the hearse and was met by four waiting men. They shouldered the huge coffin with its silver-plated fittings, and slowly shuffled with it to the open grave. It was more in keeping with a millionaire or a duke than Uncle Fred, who, at the end of his life, had got down to the bare essentials of simple things, old clothes, and humble, kindly friends.

A crowd of sightseers assembled and followed the funeral, perhaps mistaking it for the obsequies of a prince. From the town below, all the noises of fun and amusement rose and fell as the gentle wind wafted them about. The crack of rifles, the music of roundabouts, the shouts of trippers. Crowded charabancs passed the cemetery gates and a youth went by playing a harmonica.

I left my heart

In the blue-grass country...

The gate-keeper told him to shut up.

The first taxi emptied. The two women who emerged created quite a sensation. In black from head to foot, but in model hats and costumes, flown over hastily from the West End, accompanied by a seamstress to fit them. They looked, for all that, incongruous in the glorious weather, with the view of the sea behind and a crowd of sightseers full of vitality, milling around.

Then Willy, faultlessly dressed for the occasion, his hair sleek, his shoes sparkling, his clothes like those of a receptionist at a super-hotel. His secretary followed, dressed in black as well.

The brewery lorry left the remaining three cabs to their own devices and they all seemed to open at once and pour out their contents. Mrs Trimble. Mrs Nessle. And then three people who peered anxiously about as though wondering if they were in the right funeral. The waitress from the Villa Marina, the tobacconist with the large moustache, both dressed in black, and a man who looked like a tramp who had somehow got mixed up with the party. A simple fellow who delivered Uncle Fred's newspapers and could always be sure of the price of a meal from Snook whenever he was hungry. Uncle Fred's buddies.

The immediate noises subsided, but those of the town went on. People made way for the coffin and the procession. Mrs Boycott and Victoria together; Willy and his secretary; Mrs Nessle and Mrs Trimble; Littlejohn and his three friends; then Uncle Fred's humble pals, looking out-of-place and shy.

'Who are these people?'

Mrs Boycott asked it loudly, and Willy whispered something. He was quite at his ease and gazed round casually, making a slight gesture of recognition at the only good-looking one, Mrs Trimble.

It all went smoothly. The parson read the service, and Mrs

Boycott and Willy were bored and anxious to get it over. Poor Queenie was uncertain how to behave. She looked at her husband, who was now smiling to himself, and then she must have remembered her father, for she burst into a flood of tears.

The gravedigger was inviting Mrs Boycott to throw in the first handful of earth; then everybody else started seizing soil and dropping it on the coffin.

None of the women spoke to each other. They might all have been complete strangers. Or, with Uncle Fred now lying ready to receive the kindly earth, they might still have been jealous of each other about him.

Littlejohn looked round. Susie had just appeared from a town bus, panting, and too late to see anything but the crowd around the grave. She dodged between monuments and tall gravestones to keep out of sight. She wore her neat little dark costume and was flushed and pretty with hurrying. Littlejohn saw her asking a gravedigger a question and he nodded in reply. Then she pointed to another half-opened new grave, and he nodded again.

The priest's surplice flapped in the breeze. There was a brief pause as everybody seemed to wonder what to do next. Willy detached himself from the crowd, sorted out his party, and shepherded them to the gates. Queenie turned once to take another look at the grave with the wreaths and bunches of flowers piled on the next mound. The gravediggers stood by waiting to start filling in.

The official mourners and those from *Sea Vista* left for their vehicles without a word to each other, the women tottering along the paths on their high heels, Willy stroking down his sleek hair, which the wind had ruffled. He slipped his arm through that of his secretary, ostensibly to help her along, and gave her a secret smile.

The waitress and the tobacconist placed their bunches of flowers with the rest and stood for a minute beside the grave. The half-witted newspaper man, who hitherto had kept on his old felt hat, now removed it, looked down at the coffin, and shook his head in a mixture of question and rebuke at Uncle Fred for ending up in this fashion. Mrs Costain left her companions, threw in a handful of soil, and laid down her flowers... Then they all made their way to the road.

Looking back, Littlejohn could see Susie, her pony-tail of hair teased in the wind, hurrying to Uncle Fred's grave before the men got to work on it. She carried a paper bag and drew from it a single rose which she threw on the coffin. Then, her handkerchief to her eyes, she ran to catch a passing bus.

At the door of his cab, Willy was just dealing with some journalists and photographers.

There might have been others in Uncle Fred's life, but they weren't there. And he had made his last disappearance.

Trimble's grave was not far from Uncle Fred's, and half ready to receive him, too. A passing couple with a child looked at it, and the child threw away a bun he had been chewing. Before it reached the ground, a gull swooped to retrieve it. Watching it, Littlejohn saw in the graceful curving up and down of the bird, something which made him think of Trimble at his best. The skilled flight of the acrobat in the air.

At the gate, a fisherman was handing a string of fresh-caught dabs to the keeper and giving him a cod's head for his dog.

14
THE STRANGER ON CALF ISLAND

There was a lull in the noise and bustle of the town, for hunger had swept everybody indoors to eat. To look in at the front windows of the boarding-houses as you passed on the promenade was like touring round the fish-house at a zoo. Aquarium after aquarium, with the mouths moving and eyes watching you through the glass.

The promenade was quiet for the time being. A few people pottering about enjoying the peace of it, dogs tacking here and there along the causeway sniffing the walls and seats and lifting their legs without being chased away. A day-trip from Llandudno discharging a crowd of excursionists at the pier-head, a plane hovering overhead...

Littlejohn and his party returned from the cemetery by way of the seafront. Wherever they'd been, Knell, if he were driving, brought Littlejohn back that way. He seemed to think it his duty to give the Superintendent as many views of the sea as he could.

The windows of the car were all down, the warm air caressed Littlejohn's cheeks, before him stretched the panorama between Douglas Head and Onchan. Everybody seemed to be on holiday and Littlejohn wished he were the same. If he could manage to clear up the mystery of Uncle Fred's death before week-end, he could stay on for almost another week and thoroughly enjoy himself with the Archdeacon. His heart sank a bit. He had a good idea what lay ahead and he didn't like the thought of it.

On leaving Grenaby that morning, they had solemnly promised Maggie Keggin to return for lunch. Someone had brought a salmon to the vicarage the night before. No questions had been asked about its origins, but Maggie Keggin was cooking it for lunch. The Archdeacon had invited Knell and Mrs Costain to join them.

After Knell had attended at Trimble's inquest they left the town by way of the quayside and then along the old Castletown road. Littlejohn wished Knell wouldn't drive so fast. Perhaps he wanted to get to the salmon, but it didn't give anyone a chance to sit back and admire the view. That was what the Superintendent wanted. To admire the view. He wished they'd hired a landau with a horse which would just jog-trot them home. Knell had given him another sample cigar, he was puffing it contentedly, he felt relaxed, and, for the minute, Uncle Fred was miles away. They hardly seemed to have started before Knell was turning up by the little signpost... *Grenaby*. In ten minutes, they were sitting at table with the salmon, whilst from the kitchen, the gossiping voices of Mrs Keggin and Mrs Costain sounded in a continual pleasant Manx buzz.

Littlejohn was loath to start off again. At the bridge a man was idly fishing. Joe Henn, his trousers and jacket again drawn over his nightshirt, was leaning over his gate, hunting for someone to talk to, and the village cats were outside their cottage doors snoozing on the warm stones of the threshold. It wasn't fair having to work on a day like this.

They went over the hills to Port St Mary, rising to a height which gave a wide view of the south-east of the Island from the fish-tail of Castletown and Derbyhaven bays to the Mull Hills and

Port St Mary itself. Then they descended to shore level and climbed up to Cregneish again.

John Costain was still sitting up in bed, with the dog at his feet and a tall gangling man with a shock of stiff hair like a shaving brush, and a humorous long, rugged face, sitting on the chair beside him. He introduced his friend as Charlie Bridson. He had been specially commanded to appear by John Costain, for he was the fisherman whose boat Trimble had borrowed on his last trip to the Calf of Man.

Bridson, to fill in the time whilst the pair of them waited for the arrival of the police, had given Costain his midday meal, washed up after it, tidied his bedroom, and cut his hair and shaved him. A real handy man!

'If you'd been much longer comin', Charlie would have decorated the bedroom an' painted the doors and window frames,' said Costain.

Bridson was shy to begin with. He wasn't used to what he described as 'the big nobs' and Costain had had to use threats to keep him there. The Archdeacon's visits to Cregneish were few and far between and then only on special occasions. Bridson wasn't used to it at all. He shook hands mightily as he was introduced and gave Knell a peculiar look as he gripped his hand. Something about shooting after dark with flashlight illuminations on Ronagh... Bridson had been a better runner than P.C. Knell in those days, or else it might have ended in the High Bailiff's court... However, Knell didn't seem to remember, whereat Bridson smiled again.

It was obvious they were in for a 'session'. Costain's sparkling eyes betrayed that there was going to be a lot of serious talk and the ritual demanded first of all, a repast of tea and soda-cakes. After that, they got down to work. It was pleasant doing business there, with the room full of flowers, the air scented by the gentle breeze blowing from the hill-side and the gardens, the sea ahead, and the Calf basking in the sun across the Sound.

It would not do at all to report the whole afternoon's conversation verbatim. The slow caressing Manx brogue, the sharp questions of Knell, the lazy listening of Littlejohn, with here and there a word or two to clear some matter up. Charabancs full of holidaymakers passed on land and ships passed on the sea, and the droning sounds of many voices filtered through John Costain's bedroom window and tickled the curiosity of the good people of Cregneish.

'Charlie called to tell me about his boat... He missed her when he got down at the Sound on his way for crabs... '

There was an interlude whilst Charlie talked about crabs and where they were best found on the Calf. He finally said he thought some hooligans on holiday from 'over' had stolen his boat. She wasn't locked up. Just drawn up high on the rocks facing Kitterland with a sheet of corrugated iron over her to keep the water out. It was a load off his mind, sure enough, when Kinley let him' know that she was safely tied up on the Calf. Together they had crossed and towed her back across the Sound after Kinley's return from Douglas.

'What made me so mad about it was that Trimble's had her before and alwiss asked if he could teck her out. Why he didn' ask agen just puzzles me... But then, the poor fellah's dead now and past tellin'... The boat's not been damaged, so the thing's forgot.'

The man in the bed waved an excited hand.

'But that's not the end of it... Not the end of it, for sure. Charlie tells me that while I been in bed, Fred and Trimble used his boat instid o' mine to get over to the Calf.'

Bridson nodded.

'Mr Snook when he came to me about hirin' the boat, axed me not to tell John. "It might make him melancholy, leck, to think of me on the Calf enjoying myself and him in his bed an' can't move. So don't tell him... Jest lend me the boat and keep your mouth shut about me an' Trimble, leck... He didn't want John to think he'd found another pal because it might upset John.'

Just like Uncle Fred. Thoughtful... a bit too thoughtful. So thoughtful sometimes that he caused complications.

'I never heard from a sowl that Fred was goin' on the Calf just as offen as he did when him and me was around together.'

Bridson explained that he'd warned the men of Cregneish that Costain wasn't to be told on Uncle Fred's express orders.

'It wouldn' have made me jealous. Though the thought of me lying here on me back and Fred on the Calf like we used to be together, would have made me fret to be around again... He was a good mate to be around with, was Fred Snook.'

'So Trimble took your place until you were better and could help him across the Sound again?'

'That's right, Superintendent. It needs two in the boat most times. The currents is terr'ble strong some days. Trimble, of course, was a bit of a cripple and not much use. But he added weight and could steer.'

So... that was what Uncle Fred had been doing. Gallivanting with Trimble, taking his landlord on his trips to the Calf, perhaps using him to take a brief turn at the oars and then spending one of those lazy days he'd so much loved, idling about, lying in the sun, with a case of beer for refreshment and letting the time pass without a care in the world.

Perhaps Fred and Trimble had talked a lot, just as Fred and John Costain had done. Talked about old times and exchanged secrets they usually kept in dark parts of their minds and didn't bring to the light of day except when the silence of the deserted islet, the monotonous beat of the sea, the cry of the birds, and the magnetism of the complete solitude made different men of them, put their past lives and tragedies in proper perspective, and encouraged them to talk about life and how it had treated them in days past.

What had Fred told Trimble and Trimble told Fred to sow the seeds of total disaster and death for both of them?

Littlejohn brooded over it as his companions talked together, the smoke of his pipe rising blue in the sunshine flooding through the window like a limelight illuminating a stage.

'You wanted to tell me about something you'd seen through your telescope the afternoon we found Trimble's body, John?'

He suddenly remembered it and the man in the bed raised himself on his hands and pointed to the window-sill.

'The telescope's right there, sir. Teck a look through her across at the Calf.'

Littlejohn drew out the segments of the glass and put the eyepiece to his eye.

It was a good glass. He swept the country between Cregneish and the Sound with it first. He felt he could touch the farm lad on his way to bring in the cows for milking. The same with the charabanc and its load, pitched on the green turf near the café opposite Kitterland. He could plainly make out the expressions of the men and women drinking cups of tea and lemonade. In a cleft of rock hidden from the rest of the coach party, a man was kissing a woman. Either he or she belonged to someone else, for the unpleasant furtiveness of the embrace and the awkward way in which it was effected were almost comic... However, it was taking an unfair advantage to catch them in a telescope.

The Calf itself seemed as near as the garden hedge of Costain's cottage. The little harbour at the Sound, the steep path leading up to the summit, beyond which the hidden valley and the house were nestled. Telephone poles without wires climbed all the way up... Kinley was there with his boat, taking a party back to Port Erin on a round trip from Port St Mary.

'From where I was in bed, I couldn' see Cow Harbour, just over the Sound, proper. So, I didn' see Trimble get there with Charlie's boat. But I happened to sight him climbin' up and round the west side to avoid the house, leck. As if he didn' want the warden to see him. "Hullo," I thinks. "There's Trimble gettin' on the Calf without payin' for his ticket." It was late in the day and he was carrying a biggish bundle an' he climbed on and vanished in the direction of the old lighthouses over the cliff tops.'

'Did you see him again, John?'

'Yes. But not till next day. He must have stopped there all night. He came back on the skyline next afternoon... Didn' stop long, though. Then, I saw Kinley takin' a party in his boat to the South Harbour... They was out of sight when they landed, leck, but soon, I see 'em wandering around, lookin' about at the sights of the island... I see a woman right on the top near where Trimble had been. She seemed to be lookin' for someborry... Then she vanished just like Trimble did, in the same direction.'

'Did you make out who she was?'

'Naw... I never see her face proper. There was some-thin' sleechy... sneaky... about 'er. She was lookin' for something or someborry and tryin' not to look as if she was... You unnerstand what I'm meanin'?'

'I do. How was she dressed?'

'Sort o' long white coat, I seem to reckerlec'... Colour of this blanket... She looked to be wearin' sun-glasses, too. After a while, she come back the way she'd gone, hurryin' at first, and then slowin' down as though she'd seen people and didn't want 'em to think she was in a hurry or runnin' from somethin'... As soon as I heerd Trimble was dead, I thinks "oho, me lady's somethin' to do with that", and yet I couldn't say what she looked like.'

'That's all right, John. You've told us enough.'

'You know who she is?'

'I think so.'

Knell started and the Archdeacon smiled. He could wait, but Knell had a 'what are we waiting for?' expression on his eager face. Littlejohn filled his pipe and passed his pouch across first to Costain and then to Bridson, who had now settled comfortably down with his new friends and was ready to talk until the cows came home.

Littlejohn, too, felt like prolonging this interview. He looked approvingly round at the ring of honest, pleasant faces, and thought about the rest of the characters in the case, those in Douglas. Mrs Boycott and her retinue at Fort Anne, busy with Fred's affairs, trying to sort them out in a fashion which would release his fortune for their own purposes.

And *Sea Vista* with its seedy atmosphere of undischarged bankrupts; married men on a spree with women they'd tricked into spending a furtive week's holiday; Teddy-boys making the place into a bear-garden; the honeymooners of diverse ages, the man after the money, the woman pathetically clutching the last straw of late romance; a moneylender's widow posing as half an aristocrat; a servant with a diamond ring worth a small fortune; another whom the men couldn't keep their hands off. All collected by post for a holiday by a broken trapeze artist and superannuated principal boy from a pantomime.

Uncle Fred in his grave and Trimble in the morgue.

What a lot!

Littlejohn knocked out his pipe through the window and rose to his feet. The rest, except John Costain, rose, too, and the little party ended.

'I hope it's helped you, Superintendent. And I hope more than that, that you'll come agen to see me before ye go back to London.'

'You've been a great help, John... A very great help. And I'll promise to come and have a real afternoon's *cooish* with you in a day or two. You shall tell me some of your tales of the sea and we'll eat soda-cakes, drink tea, and forget crime.'

Knell dropped Littlejohn and the Archdeacon at the vicarage. They'd had enough for one day, and a rest was due to all of them.

'I'll be glad if you'll have us picked up about ten in the morning, Knell, and could you arrange for us all to meet somewhere about eleven? By all, I mean all the characters in the affair. Mrs Nessle, Mrs Trimble, Susie, Finnegan, and Mrs Boycott and her daughter and son-in-law. Miss Crawley will leave by the morning boat and you needn't bother about Maria. She'll only upset people.

I want a talk with them all together... If you could arrange for it to be held in the private room the Boycotts occupy at Fort Anne, it would be preferable. *Sea Vista* will be humming with new arrivals and it will be too diverting... The hotel room is quiet.'

'I'll see to it, sir.'

'Till tomorrow, then, Knell, and put Uncle Fred and all his affairs out of your mind till we meet. Take a rest from him.'

'I'll try.'

'Good-bye, Knell... And thank you.'

'Thank *you*, sir.'

There was something a trifle emotional even in this temporary parting. It seemed to arise from the bond of affection which had been forged between the junior police officer and his superior. But then, the whole Uncle Fred affair had been teeming with emotion of all kinds. Buckets of it...

There was an old seat in the sunshine in the vicarage garden, and when dinner was ready, Maggie Keggin seeking her master and Littlejohn, found them both sleeping, side by side, in the last of the evening light.

'Wake up, the pair of ye... Ye'll both be gettin' your deaths of cold in this everin' air... And dinner's ready and it's pigeons and they won't wait.'

Someone had sent the Archdeacon a bottle of Richebourg, '48, and he opened it with the meal. It stimulated them both and they talked a lot and it encouraged the Archdeacon to ask Littlejohn to tell him everything about the case and who'd murdered Fred Snook.

'I'm sorry, sir. Although I've made up my mind by instinct, I can't tell a coherent tale yet. There are one or two missing links and I'm a bit confused.'

'What about a game of chess, then? It will take your mind off it all and meanwhile get your subconscious to work.'

They played for an hour in front of the log fire and then they drank a glass of port, which was the Archdeacon's speciality and came from a village grocer who had once supplied it to a famous Bishop of Sodor and Man. Littlejohn telephoned home to his wife and arranged for her to join him there at the week-end. The clock struck midnight and the two of them prepared to retire.

'For all the work of the day, Littlejohn, it's been a pleasant one... a happy one... because of your company. To my way of thinking, when two men get together and have much in common, their comradeship is the nearest thing to heaven we can find here.'

Littlejohn paused with one foot on the bottom step of the stairs.

Uncle Fred and Costain... And then Uncle Fred and Trimble.

'Could we go back to the fire, sir? I can see it all now... '

Half an hour later they were still talking when the telephone rang. Of course, it was Knell! Apologetic as usual.

'Susie's tried to murder Mrs Trimble. Stabbed her with a knife. Luckily, it was a flesh wound; she wakened up just as she was attacked in bed... What do we do, sir? Do we stop all those goin' by the morning boat, from leaving?'

Littlejohn sighed.

'Can you send a car for me, Knell? I'd better come along.'

Why did it always have to happen late at night!

15
THE LAST NIGHT

It was about two o'clock in the morning. The policeman stationed at the door of *Sea Vista* saluted Littlejohn and the Archdeacon.

'Inspector Knell's upstairs waiting for you, sir.'

The promenade lights were on in an attenuated way, every other one illuminated. The only sounds came from the direction of the harbour, where a cargo boat was being loaded and a skeleton staff was astir for the midnight passenger excursion from Liverpool, due in Douglas about five o'clock. Odd street lamps shone here and there. In the distance the sound of the tide beating on the promenade wall. The intermittent beams of Douglas Head lighthouse flickering across the distant water.

It was a warm night. Windows of hotels and boardinghouses wide open. Now and then, the shouts of some late reveller broke the silence. Otherwise, everybody seemed asleep. Rows and rows of them, tier upon tier. Some of them even sleeping in bathrooms and on billiard-tables, for Douglas was packed out.

One or two lights were on in bedrooms of *Sea Vista*. Uncle Fred's old room was in darkness and was now occupied by the evangelical-looking lodger, who kept asking everyone if they'd been saved. Now, the Teddy-boys got it in first and asked *him* if *he'd* been saved, and he didn't like it. There was a light in No. 3, and as Littlejohn climbed the stairs he could hear the dismal sound like chanting going on between the honeymooners. Mullineaux appeared at the door as he passed. He wore a raincoat over his pyjamas and stood in his bare feet. Without his large glasses, he looked a different man and his face wore the strained, flabby expression of worry and sleeplessness in the small hours.

'This won't stop us getting the morning boat?'

'No.'

'Oh, thanks... Thank you very much.'

He went inside and shut the door of No. 3, and the chanting, this time presto and in a higher delighted key, started again.

Dirty shoes outside the bedrooms; a whole shopful of them at the Greenhalghs'. No Trimble to clean them. A small boy came and did it at seven, before he went to school.

Knell was waiting for them in No. 6, the Trimbles' old bedroom. The lights were on, pink shades and tassels, casting a restless glow on the figure in the bed. It was Mrs Trimble and, considering what she'd been through recently, she looked remarkably well, albeit a little pale. Her hair was tidy and there was even lipstick on her mouth. It might have been a stage bedroom.

Modern furniture in light oak, a good carpet on the floor, and all kinds of odds and ends and bric-à-brac scattered around. Cheap little porcelain figures, dolls dressed in coloured silks, small framed sentimental prints up and down the walls and, over the fireplace, now bricked-up and with an electric heater inserted under the mantelpiece, a perfect picture-gallery of variety artists, old friends of the Trimbles, judging from the affectionate superscriptions. 'All our Love to Gracie and Ferdy, Mai and Joe' – a couple of jugglers. 'With eternal gratitude and affection, Ed. and Fi.' – a pair in evening dress, the man playing a piano and the girl sitting on the top... Another photograph of Trimble in tights, dark moustache bristling, muscles rippling, standing at the foot of a trapeze; Mrs Trimble, dressed as Dick Whittington, tights and all, smiling from ear to ear at the stage cat sitting tailor-wise at her feet. In the background a cardboard milestone, 'London, 10 miles.'

Knell was perched uncomfortably on a bedroom chair. He looked like a guilty party himself, moodily waiting for justice to tap him on the shoulder. There were dark shadowy rings under his eyes and his quiff sagged despondently. He smiled and bucked up when he saw Littlejohn.

'I'm glad you're both here, sir... Susie came in the room and tried to stab Mrs Trimble... Or that's what Mrs Trimble says. Susie denies it.'

'Where is Susie?'

'She's in the kitchen. I thought it best not to leave her on her own. One of our men is there with her.'

'Nice for him.'

'Beg pardon, sir.'

'Don't heed me. I was just being funny. How did it happen?'

There was a moan from the bed. Littlejohn went to the bedside.

'How are you feeling, Mrs Trimble?'

'Not so bad. It was the shock more than anything else.'

She smiled bravely, the sort of smile Littlejohn thought she might have given the stage cat when, as Dick Whittington turned adrift away from London, she sat on the milestone and told him to cheer up and be brave. And the cat would answer *Meeouw*.

'Where is the wound?'

'At the top of my arm.'

She pushed back the bedclothes and displayed a pink night-gown with hardly any top, and a bare arm, shapely and trussed-up in bandages from shoulder to elbow.

'She tried to stab me in the chest and fought like a tiger. If I hadn't fought back and shouted for help, which came just in time, she'd have killed me.'

Meeouw!

Somehow it all sounded stagey and melodramatic.

'Tell me just what happened.'

Mrs Trimble, lying on her back, stretched out her arm again and made clutching movements in mid-air above the bedside table. This was to indicate to Knell that she wanted a dose of what smelled like brandy and water contained in a large glass there. Knell put the mixture to her lips and she drank half of it.

'I came to bed early. After the funeral and the inquest... and I can tell you, the Coroner put me through it... I was whacked and I got to bed about nine... Everybody was out except Miss Archibald and the two servant girls... Is that you, reverend? Don't stand there looking a stranger. Draw up a chair and make yourself at home.'

'Thank you, Mrs Trimble. How do you feel?'

'Not so bad, sir... Not so bad that I need praying for yet, if you understand what I mean without me being unreverent.'

'Well, Mrs Trimble?'

'Sorry, Superintendent... Where was I? I came to bed about nine. I made myself a hot toddy, drank it, and fell off. I must have been asleep a good two hours when someone singing outside half woke me... It was then I had that funny feeling you sometimes get, even when you can't see, that somebody's in the room... I put on the bedside light, and there stood Susie, a knife in her hand and an awful murderous look in her eyes. She didn't give me a chance even to sit up in bed, but came for me... We struggled and I screamed. I caught her hand, the one with the knife, between my two hands and turned the blade from my chest, and she gave a jerk and it made a deep cut in my shoulder... Then somebody came in the room. It was one of the boys from the end room. He'd come up for his accordion, and next, Mrs Nessle arrived... Then others... I fainted. Give me another little drink, Mr Knell, please. I shall never forget it till my dying day... the look in her eyes as the light went on.'

Meeouw!

Littlejohn knew he wasn't being fair treating it all with a pinch of salt and inwardly smiling grimly, but he couldn't help it. He needed Susie's tale before coming to a conclusion.

'Why in the world would the girl want to kill you, Mrs Trimble?'

The Archdeacon spoke, eagerly keeping the tale on the boil.

'She wanted to keep me quiet. If I told all I know, she'd be on the carpet for Fred Snook's murder.'

Littlejohn turned quickly.

'What's this, Mrs Trimble? Have you been keeping something from us...? If so, why?'

The body in the bed moved voluptuously under the sheets. The face framed by the pillows assumed a compassionate, almost motherly look.

'I didn't want to say anything without being sure. Both my late husband and me were very fond of Susie. She was like one of our own flesh and blood. But, after my husband died and I put two and two together, I began to see daylight. I asked her a few questions when I got home from the inquest today and she knew that I knew all about it.'

'Well, you'd better tell me everything at once. This is very serious and you might have wasted us a lot of time by withholding it... What is it?'

'The day Uncle Fred died... I was out watching the carnival.'

'Alone?'

'Yes. I went on my own.'

'Did anybody see you?'

'I can't tell you. There were thousands of people all crowded together. I'm sure I couldn't tell one from another. Why?'

'Go on.'

'The visitors all went to the carnival right after dinner. Mr Trimble stayed behind, minding the place, and Susie, too. Somebody had to be here to look after the tea. Uncle Fred was in his room. That's all. Just the three of them. On the day before he met his death, my husband happened to mention that on the day of the murder he'd seen Uncle Fred and Susie going upstairs, had quietly followed them up, and found they were in Susie's room. He didn't know what was going on there, but he guessed, and I'll bet he was right, too. The little devil! Next thing, Uncle Fred staggers down the stairs and out at the front door... Give me another drink, please, Mr Knell.'

She gulped greedily. Her face was pink with excitement. 'Now, I never thought anything about it at the time, and then, funnily enough, as we were coming away from the funeral, it struck me. Uncle Fred might have been stabbed here. See what I mean? He might not have died right away, but staggered out and died on the prom. It was then it dawned on me how it had all happened. Susie had quarrelled with him in her room, after... after... At any rate, she'd quarrelled with him and stabbed him.'

'What with?'

'I don't know. Perhaps the knife she tried to kill me with. It belongs in the kitchen. A paper-knife... she has one that one of the visitors once gave her, one he won in a dancing competition at the Palais... Or even a table knife, she might have had there.'

'Did you tell her your suspicions?'

'Yes. This afternoon in the kitchen. We were alone for a bit. I just asked her what she and Uncle Fred were doing in her room the afternoon he died and if they'd quarrelled and she'd tried to stab him. She didn't say a word. Just went out with a jam-cake in her hand and put it in the dining-room. As if I'd not spoken at all. But she knew I knew... That's why she tried to silence me.'

'What kind of a weapon did she use when she came for you?'

Knell produced it from his pocket, wrapped up in tissue paper. A small game-carver ground down by use to a fine short blade. It was stained with blood.

'A murderous-looking weapon!'

'I thought so when she came for me waving it.'

Littlejohn picked up his hat.

'Let's go and have a word with Susie, now.'

'She denies it all. Naturally, she will do. But don't believe her, Superintendent. She's a deep one. She's been hankering after Uncle Fred for a long time and he fell for her and then he must have cooled off. It's as plain as the nose on your face why she went for him. She hated him for jilting her. She even denies she tried to kill me. Is it likely I'd make this mess of myself and cook up a tale? Why should I? You'd think me potty if I started trying to kill myself, even if Trimble's death has made life not worth living any more. I'm not the sort to kill myself. I've more pluck than that. No. She was afraid I'd tell the police and she wanted me out of the way. If she'd succeeded, you would have suspected anybody but her. With a house full of lodgers, some of them not above suspicion, I must admit, the police wouldn't think of suspecting our innocent little Susie... She's a dark horse, that one, though I must say, if she hadn't tried to do away with me, I might have shielded her... I'd have gone a long way for her, at any rate. So, you be careful if you're asking her questions. She's the sort who'll lie to save her neck, just as anybody else would do.'

Knell stayed behind again and was joined by Mrs Nessle, anxious to do all she could to prove she was a friend in need. She and Mrs Kelly, from next door, had undertaken shifts of watching the patient's health, whilst Knell saw to it that she remained safe.

Down below, Littlejohn found Susie asleep in a chair, with the bobby in charge of her reading the day-before-yesterday's paper in an armchair by the stove. Susie was physically and emotionally exhausted and all her beauty had vanished. Her hair had slipped from the little clips which usually held it in place, and hung limply framing her pale face. There were dark rings under her eyes, and the lipstick had rubbed and smudged on her small mouth showing the anaemic pink of the lips. She was breathing heavily through her mouth which was slightly open, and the breath which escaped blew up and then down a little curl which hung over her cheek.

The policeman sprang to his feet and apologized. He was in his shirt sleeves and smoking a cigarette. His shoes were unlaced... He started to straighten himself up, but Littlejohn stopped him.

'Don't bother. Make yourself comfortable. It's late and regulations don't matter.'

At the sound of voices, Susie's eyes slowly opened. She smiled slightly and then remembered her plight. She passed her hand across her forehead and hair, softly teasing it into a semblance of order. It was the eyes which made the face, however. Open now, they illuminated it, the angles of the jaw tightened, the bones seemed to stiffen, and she was good-looking again. She glanced from the Superintendent to the Archdeacon and then back again.

'I'm so glad you're both here. I don't seem to have a friend in the world, now. I just can't get anybody to believe what I say, but I swear it's true.'

'Tell us your version of what's happened tonight. Do you smoke?'

Littlejohn passed his case to her and then to the constable, and lit all three cigarettes with his lighter. Susie inhaled deeply and gradually relaxed. She smiled faintly again at Archdeacon Kinrade. She pointed at him.

'I know *he'll* believe me. He knows the difference between the truth and a lie.'

'What happened?'

'It just bewilders me. It's so ridiculous of her to lie like that. But I see quite plain that it's between her and me, and as she's the oldest and the boss, I'm likely to suffer. It's just this. This afternoon when I was getting teas ready, she came in the kitchen and said her late husband just before he died said that Mr Snook was in my bedroom, and up to no good with me, the very last thing he did in this house before he went out and died. She also said, in her opinion, he'd been stabbed when he left the house and fell dead on the promenade from bleeding to death. She said I'd done it when he was in my room with me. I naturally thought the shock of her husband dying, and the inquest and such, had turned her a bit queer. So I didn't argue. I just left the kitchen and went on with the teas in the dining-room.'

She took another puff at her cigarette and looked round at the men's faces to see if her tale was going down well.

'And then?'

'After tea, we cleared up, and then Mrs Trimble arrived. She'd been out for a walk or something and said she was going up to bed. She'd have a good sleep, she said. And she says, "And you, Susie, bring me up a large rum and milk on your way to bed." It's the last night for a lot of them and I didn't get finished till about eleven. Even then, some of them weren't in, but it's Maria's turn to stay and lock up, so I took the rum and milk up to Mrs Trimble's room. When I got in and switched on the light, it didn't light up. That was the one over the dressing-table. I knew there was another on the bedside table, so I walked over to it in the dark. Mrs Trimble seemed to be breathing regular, so I was quiet about it. Just as I put out my hand to the lamp, she got hold of my arm and started to scream. She'd something in her hand as she gripped me and when I managed with my free hand to put on the light, I could see it was a knife. She was bleeding and I don't know whether I did it or she did it, but it was at the top of her arm and she shouted I'd tried to kill her. People rushed in, she fainted, and the police were sent for. But I swear I'd no knife in my hand when I entered the room. Why should I want to kill her? She's never really done me any wrong.'

'She says you were afraid she'd tell the police that you'd killed Uncle Fred.'

'That's what I gathered, thinking it out while I've been sitting with Charlie here.'

The bobby blushed to the roots of his hair. His hands even blushed.

'I'm the man on the beat here, sir. We've known one another for a long time. I come in now and then for a bite of supper when it's not the busy season.'

The look he gave Susie showed that he, for one, was on her side.

'You do, do you, Charlie?'

'Yes, sir.'

Poor Charlie stood at attention, wondering how he'd fare when reports were made.

'Well, Charlie, will you kindly go and ask Inspector Knell to remove the bulb from the fitting over the dressing-table, and bring it, together with the glass from which Mrs Trimble's been drinking, down to me? Just that, as quickly as you can.'

He turned to Susie.

'Did anybody try the light over the dressing-table after the rescue party arrived?'

'I don't know. Vincent, the boy who plays the accordion in Number 8, was the first to appear and separate us. Then Mrs Nessle came in. Vincent held me, while Mrs Nessle went to the top of the stairs and called down for help. I remember... Mrs Trimble kept shouting, "Take her out of here," so Vincent pushed me on the landing till the others arrived. Then I was taken down...'

'The room was empty for a minute after Vincent took you out?'

'Yes. It took a minute or two for the others to get up. They were making such a noise... It was their last night and some of them were a bit lit up... Vincent stood holding me outside.'

'Now, just one more question, Susie. How was Uncle Fred killed?'

'They said he'd been stabbed in the back.'

'What with?'

'The papers said it might have been a bread-knife. I don't know. Why?'

'Have you a paper-knife in your room?'

'Yes, sir. You don't think... It was one a lodger gave me. He'd won it dancing. It's on my dressing-table, as a sort of ornament. It looks good, you know... all silver like...'

'Go and get it, Susie.'

'Alone?'

'That's all right.'

She was quickly up and quickly back again, this time accompanied by P.C. Charlie, who tenderly piloted her before him into the room. She carried the knife, he the light-bulb and glass.

'Take them both to the station and if there's anybody there who understands fingerprint work, compare those on the glass with any on the bulb. Be careful. The bulb's dusty and the prints look fresh... Please go now, Charlie, and be quick, and telephone the result.'

After doing himself up respectably, shoes, tunic and hat, Charlie was off.

The paper-knife was a good stainless steel affair, like a dagger, with a leather handle. It was shining, clean and dry.

'It was in its usual place?'

'Yes. I'm going to be all right, sir? You do believe me.'

'Don't excite yourself, Susie. One way or another, it will soon be over. You'd better make yourself a cup of tea. You look all-in and I'm sure the Archdeacon and I will be glad to share one with you.'

As she filled the kettle and set it to boil, they sat there with absolute silence in the house around them. Everybody seemed asleep. Littlejohn went into the hall. There he could hear some snores from the floors above. The honeymooners had ceased their chanting, the eternal accordion was silent, and the Greenhalgh children at peace for a change. Somewhere, a half-turned-off tap was whistling...

Then, suddenly, the sound of padding footsteps, and Knell appeared around the balusters. He was in a hurry. He expressed a wish, in pantomime, to speak earnestly with Littlejohn and when he reached him whispered hoarsely:

'Mrs Trimble's coming down... We can't stop her. She's getting rough... Mrs Nessle's trying to pacify her. She wants to know what Susie's telling you.'

It was dim in the passages and staircase. One light only in the hall. Suddenly, the lot were illuminated by someone switching on above. Mrs Trimble appeared, fastening as she descended the innumerable buttons which ran down the front of her long, trailing house-coat.

'I won't stay there while she tells you a lot of lies... I'm coming down.'

She shouted at the top of her voice and the noise rang round the stairs and corridors. Voices, doors opening, shafts of light shooting from rooms and holding in their beams half-clad, sleepy, exasperated figures. Two of the Greenhalgh children began to wail dismally and finally Greenhalgh himself appeared, dishevelled and hideous after a final holiday binge and a brief drunken sleep.

'What the hell's goin' on? How much longer is this goin' to last? Hey! You the police? Somebody's pinched my raincoat. I want to report it. I hung it on the 'atstand when we arrived and 'aven't needed it since. And when I came to pack it, I found it 'ad been swiped...'

The rest was drowned by the voice of the man so anxious about salvation, thundering texts and exhortations from the floor above. Greenhalgh told him to go to hell. The heads of the Teddy-boys, tousled and oily, appeared, too, at the top landing, but their attention was quickly diverted by the arrival of Maria from her attic, clad in almost transparent pyjamas and looking like a wraith from the Folies Bergère.

From behind the door of No. 3, a dull free-chant arose, like a crowd of monks singing a midnight Mass. Miss Arrow-brook, to whom Mrs Nessle had transferred her ministrations, was asking for a doctor to stifle one of her *does*.

Only Finnegan, the sinner, the seducer, seemed at peace. His snores burst rhythmically from the gap under his attic door. Now and then, the steady tide of his harsh breathing broke and seemed to stop. Then it was resumed with redoubled fury.

The telephone bell rang. All the spectators on the stairs and in the doorways held their breath. The Mullineaux even stopped their litany and crouched listening. Finnegan alone took no heed. He snored on like a great furnace, gulping-in air, until Maria tapped on his door. There was a pause and then a shout.

'All right. I'm waken. I'll 'ave early mornin' tea for once, seein' I'm crossin' by the first boat.'

He'd mistaken the noise for his customary *knock*! Then, he must have seen it wasn't daylight. They could hear him thinking it out. The snoring started all over again, this time accompanied by shrill whistling.

The telephone message was a brief one. Mrs Trimble's prints on the glass tallied with those on the bulb. She'd obviously removed it herself. There was one other set they couldn't identify. Littlejohn grinned. Knell's!

'That's all for the present,' called Littlejohn blandly to the audience on the stairs. 'You'd better go back to bed and get some sleep.'

'Wot the hell's it all about?'

Greenhalgh was cut short by the evangelist, who heaped biblical texts, threats and abominations upon him until, drowning in a sea of divinity, he fled to the bosom of his family, where he smacked two of them soundly, thus relieving his feelings. The people and the noises died away and all that remained in the stillness was the snoring of Finnegan and the midnight Mass of the Mullineaux...

Back in the kitchen, Susie and Mrs Trimble faced each other in silence. The Archdeacon, apparently as fresh as a daisy, in spite of the hour, at which first light was now appearing across the sea, had ordered them to be quiet in a manner which filled their superstitious souls with a feeling of dire consequences if they disobeyed.

Littlejohn's reappearance broke the spell.

'Isn't it time you stopped messing about and arrested her for murder, Superintendent? I won't have her here another minute. The police-station's the place for her... And I hope she swings for all she's done.'

Mrs Trimble, majestic in her blue house-coat, her finger pointing at the culprit like a pantomime Lady Macbeth, drew herself up in majesty and demanded justice.

The melodrama was spoiled by an intrusion. Mrs Nessle, wearing a long flowered dressing-gown which, for elegance, put Mrs Trimble's robe to shame, opened the door apologetically. She looked tired and very old after her vigil during which the powder and paint had worn from her face and revealed the pathetic ravages of the years.

'Please excuse me... Miss Arrowbrook is very unwell. I think we ought to get a doctor. I know she's a hypochondriac but I, personally, am not prepared to take the responsibility.'

Miss Arrowbrook! Littlejohn frowned. Miss Arrowbrook, the invalid, the *malade imaginaire,* whom everybody laughed at and ignored. The woman who went her silent way, constitutionals, doctors, quack medicines... and nobody cared. The poor soul nobody wanted to bother with, because she was a bore. She ate at a little table by herself, came and went alone, avoided the rest, lowering her eyes as she passed... In fact, the invisible woman, the nonentity, the one who didn't count. And Littlejohn realized that he'd behaved exactly as everyone else did. He'd treated her as though she didn't exist... A flush of self-reproach filled him. He took a clean glass and the whisky bottles from the tray on the table, whence some of the favoured addicts of *Sea Vista* had been refreshing themselves after hours, in secret, because the licence didn't embrace spirits.

'Will you come up with me, Archdeacon...? And you, please, Mrs Nessle?'

Miss Arrowbrook's room was woefully different from the

Trimbles' next door. A shabby mat covered the linoleum and the heavy oak furniture was drab and second-hand. Miss Arrowbrook was sitting up in bed under a glaring lamp shaded by a dusty parchment cover. She revived when the men entered.

'Mrs Nessle! I didn't ask for a minister... And who is this?'

'I'm a police officer, here on duty, Miss Arrowbrook, and I heard you were ill... I wondered if I could help until a doctor arrives... This is the Venerable Archdeacon of Man, who also wishes to help.'

The atmosphere changed. Miss Arrowbrook liked attention in spite of her retiring ways. She almost bowed herself out of bed at the parson, whilst, with one hand, holding a plain nightdress closely to her throat.

'It is kind of you.'

'Take a little of this.'

Littlejohn poured out a couple of fingers of whisky and offered her the glass. She sipped and savoured the contents and then swigged it off. Her colour rose right away.

'This is the medicine which Mr Snook used to give me when I had my turns. It always did me so much good. He would never tell me what it was. A little secret of his own, he always said.'

She still sat there, gaunt and awkward, with brown circles under her grey eyes, her greasy nondescript hair awry, her thin pale hands picking at the bedclothes.

'Miss Arrowbrook, did the police ask you where you were on the afternoon of Mr Snook's death... at, say, about three o'clock?'

She put both hands over her heart as though suffering from palpitation. Her eyes turned beseechingly to Littlejohn.

'Yes,' she whispered. 'I was very upset about it all. It put me back quite a lot. I'd been feeling better.'

'And you told them you were out in the town, didn't you?'

'Yes.'

'Were you?'

Her eyes grew panic-stricken and she looked at first one of the surrounding group and then the other, seeking a single ally or a pitying glance.

'Please tell me, Miss Arrowbrook, one way or the other. Nobody's going to hurt or reproach you. In fact, only the three of us here need know.'

'I do not tell lies. I must emphasize that. I am a truthful person. But when the policeman asked me, I was afraid. You see, I simply could *not* appear in court to give evidence. My heart would not allow me. I would have another of my attacks right in the witness-box.'

'There's no question of that, I assure you, Miss Arrowbrook. Just the truth and you'll not be worried. It won't be mentioned to you again. You have my word for it.'

The lonely figure in the shabby bed grew more composed.

'Do you mind if I have another dose of the cordial? It has done me so much good. What is it, may I ask?'

'Scotch whisky, Miss Arrowbrook.'

She thrust aside the glass in horror.

'But I am strictly temperance! I cannot touch it. I have signed the pledge of the Band of Hope... I did wrong in taking the last dose you gave me.'

The Archdeacon intervened.

'This is purely a medicine, Miss Arrowbrook. I assure you, you do no wrong in taking it. Why, a doctor may, unknown to you, even include alcohol in a prescription... Come now.'

'You really think I am doing right? You are a clergyman and would not trick me, I know.'

'You must take it in medicinal doses. It will do you much good.'

A pause whilst she laboriously pondered the problem.

'Very well.'

She drank off the whisky again and nodded sagely.

'It is very beneficial. And now, if you promise, I will tell you what happened. I did go out, but the crowds were so dense that it brought on one of my attacks of breathlessness and palpitation. I came to my room... '

'At what time, please, and did anyone see you?'

'It was just after half past two. The front door was loose and I hurried to my room as best I could, for I didn't want to faint. I got in bed.'

'Then?'

'I laid in bed getting my breath back. Someone came upstairs shortly after me. It was Mr Snook and Susie. I heard their voices. I couldn't tell what they were saying; they spoke almost in whispers. They passed my door and then I heard them go up to Susie's room in the attic... I must confess I was horrified!'

'How long were they there?'

'I can only guess. About ten minutes. Then I heard one of them descending. It must have been Mr Snook, judging from the footsteps.'

'Yes?'

'After Mr Snook and Susie had gone to the attic, I heard a door open and close softly on the floor below.'

'Can you say which room?'

Miss Arrowbrook looked distressed and gripped the clothes again, looking all the time at Mrs Nessle, who was standing at the foot of the bed, listening, saying nothing.

'Why are you looking so queerly at me?'

'It was your room, Mrs Nessle. I'm sorry, but it was... '

'Mine! But I was out at the time. I went to the crowning of the carnival queen. I was with a friend. She will tell you I was... You must be mistaken.'

The thin lips of the figure in the bed tightened.

'I'm quite sure. I have a good sense of direction. During the war, when I lived with my dear father in London, I could always tell exactly *where* the German planes were in the sky at night. He used to rely on me and we would emerge from the air-raid shelter when I said they'd passed over. I was never wrong.'

'Well, you're wrong this time, my girl.'

'No, I'm not.'

Littlejohn intervened in what looked like developing into a bitter and protracted duel.

'Does anyone come in and out of the rooms during the day? I mean, after the usual morning tidy-up.'

Mrs Nessle's eyes opened wide.

'Why... Yes. Someone did go in my room that day. When I got up and pulled back the curtains that morning, they stuck, and I tore two of the hooks from the material in my struggles. I told Mr Trimble and he said he'd see to it. They needed stitching. It hadn't been repaired when I went up to wash before lunch, but when I returned for tea, the hooks had been stitched back again... Yes, that's right.'

'And after the door opened and closed, Miss Arrowbrook?'

'Someone climbed the stairs and stood in the passage outside my door. I knew it. I'm good at sensing things like that. My dear father always said I was clairvoyant.'

'Any idea who it was?'

'No. But I think there was a sound of someone sobbing or out of breath. That's what it was like, two big gulps... You understand? Then, I heard Mr Snook come down. Whoever it was must have gone back to the top of the stairs. As he got there, I heard voices. I think he said, "What are you doing here? I thought you'd gone to the carnival." Or something like it. And then a low voice just said a few words and I heard a sound like a... like a mixture of a loud grunt and a cry. Either Mr Snook struck someone, or they struck him. It was a noise like one makes...'

'What then?'

'Mr Snook sounded to go down the stairs. His heavy footsteps, you know...'

'What about the other unknown person?'

'He or she went in the room next door... the Trimbles'. I heard the water running and then quick footsteps coming from the room and hurrying down the stairs to the front door, which I heard close. Susie came down soon after... That was all.'

'Thank you, Miss Arrowbrook.'

'And I won't be needed in court or get into trouble about not telling the police?'

'I give you my word.'

'Thank you. And it will be all right, Archdeacon, my taking the cordial... the whisky, as medicine?'

'Of course.'

And then, as though she hadn't said anything which could hang anybody, Miss Arrowbrook lowered herself beneath the sheets, Mrs Nessle, with trembling hands and contorted features, tucked her in, and she fell asleep.

16

THE LONG TRAIL HOME

'What have you been doing up there all this time? Keeping us all standing about here like a lot of fools in the middle of the night! It's nearly dawn.'

Mrs Trimble was overwrought and in a rage. She had now grown dishevelled, too, and her sagging cheeks and the lines of fatigue round her mouth and eyes added ten more years to her appearance.

'Shall we all sit down for a minute or two?'

Susie looked almost asleep as she stood, uncertain what to do, leaning against the table, her hands clasped tightly, with the constable, who had returned, hovering about her. Knell was sitting by the stove with Mrs Trimble occupying the only other chair in the place. Knell hastily bowed the Archdeacon into his seat and Charlie, the bobby, hurried quietly to the lounge and brought in chairs for Littlejohn, Susie and the Inspector.

'There's no sense in settling down here at this hour of night. We all want to get to bed. I've had a bad time and it's taken it out of me. What do you want to know now? Haven't we answered enough questions? It's time you took Susie to the police-station and charged her with attempting to murder me and, if I'm not mistaken, stabbing Fred Snook, too.'

'But she didn't kill Snook. That's what I'm coming to. I'm just going to tell you all what we've found out in the course of our inquiries and you can correct me if I'm wrong. It's got to be settled now. All the boarders leave by the nine o'clock boat. It's got to be over by then.'

A look of wild uncertainty came into Mrs Trimble's eyes and she ran two hands across her forehead.

'I'd forgotten the day. Don't take any notice of me. I've been through hell lately, with Snook, Mr Trimble, and now this little ungrateful devil... What were you saying?'

'Ten years ago, Fred Boycott ran away from his wife. He was tired of the life she led him and even willing to leave all his money and his nice home behind to get a bit of peace. He went off with another woman and settled in Leicester under the name of Snowball, so that he couldn't be traced. There they lived for two or three years. They didn't get on for long. She nagged him and he found he'd jumped out of the frying-pan into the fire. He ran away again...'

'I don't know what all this has to do with us... Uncle Fred never told us much about his past, so I can't confirm what you're saying. Anybody want a drink? No? Then I'll help myself... I'm dead beat.'

Mrs Trimble groped about for words and then for the bottle, which came to light in a cupboard. She poured herself a liberal dose of gin and drank half of it in one gulp. Then she sat down and crossed her legs.

'... We don't know where Uncle Fred fetched up just after leaving his girl in Leicester. But around eight years ago, he found the Isle of Man, changed his name again, to Snook this time, and discovered here the peace he'd always sought. The place got hold of him and he used to cross backwards and forwards, calling to see a friend he'd made after his own heart, John Costain of Cregneish, who owned a boat. Together they spent idyllic days on the

Calf and around the village of Cregneish. Uncle Fred was happy at last with his boat, his fisherman companion, and the lazy times they spent together. But he hadn't much money. His love affairs and his running away from his women had cost him too much. He'd only enough to live on modestly. Then, one autumn, when all the hotels and places in the south near Cregneish were closed and there were only one or two open in Douglas, he turned up at *Sea Vista*.'

'Who told you this? But it's true. He came in November, of all times. And here he stayed ever after.'

Mrs Trimble, having drunk all her gin, was now less depressed and more talkative. She seemed proud to tell them all that Uncle Fred had chosen *Sea Vista* out of all the places he could have found.

'There was one thing lacking in Fred Snook's life. A woman. He was always fond of women and even the beauty and peace of the Island and the friendship of Costain couldn't make up for that. At *Sea Vista* he found what he sought. Otherwise, he wouldn't have stayed so long. He'd have moved nearer to the Calf of Man and his friends at Cregneish. What he found here made him stay.'

Mrs Trimble, groping in the cupboard for more gin, turned as she filled her glass up and smiled.

'Yes... And it wasn't Susie, either.'

They all jumped and looked at her strangely. She didn't seem to care where the tale was leading. It looked as though her mind was going, or else she'd had a lot more to drink than they thought. She sat down.

'Go on, Super. I want them all to listen to this.'

'*Sea Vista* was owned by Mr and Mrs Trimble, who came here when they left the stage. He'd been a handsome man and quite a top-ranker in the circus and vaudeville world. She'd been a variety artist and pantomime principal boy.'

'Right again. I was good in my time, too. I could have married into the gentry, but I preferred Ferdy... He was a good trouper. He understood me.'

She started to cry. Tears rolled down her cheeks and she wiped them away with the sleeve of her gown.

'Trimble was a wreck when he came here. He'd had a bad fall. He never performed again after it. He went to seed. A shadow of his old self. Loafing about, doing domestic work in his boarding-house, and tippling on the sly.'

'Here! Whatever he was, I won't have you speak ill of him now. He's dead. Let him rest.'

'Did *you* let him rest, Mrs Trimble, when he was here? He worked all the time. He was only half a man after his accident. You were still very good-looking and attractive. Fred Snook fell for you completely. There was soon an affair going on between you behind Trimble's back, although I wonder if he'd have cared if he'd found out.'

'Of course he would. He loved me to the end. And don't you try to take my good name away. Fred Snook and me would have been married if Trimble hadn't been alive. And from all accounts, he should have died long ago. After his accident, the doctors gave him a year. That's why he didn't care about anything. He wore a sort of harness to keep his back in shape and the doctors said his backbone might go at any time and he'd pop off like that.'

She snapped her fingers and took another drink.

'So, you see, he'd a right to his drink, as much as he wanted. It was his only pleasure. Uncle Fred being about the place made it easier for him. He'd somebody to talk to all the year round, instead of moping in this empty barn all the off-season... He accepted things as they were. And we were all happy together, until this little devil set her cap at Uncle Fred. Yes... I mean you. You needn't look so innocent. And when Fred didn't fall for her, she killed him in a rage.'

'You know very well, Mrs Trimble...'

'Be quiet, Susie, please, and let me go on. Life here became settled, as you say, Mrs Trimble. The lazy, easygoing way suited Fred. He went off regularly on his trips to the Calf and out in the boat, and came home to the bosom of Trimble's family when the happy day was over and it was as inconsequential here as it was elsewhere. Then two things happened. He took a fancy to Susie.'

'Never! He wanted only me right to the end. He loved me, did Fred, and he wouldn't let me down.'

She burst into tears again, sniffing, blubbering and weeping in her gin. It was painful. Littlejohn wished there wasn't such an audience there to see it working out, but they were essential for what he'd got in mind.

'He didn't fall in love with Susie really. But he thought her too nice a girl to be spending her time in a place like this, half alive, waiting on all kinds of second-rate people in the season, wasting her time sitting around in winter. Gradually becoming as idle and ineffective as he'd become himself. He planned to make something better of Susie and he was ready to help her with the last of the money he possessed. He gave her a ring which was his mother's, a very valuable one, which, if anything happened to him, she was to use to educate herself. Meanwhile, he did what he could in his own tinpot way, to make her more of a lady.'

Susie was sobbing now. But Mrs Trimble wasn't. She was furious.

'You little cheat! You never told me about the ring. I knew he was always trying to tidy you up... and you needed it when you came here, my girl. A proper little guttersnipe, you were... And you can't say I didn't do my best to make you better. Can you now?'

Susie looked at her without answering, tears still rolling down her pale haggard cheeks.

'The other thing was, John Costain was taken ill. He took to his bed last autumn and is still there, out of commission. Uncle Fred was a sociable man. He wanted somebody comfortable, on his own free-and-easy wave-length to talk to, somebody to whom to express his feelings about the wonder of the country, the sea and the birds, somebody to tell about his past miseries and how he'd now settled down and was happy, idling and passing timeless days in peace. He tried Trimble. He took Trimble off with him on his jaunts, and Trimble, instead of loafing and drinking at home in the off-season, gradually found that Uncle Fred's company and simple pleasures suited him, too. They became chums, exchanged confidences, spent glorious hours together... And Uncle Fred began to like and understand Trimble. This decrepit acrobat wasn't only the man who shuffled and tippled his time away at *Sea Vista*, despised by his wife and a figure of fun to his boarders. He was a man who'd seen a lot of life and found it inadequate, just as Uncle Fred had done. Trimble talked to Fred about his own colourful past and his adventures. Together they were happy. Uncle Fred's conscience started to trouble him. He grew to regret his affair with Trimble's wife behind his back. It didn't seem right. He started to avoid and cold-shoulder Mrs Trimble and she thought it was all due to Susie. She didn't understand Uncle Fred, *or* Trimble for that matter.'

Mrs Trimble didn't say a word. She just gaped at Littlejohn, as though she couldn't understand what he was talking about. Under the drink she'd taken, her thoughts must have been hard to collect. Like looking through a mist. She got up to get another dose from the bottle.

'That will do, Mrs Trimble. You've had enough. Please sit down.'

The parson intervened and gently led her back to her chair. She flopped down like a sack in it, too taken aback to protest. She moved to the table and, sitting up to it, put her elbows on it and her head between her hands. Susie made an uncertain gesture of placing her hand on Mrs Trimble's shoulder, perhaps out of sympathy or to encourage her. She jumped and pushed her off.

'Get away from me, you little rotten brat! Leave me alone.'

'Last Saturday among the boarders there arrived Finnegan

with Miss Crawley. Miss Crawley was the sister of Fred Snook's woman in Leicester long ago. She had died and left a daughter, Fred's daughter. Miss Crawley had traced Fred here with the help of her friend, Finnegan. Finnegan, a disreputable chap at best, saw his chance to pester Fred, disturb the peace he'd found, and briefly, blackmail him. Between the two, the child in Leicester – and remember, Fred was fond of children, first his own daughter Victoria, and now little Bertha in Leicester – and Finnegan pestering, he found he must have money, and a fair amount. He thought of Susie's ring and asked her to let him have it. In exchange, he'd give her some cash from securities he'd sell. The ring was immediately convertible into money; the securities would take a little time. This happened on Monday, after lunch, with all the lodgers going out to the carnival.'

Mrs Trimble stood up suddenly, panting, fighting for air. She looked ready either to faint or have a fit. Then, she saw Susie, reached out her hands for her, drew her to her, and buried her head in her breast.

'You didn't take him from me, Susie... did you...? You didn't...'

She sounded to be choking, speaking into the cloth of the girl's dress. In all his career, Littlejohn had never known anything so distasteful. It was horrible, but it had to be finished.

'Susie took Fred upstairs to get the ring. When she looked at it again she didn't want to part with it. They argued. She wept. He persuaded her, and finally came away with it. Down the attic steps. And, waiting for him below, was someone with a pair of scissors. Someone who'd been mending the curtains in Mrs Nessle's room. Someone who thought the worst about Uncle Fred's being in Susie's bedroom, who met him in a rage, leapt at him in the dark corridor, and stabbed him in the back. Take that! He took it, knew who'd done it, and tried to protect her to the last by struggling as far away from *Sea Vista* as he could. With the mists gathering round him, he snatched Greenhalgh's raincoat from the hall-stand, covered his bleeding back with it, and dragged himself to the promenade where, after being jostled and trampled upon by the rabble of a carnival, he died.'

Mrs Trimble, sobbing and clutching Susie, turned and looked up.

'And me thinking all the time...'

'You thinking it was Susie who'd stolen his affection?'

Susie kept holding her, although she looked ready to drop herself. The shadows under the girl's eyes were deeper than ever. Charlie, the bobby, in his turn, put a compassionate hand on her thin shoulder and pressed it.

Mrs Trimble had lost the thread of what was going on. First she clung to Susie, then she flung her off again. Finally, Susie fainted, just quietly folded up and ended hanging, her hair over her face, across Charlie's arm.

'Take her away and look after her, Charlie. I think Mrs Nessle's about. Find her and tell her to put Susie to bed.'

Strangely enough, Charlie seemed delighted. Susie married him in the autumn, and Knell gave her away at church!

Littlejohn wished he could pack up and go for good. Instead, there were the unpleasant formalities of arresting Mrs Trimble after the case had been brought home to her and her guilt finally established.

There were just the three of them with her now; Knell, haggard and struggling to keep awake and alert, and the Archdeacon, his kind eyes on Mrs Trimble, wondering how he could help her. She raised her face from the table where she had been lolling since Susie's collapse. Her forehead and cheeks were bathed in tears and sweat.

'I'll tell you, Mr Kinrade. I'll tell you... I can confess it all to you... You've always been kind about things... You'll understand all about it and not blame me. I heard them go up to her room. I thought only one thing. How was *I* to know about the ring and he needed the money? When he came down from the attic, he looked so satisfied with himself that I saw red. I'd been sewing. I'd the scissors in my hand. I struck at him without a word and then I said "take that"... He caught my arm and stopped the blow. We struggled... I must have been so mad, it gave me strength. Before I knew what I'd done, he was staggering down the stairs and he went out. There was blood on my hands. I went up and washed it. Then I followed him. I didn't know he was dying. I didn't even know I'd wounded him, if it hadn't been for the blood... He was nowhere about. There was a crowd on the promenade. I got mixed up in it and I couldn't get away. Later, I heard he was dead. I was afraid. I kept quiet... That's all there is to it.'

She was clinging to the Archdeacon now and he was holding her gently by the shoulders.

'But your husband knew, didn't he?'

'Yes, reverend. He was in at the time, knew where I was, and put two and two together. He told me he knew and that he would keep quiet.'

'But the strain was too much for him, wasn't it?' said Littlejohn gently. 'He felt he'd break down under questioning. He was afraid of himself. After I questioned Susie in private, he thought she'd given vital information. So he bolted to where he'd once had peace with Fred. You guessed where he'd gone. You followed him.'

'That's it... I wanted to know what had become of him and why he'd gone. But I thought I'd be followed.'

'So, you disguised yourself in sun-glasses and an old wig from the stage properties you'd kept. Then you burned the wig and coat you wore, and unluckily set the chimney on fire.'

'Yes... You seem to know it all... I didn't kill Ferdy. I found him on the Calf near the old lighthouse. He'd been drinking. He was standing on the cliffs staring out to sea with a wild, queer look. When he saw me, he just said, "Go away... I can't bear it any more," and he tried to run. He was never safe on his feet and he just crumpled up and fell... He slid down the rocks and over the edge of the cliff. I could see him stretched out below, awful and still. I knew he was dead. I ran back to join the boat that was ready for leaving and I hurried back home. I was afraid of what they'd do to me if I was found out. I didn't kill Ferdy, but they'd have said I pushed him. I wouldn't have done that to him.'

'And you made up your mind to try and get away with it, Mrs Trimble?'

She looked at him with eyes which seemed dead.

'While I thought Susie had taken Fred from me, I made up my mind to keep it dark. I thought Fred had deserved it. As for her...'

'When you thought we might find out about you, you tried to engineer a theatrical scene and make it look as if Susie wanted to kill you, as well. It was your idea of revenge and it was a very poor one. She might very easily have been suspected of killing Uncle Fred. She was the only one, besides your late husband, who was thought to be indoors at the time Fred was stabbed. But we found another witness who heard all that went on and her testimony put Susie in the clear and made it almost certain that you were the culprit.'

'Who was that? Nessle?'

'Miss Arrowbrook.'

'I forgot her and her funny ways! First she's in, then she's out. You never know where she is two minutes together. So, she split on me, did she?'

'No. I had to drag it from her.'

'Well... so long as Susie and Fred weren't... Well, now I know Fred still loved me when he died and I don't need any revenge on Susie, it's easy to confess. I want to atone and take my punishment for what I did to Fred.'

The idea of punishment hadn't struck her before and now she sat frozen.

'They'll not... they'll not say it's murder and... and...'

She was on her feet again, raving, her eyes popping.

'Not that... They'll not...'

They didn't. She got a good lawyer, who emphasized the fight on the dark stairs, the domestic bliss of *Sea Vista* until Uncle Fred arrived, the seduction of the accused, with Mrs Trimble, now neat and trim, playing a part for the jury... It was manslaughter; four years.

Formalities, a caution, and the words preceding arrest, and then Mrs Trimble went quietly away with Knell and Charlie in a police-car.

Littlejohn and the Archdeacon drank a cup of tea made by Mrs Nessle, who was still about. Miss A. arrived at five o'clock and after being informed that Mrs Trimble had gone, took a hold of matters, and started the little boarding factory of *Sea Vista* throbbing again, making out bills for the departing, cooking breakfasts for early arrivals, seeing that guests were knocked up and early tea served.

As Littlejohn and the parson left, dawn had broken over the silent town. The tide was in and a chill early wind swept the long promenade. The early sun was shining on the eastern slopes of the little hills of Man behind Douglas. At the pier, the midnight boat from Liverpool was tied up and the first arrivals of the new week of holidays were crowding off. Buses and porters already afoot were picking them up. A taxi drew-up at *Sea Vista* and a little fat man in flannel trousers and blazer, and wearing a white soft hat, jumped out. He had the sodden look of one who'd been up all night on the boat and had amused himself all the way in the bar.

'Hello, hello... Here we are again! Good old *Sea Vista*. You leavin' to queue for the first boat out? Bit early, aren't you? All the same, it's as well to get it over.'

He wouldn't shut up, and looked like being the life and soul of next week's party.

'Hear there's been a spot of trouble. Old man lodging here, died in the carnival... How's old Trimble?'

'Dead,' said Littlejohn. 'They're burying him today.'

It seemed a damned shame to greet the fellow thus, but he wouldn't stop talking. He crumpled up.

'Wot!'

'It's all right. The place is in good hands. They're carrying on... Mind if we take your taxi?'

They heaved out his suitcase and went back to the police-station in his hired car. Then, home.

They drove slowly, along the old road which wound its way between sod hedges golden with gorse, past white farms just awakening, through wooded valleys alive with early birdsong, and skirted Castletown, still sleeping under the shadow of its granite castle. *Grenaby.* The little signpost pointing in the direction of the brown southern hills and the wild rising roads to the Round Table, with the hidden village nestling sheltered in the middle of the wilderness in a clump of great old trees.

Littlejohn couldn't help thinking of Uncle Fred, the man who thought he'd found peace, when all the time he'd touched off a series of dramatic events which ended in wholesale tragedy.

There was a smell of ham and eggs on the air around the parsonage when they arrived. During the day, as the boats and planes took away departing holidaymakers and as quickly brought in eager replacements, Littlejohn and the Archdeacon sat on the garden bench, beside the large century-old fuchsia and shaded by old trees, and slept the hours away, making up for a lost night's sleep. Thus Mrs Littlejohn found them when she arrived with Meg, the dog, on an unexpectedly early plane. The bobtail's soft nose thrust between his hands awoke Littlejohn to a new day and the beginnings of his real holiday.

ABOUT THE AUTHOR

George Bellairs is the pseudonym under which Harold Blundell (1902–1982) wrote police procedural thrillers in rural British settings. He was born in Lancashire, England, and worked as a bank manager in Manchester. After retiring, Bellairs moved to the Isle of Man, where several of his novels are set, to be with friends and family.

In 1941 Bellairs wrote his first mystery, *Littlejohn on Leave*, during spare moments at his air raid warden's post. The title introduced Thomas Littlejohn, the detective who appears in fifty-seven of his novels. Bellairs was also a regular contributor to the *Manchester Guardian* and worked as a freelance writer for newspapers both local and national.

THE INSPECTOR LITTLEJOHN MYSTERIES

FROM OPEN ROAD MEDIA

Printed in Great Britain
by Amazon

51460330R00142